SANJAY DESHPANDE

IN DEFENSE OF THE REALM

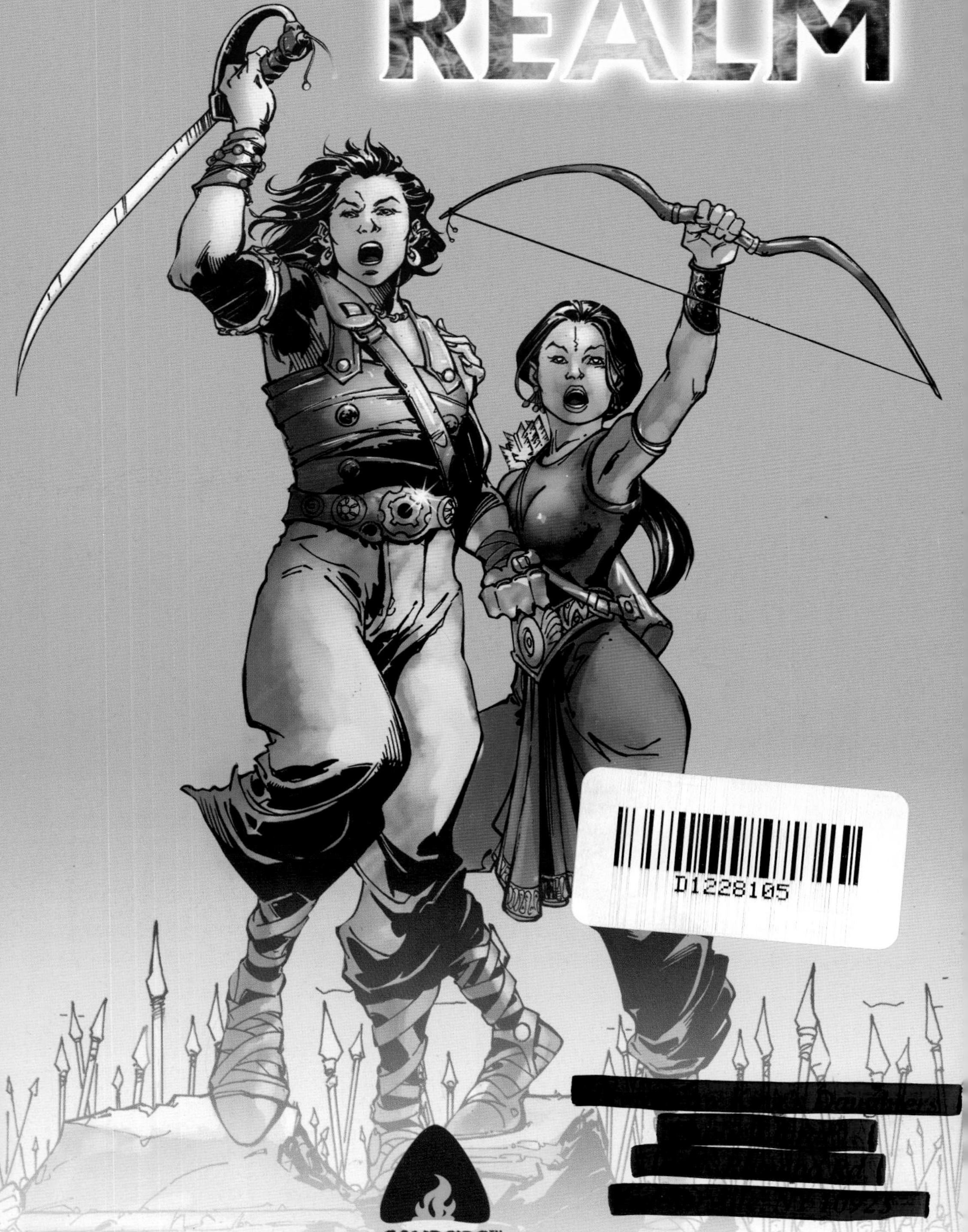

CAMPFIRE™

KALYANI NAVYUG MEDIA PVT. LTD.
New Delhi

IN DEFENSE OF THE REALM

Sitting around the Campfire, telling the story, were:

ILLUSTRATOR **LALIT KUMAR SHARMA**

INKER **JAGDISH KUMAR**

COLORIST **VIJAY SHARMA**

LETTERER **LAXMI CHAND GUPTA**

EDITORS **EMAN CHOWDHARY & ADITI RAY**

EDITOR (INFORMATIVE CONTENT) **RASHMI MENON**

PRODUCTION CONTROLLER **VISHAL SHARMA**

ART DIRECTOR **RAJESH NAGULAKONDA**

COVER ART & DESIGN

JAYAKRISHNAN K. P.

CAMPFIRE™

www.campfire.co.in

Published by Kalyani Navyug Media Pvt. Ltd.
101 C, Shiv House, Hari Nagar Ashram, New Delhi 110014 India
ISBN: 978-93-80028-64-4
Copyright © 2011 Kalyani Navyug Media Pvt. Ltd.
All rights reserved. Published by Campfire, an imprint of Kalyani Navyug Media Pvt. Ltd.

Printed in India at Rave India

ABOUT THE AUTHOR

Sanjay Deshpande

The author, an archeologist and heritage consultant, was born in 1965 in Nagpur, India. He grew up in Mumbai (formerly known as Bombay), but spent his formative years in the Philippines and then U.S.A. He later went to the Universities of Toronto and Texas where he specialized in the search for oil and gas.

In 1992, he was offered the opportunity to excavate as part of the Archaeological Survey of India's excavation at the 5000-year-old Harappan Civilization city of Dholavira on the island of Khadir in the Great Rann of Kutch. He excavated at Dholavira till 1998 and dug out parts of the city, the citadel, and the cemetery complex, as well as parts of the reservoir system, including a water storage tank and a dam.

After getting married in 1999 to a fellow archeologist, Deshpande and his wife joined the joint Deccan College and University of Pennsylvania team excavating at the Ahar Culture site of Gilund (2500–1700 B.C.), where they found many new facets of that culture. The most important of these include the presence of a written script, the oldest *tandoor* (clay oven), the oldest 'Nandi' bull figurine, and a beautifully maintained road with wheel tracks and repaired potholes.

Since 1999, he has also been actively working to promote, preserve, and protect the vast cultural and natural heritage in and around the city of Pune where he lives. He is also an active photographer and trekker who enjoys exploring new places.

INDUS VALLEY

How does one write about the unknown? This is the very question that I faced when I began writing this novel.

Talking about the Indus Valley Civilization, we know a lot about how they lived, but there is so much more that we do not know. We know the civilization covered an area four times larger than Mesopotamia, or Ancient Egypt. We know that they lived in villages, towns, and cities just like people do today. In many ways, they were exceptional—their well-planned towns and cities were all fortified with high and thick walls. We find few weapons and only the rare evidence that suggests that there may have been warfare. Similarly, there is little evidence of poverty, which surely must have been there. Unlike all their contemporaries, Harappan cities had proper sewage systems—a feature that was to become commonplace elsewhere only 3,500 years after their world collapsed around 2000 B.C.! We have found evidence that the people were craftsmen, farmers, traders, and animal herders. They built dams, had rain water harvesting systems, and complex domestic and international trade networks that stretched throughout South Asia, the Middle East, and as far as Egypt.

Interestingly, while the entire Harappan world had a uniform system of weights, planned cities, and towns, standardized types of pottery, seals, script, and construction bricks, that speak of authority and control, there is practically nothing known about their rulers. While their neighboring rulers were building pyramids, temples, great monuments, and filling their graves with their land's gold, the Harappan rulers did nothing of the sort. No great monuments, palaces, temples, or graveyards full of gold have been found. It is as if the concept of a ruler and the ruled was completely different there. Unfortunately, their written records, which could have shed some light on this, seem to have been written mostly on perishable materials. And whatever writing has been found is all on personal artefacts and has not been deciphered yet.

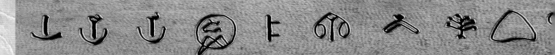

CIVILIZATION

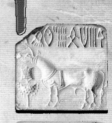

All this means that with the exception of Sargon, all the characters in the story are fictional. In fact, we do not even know what the Indus Valley people called themselves or their cities. Perhaps the invasion happened—after all Sargon did boast that he had made the boats of Dilmun (Bahrain), Magan (UAE/Oman), and Meluha (Indus Civilization) dock at the ports of Akkad. But in truth, we do not know. The rest of the material in the novel—the ships, cities, countryside, markets, the religious customs, the stuff of everyday life—is, however, all exactly as archeologists believe it to have been then.

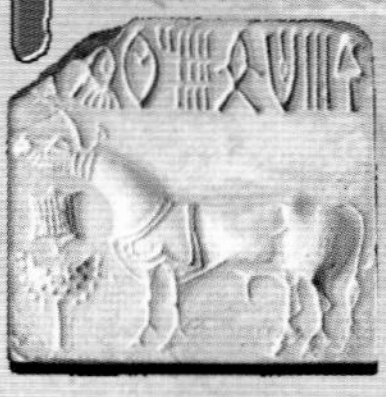

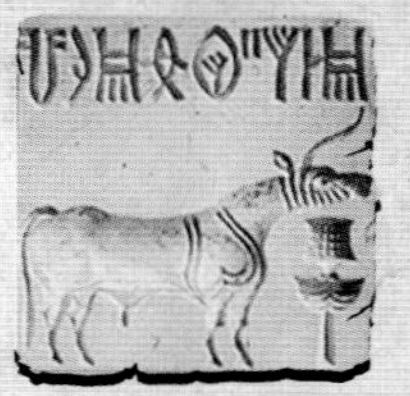

A few final points: the horse may or may not have been present—the evidence is disputed; the story of the comet derives from the belief among some scientists that around 3100 B.C., a large meteor or comet slammed into the Indian Ocean and may have marked a period of great tumult and disaster.

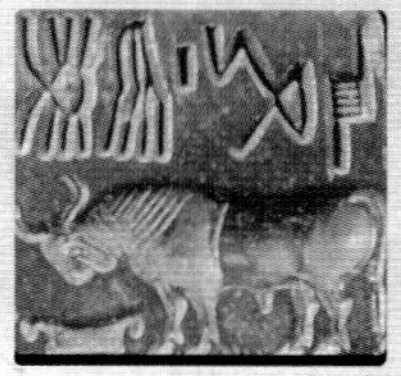

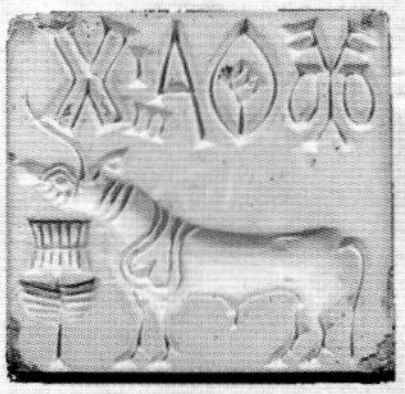

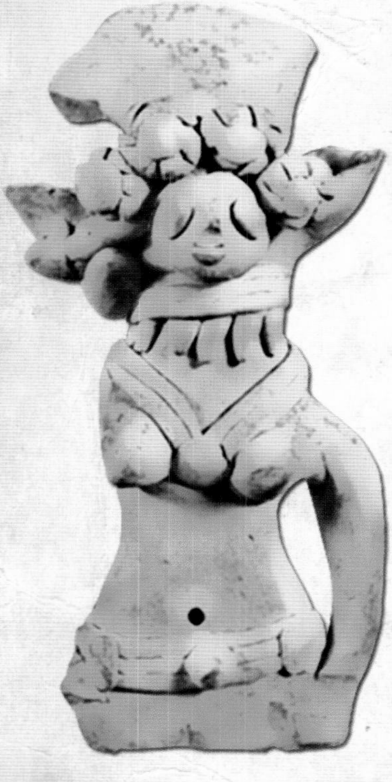

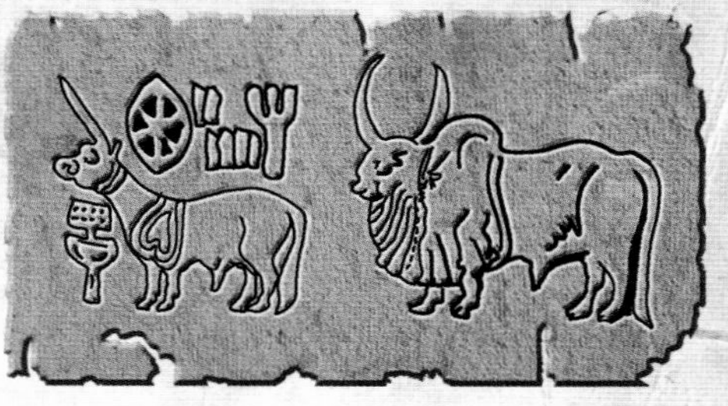

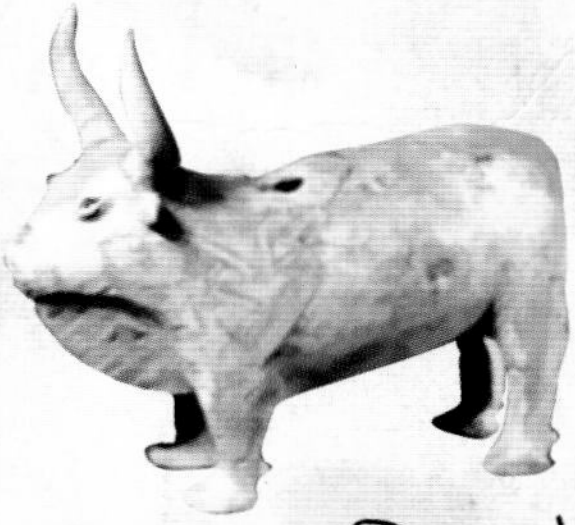

Sanjay Deshpande

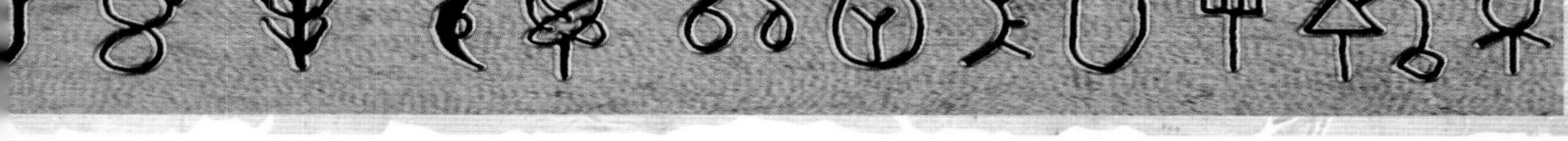

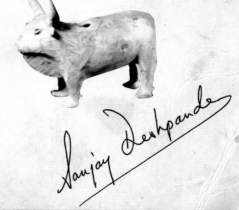

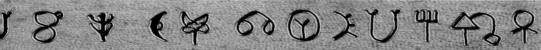

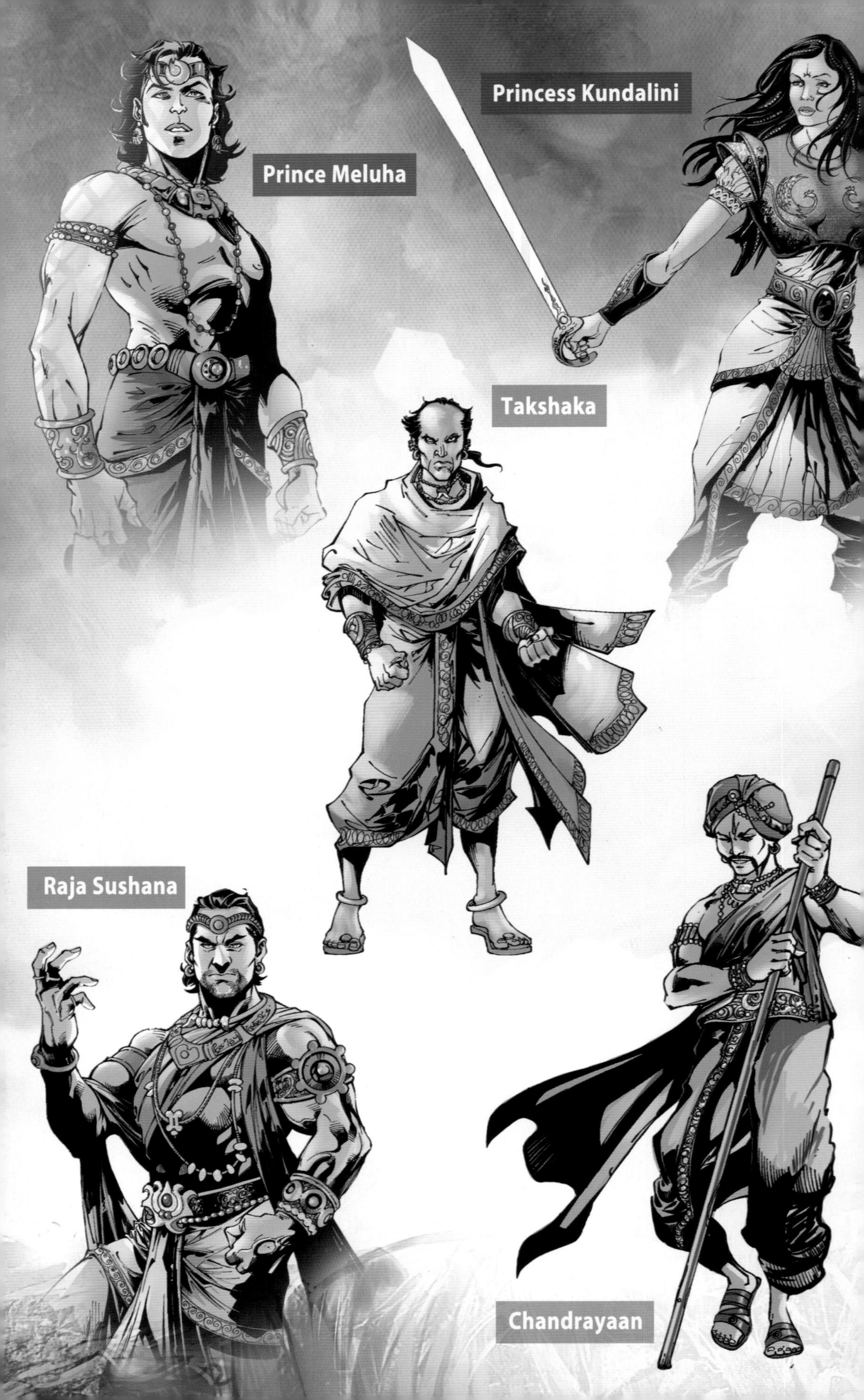

Princess Kundalini
Prince Meluha
Takshaka
Raja Sushana
Chandrayaan

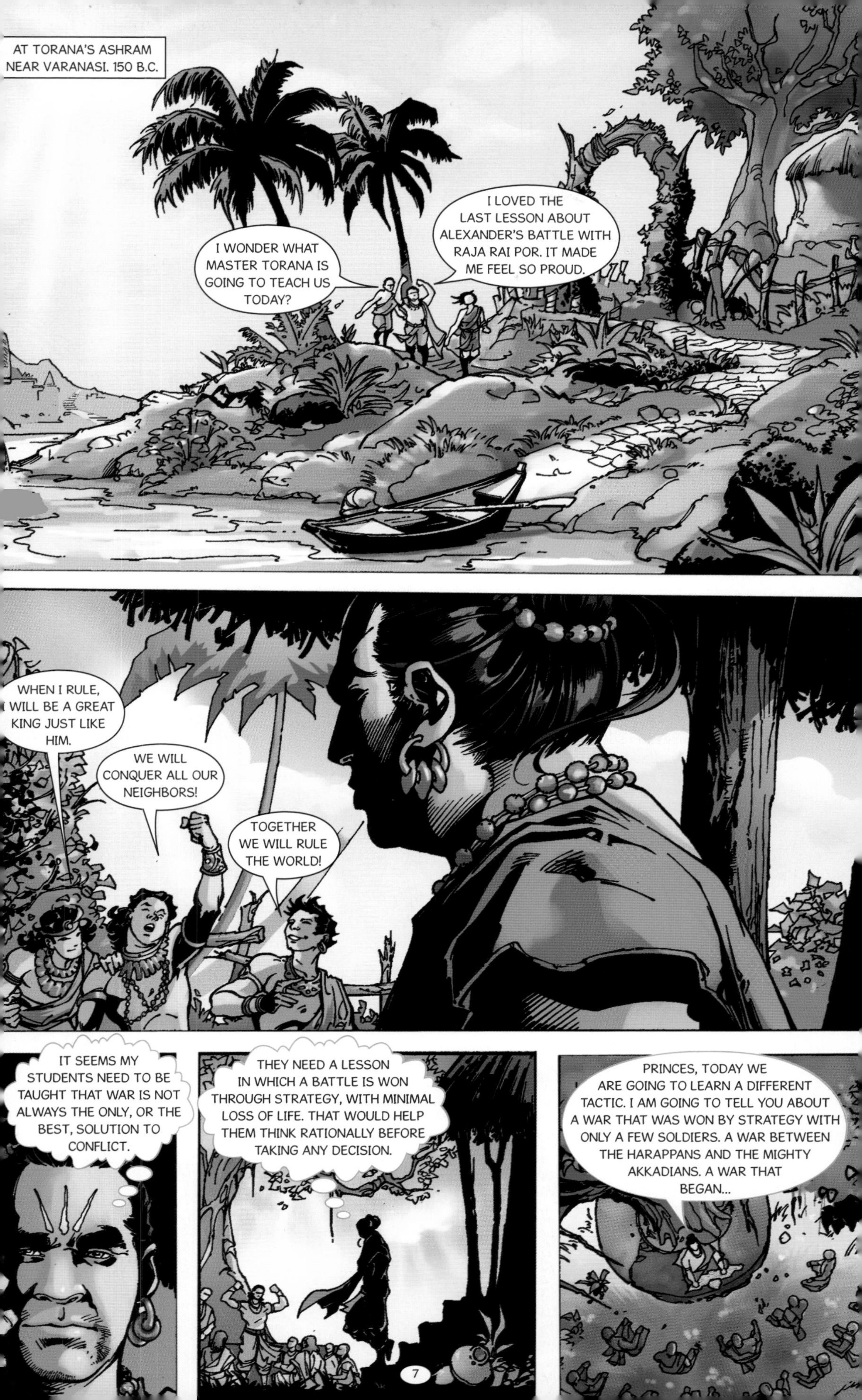
AT TORANA'S ASHRAM NEAR VARANASI. 150 B.C.
I WONDER WHAT MASTER TORANA IS GOING TO TEACH US TODAY?
I LOVED THE LAST LESSON ABOUT ALEXANDER'S BATTLE WITH RAJA RAI POR. IT MADE ME FEEL SO PROUD.
WHEN I RULE, I WILL BE A GREAT KING JUST LIKE HIM.
WE WILL CONQUER ALL OUR NEIGHBORS!
TOGETHER WE WILL RULE THE WORLD!
IT SEEMS MY STUDENTS NEED TO BE TAUGHT THAT WAR IS NOT ALWAYS THE ONLY, OR THE BEST, SOLUTION TO CONFLICT.
THEY NEED A LESSON IN WHICH A BATTLE IS WON THROUGH STRATEGY, WITH MINIMAL LOSS OF LIFE. THAT WOULD HELP THEM THINK RATIONALLY BEFORE TAKING ANY DECISION.
PRINCES, TODAY WE ARE GOING TO LEARN A DIFFERENT TACTIC. I AM GOING TO TELL YOU ABOUT A WAR THAT WAS WON BY STRATEGY WITH ONLY A FEW SOLDIERS. A WAR BETWEEN THE HARAPPANS AND THE MIGHTY AKKADIANS. A WAR THAT BEGAN...

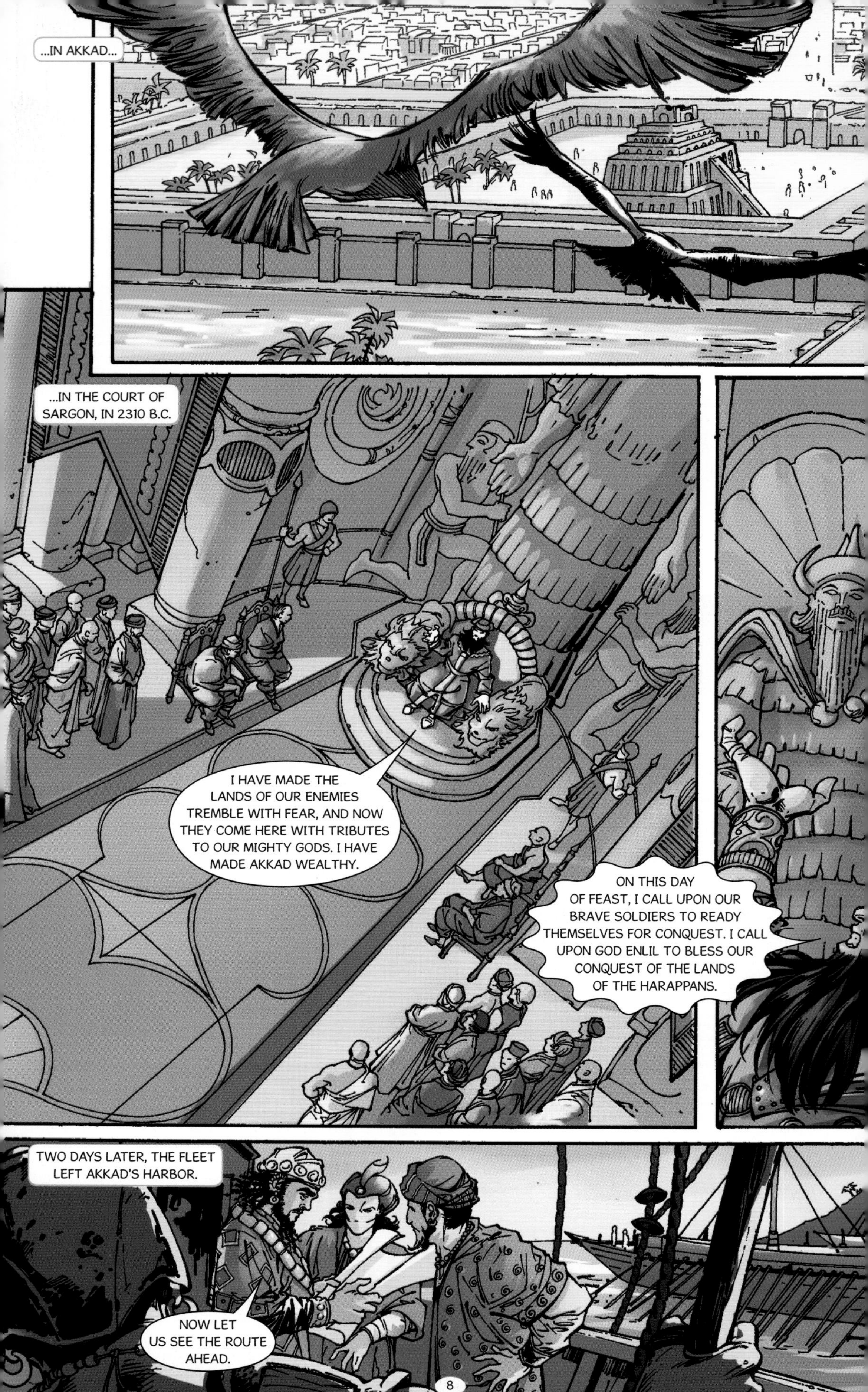
...IN AKKAD...
...IN THE COURT OF SARGON, IN 2310 B.C.
I HAVE MADE THE LANDS OF OUR ENEMIES TREMBLE WITH FEAR, AND NOW THEY COME HERE WITH TRIBUTES TO OUR MIGHTY GODS. I HAVE MADE AKKAD WEALTHY.
ON THIS DAY OF FEAST, I CALL UPON OUR BRAVE SOLDIERS TO READY THEMSELVES FOR CONQUEST. I CALL UPON GOD ENLIL TO BLESS OUR CONQUEST OF THE LANDS OF THE HARAPPANS.
TWO DAYS LATER, THE FLEET LEFT AKKAD'S HARBOR.
NOW LET US SEE THE ROUTE AHEAD.

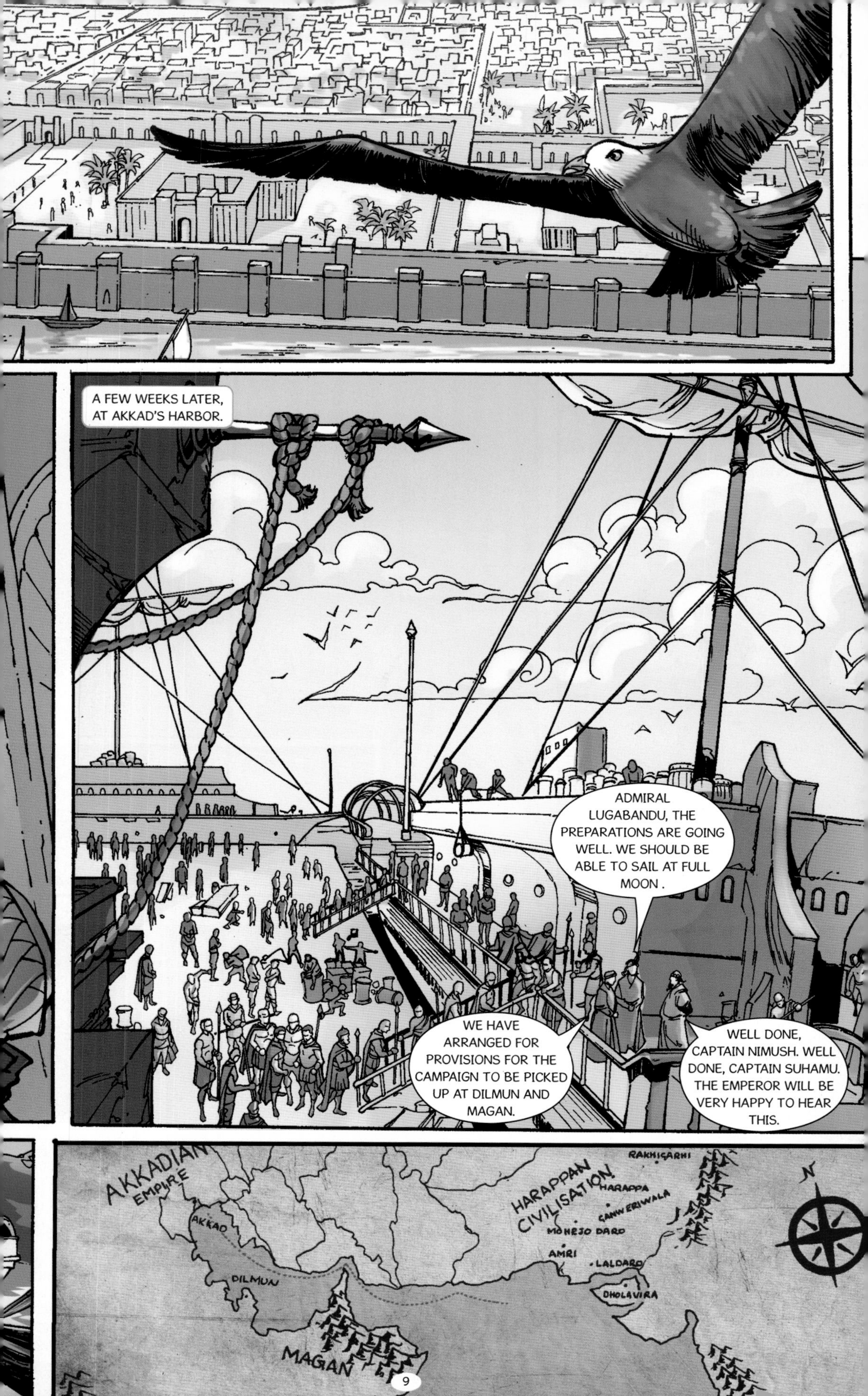
A FEW WEEKS LATER, AT AKKAD'S HARBOR.
ADMIRAL LUGABANDU, THE PREPARATIONS ARE GOING WELL. WE SHOULD BE ABLE TO SAIL AT FULL MOON .
WE HAVE ARRANGED FOR PROVISIONS FOR THE CAMPAIGN TO BE PICKED UP AT DILMUN AND MAGAN.
WELL DONE, CAPTAIN NIMUSH. WELL DONE, CAPTAIN SUHAMU. THE EMPEROR WILL BE VERY HAPPY TO HEAR THIS.
AKKADIAN EMPIRE
AKKAD
DILMUN
MAGAN
HARAPPAN CIVILISATION
RAKHIGARHI
HARAPPA
GANWERIWALA
MOHEJO DARO
AMRI
LALDARO
DHOLAVIRA
N

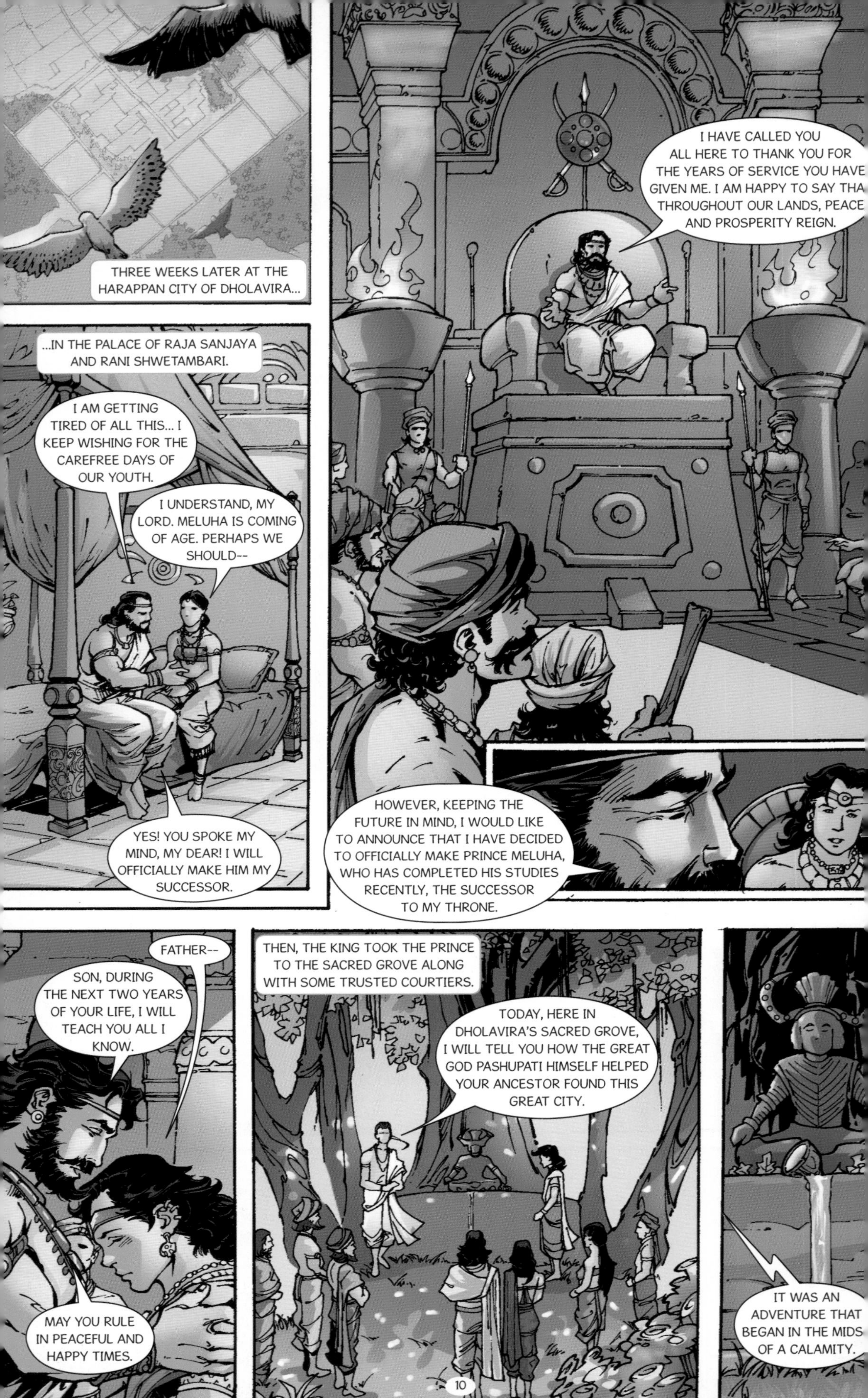
THREE WEEKS LATER AT THE HARAPPAN CITY OF DHOLAVIRA...
...IN THE PALACE OF RAJA SANJAYA AND RANI SHWETAMBARI.
I AM GETTING TIRED OF ALL THIS... I KEEP WISHING FOR THE CAREFREE DAYS OF OUR YOUTH.
I UNDERSTAND, MY LORD. MELUHA IS COMING OF AGE. PERHAPS WE SHOULD--
YES! YOU SPOKE MY MIND, MY DEAR! I WILL OFFICIALLY MAKE HIM MY SUCCESSOR.
I HAVE CALLED YOU ALL HERE TO THANK YOU FOR THE YEARS OF SERVICE YOU HAVE GIVEN ME. I AM HAPPY TO SAY THA THROUGHOUT OUR LANDS, PEACE AND PROSPERITY REIGN.
HOWEVER, KEEPING THE FUTURE IN MIND, I WOULD LIKE TO ANNOUNCE THAT I HAVE DECIDED TO OFFICIALLY MAKE PRINCE MELUHA, WHO HAS COMPLETED HIS STUDIES RECENTLY, THE SUCCESSOR TO MY THRONE.
FATHER--
SON, DURING THE NEXT TWO YEARS OF YOUR LIFE, I WILL TEACH YOU ALL I KNOW.
MAY YOU RULE IN PEACEFUL AND HAPPY TIMES.
THEN, THE KING TOOK THE PRINCE TO THE SACRED GROVE ALONG WITH SOME TRUSTED COURTIERS.
TODAY, HERE IN DHOLAVIRA'S SACRED GROVE, I WILL TELL YOU HOW THE GREAT GOD PASHUPATI HIMSELF HELPED YOUR ANCESTOR FOUND THIS GREAT CITY.
IT WAS AN ADVENTURE THAT BEGAN IN THE MIDS OF A CALAMITY.

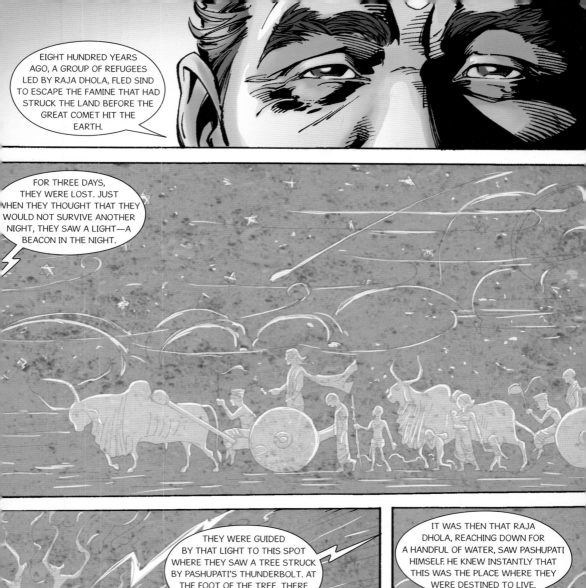

EIGHT HUNDRED YEARS AGO, A GROUP OF REFUGEES LED BY RAJA DHOLA, FLED SIND TO ESCAPE THE FAMINE THAT HAD STRUCK THE LAND BEFORE THE GREAT COMET HIT THE EARTH.

FOR THREE DAYS, THEY WERE LOST. JUST WHEN THEY THOUGHT THAT THEY WOULD NOT SURVIVE ANOTHER NIGHT, THEY SAW A LIGHT—A BEACON IN THE NIGHT.

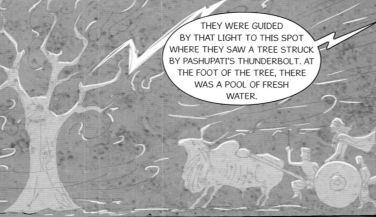

THEY WERE GUIDED BY THAT LIGHT TO THIS SPOT WHERE THEY SAW A TREE STRUCK BY PASHUPATI'S THUNDERBOLT. AT THE FOOT OF THE TREE, THERE WAS A POOL OF FRESH WATER.

IT WAS THEN THAT RAJA DHOLA, REACHING DOWN FOR A HANDFUL OF WATER, SAW PASHUPATI HIMSELF. HE KNEW INSTANTLY THAT THIS WAS THE PLACE WHERE THEY WERE DESTINED TO LIVE.

WITH THE WATER FROM THIS SACRED POND, MAY PASHUPATI WASH AWAY YOUR SINS, AND GUIDE YOUR FOOTSTEPS FROM THIS DAY ONWARD.

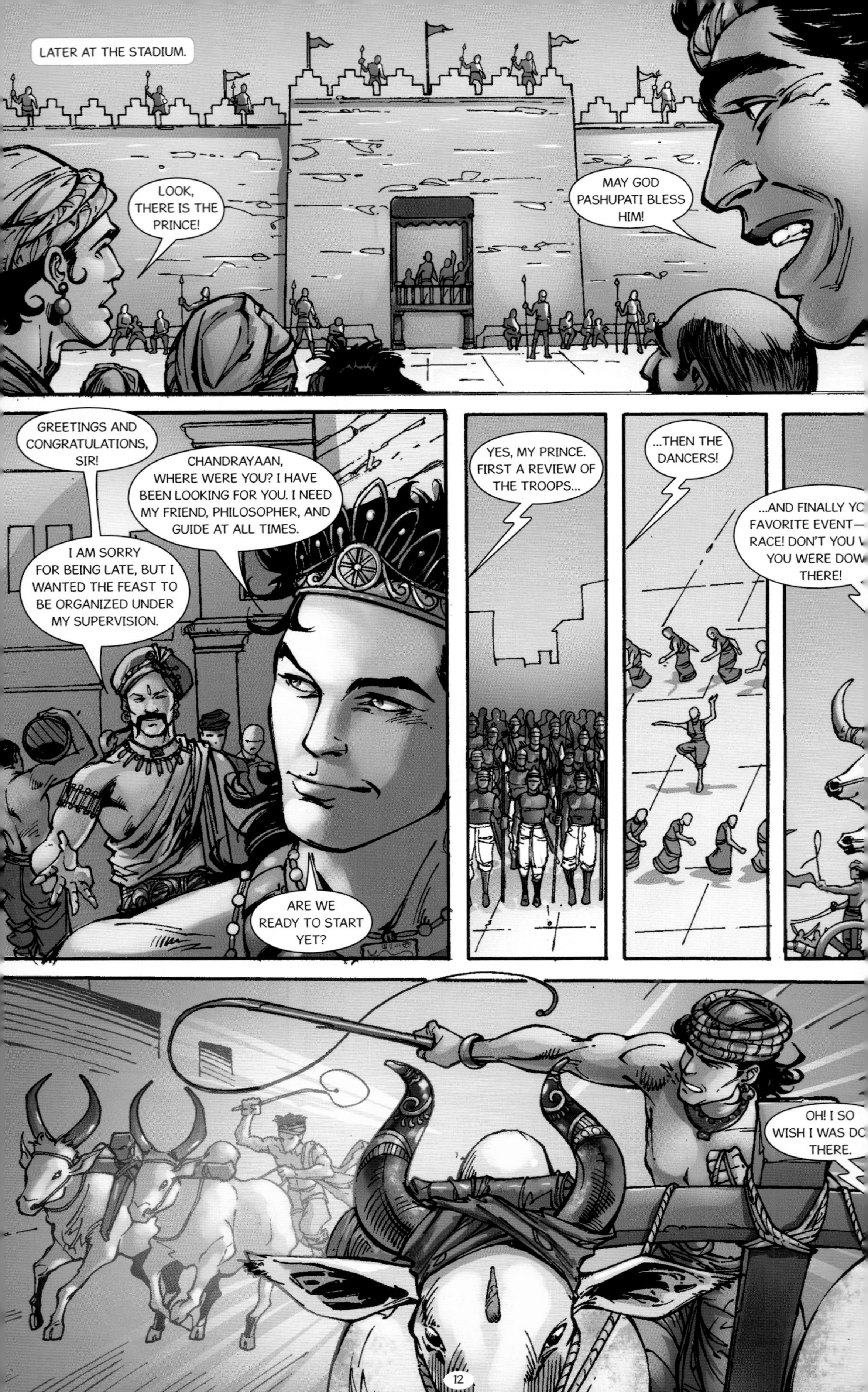
LATER AT THE STADIUM.
LOOK, THERE IS THE PRINCE!
MAY GOD PASHUPATI BLESS HIM!
GREETINGS AND CONGRATULATIONS, SIR!
CHANDRAYAAN, WHERE WERE YOU? I HAVE BEEN LOOKING FOR YOU. I NEED MY FRIEND, PHILOSOPHER, AND GUIDE AT ALL TIMES.
I AM SORRY FOR BEING LATE, BUT I WANTED THE FEAST TO BE ORGANIZED UNDER MY SUPERVISION.
ARE WE READY TO START YET?
YES, MY PRINCE. FIRST A REVIEW OF THE TROOPS...
...THEN THE DANCERS!
...AND FINALLY YO FAVORITE EVENT— RACE! DON'T YOU YOU WERE DOW THERE!
OH! I SO WISH I WAS DO THERE.

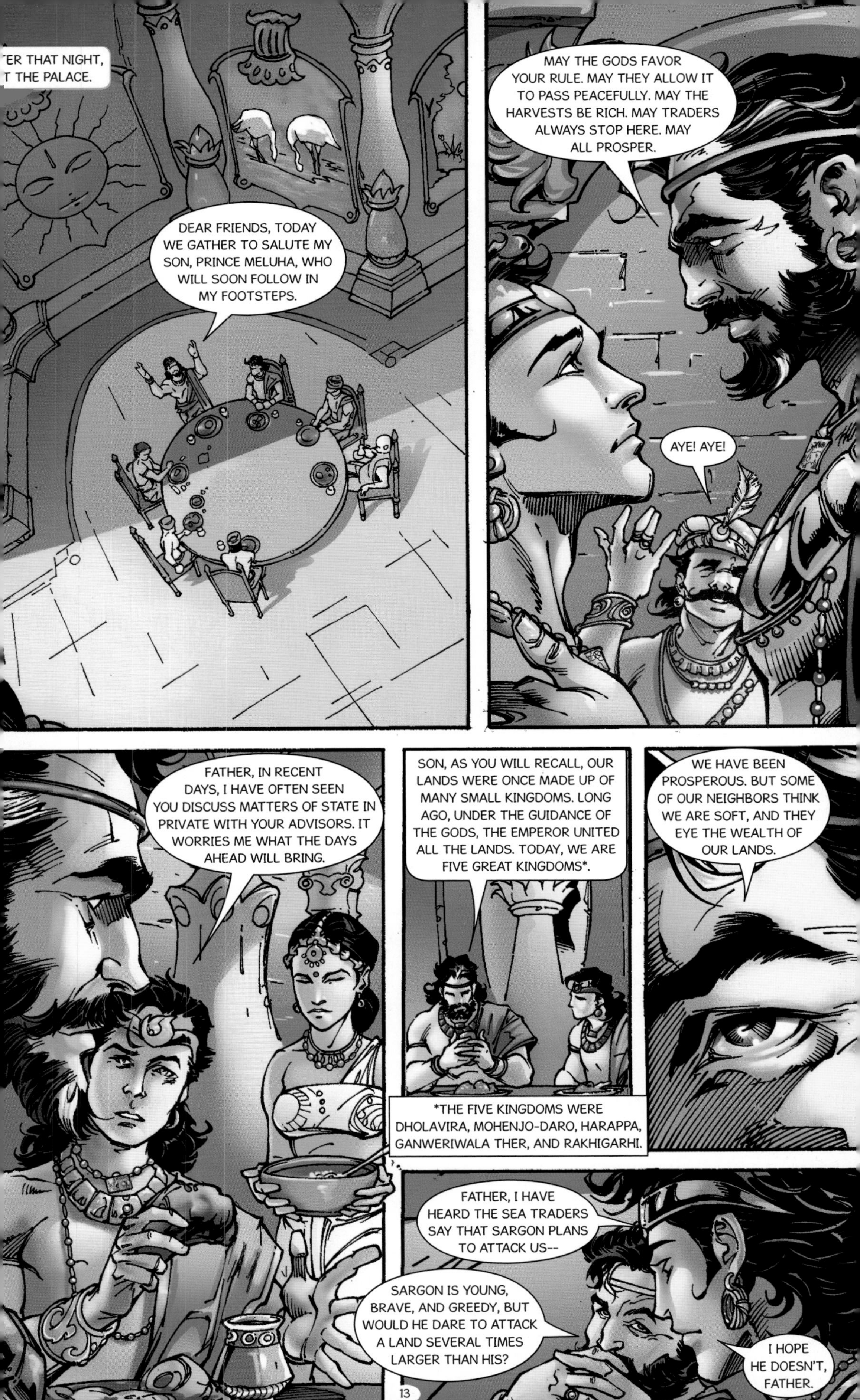

'ER THAT NIGHT, T THE PALACE.
DEAR FRIENDS, TODAY WE GATHER TO SALUTE MY SON, PRINCE MELUHA, WHO WILL SOON FOLLOW IN MY FOOTSTEPS.
MAY THE GODS FAVOR YOUR RULE. MAY THEY ALLOW IT TO PASS PEACEFULLY. MAY THE HARVESTS BE RICH. MAY TRADERS ALWAYS STOP HERE. MAY ALL PROSPER.
AYE! AYE!
FATHER, IN RECENT DAYS, I HAVE OFTEN SEEN YOU DISCUSS MATTERS OF STATE IN PRIVATE WITH YOUR ADVISORS. IT WORRIES ME WHAT THE DAYS AHEAD WILL BRING.
SON, AS YOU WILL RECALL, OUR LANDS WERE ONCE MADE UP OF MANY SMALL KINGDOMS. LONG AGO, UNDER THE GUIDANCE OF THE GODS, THE EMPEROR UNITED ALL THE LANDS. TODAY, WE ARE FIVE GREAT KINGDOMS*.
*THE FIVE KINGDOMS WERE DHOLAVIRA, MOHENJO-DARO, HARAPPA, GANWERIWALA THER, AND RAKHIGARHI.
WE HAVE BEEN PROSPEROUS. BUT SOME OF OUR NEIGHBORS THINK WE ARE SOFT, AND THEY EYE THE WEALTH OF OUR LANDS.
FATHER, I HAVE HEARD THE SEA TRADERS SAY THAT SARGON PLANS TO ATTACK US--
SARGON IS YOUNG, BRAVE, AND GREEDY, BUT WOULD HE DARE TO ATTACK A LAND SEVERAL TIMES LARGER THAN HIS?
I HOPE HE DOESN'T, FATHER.

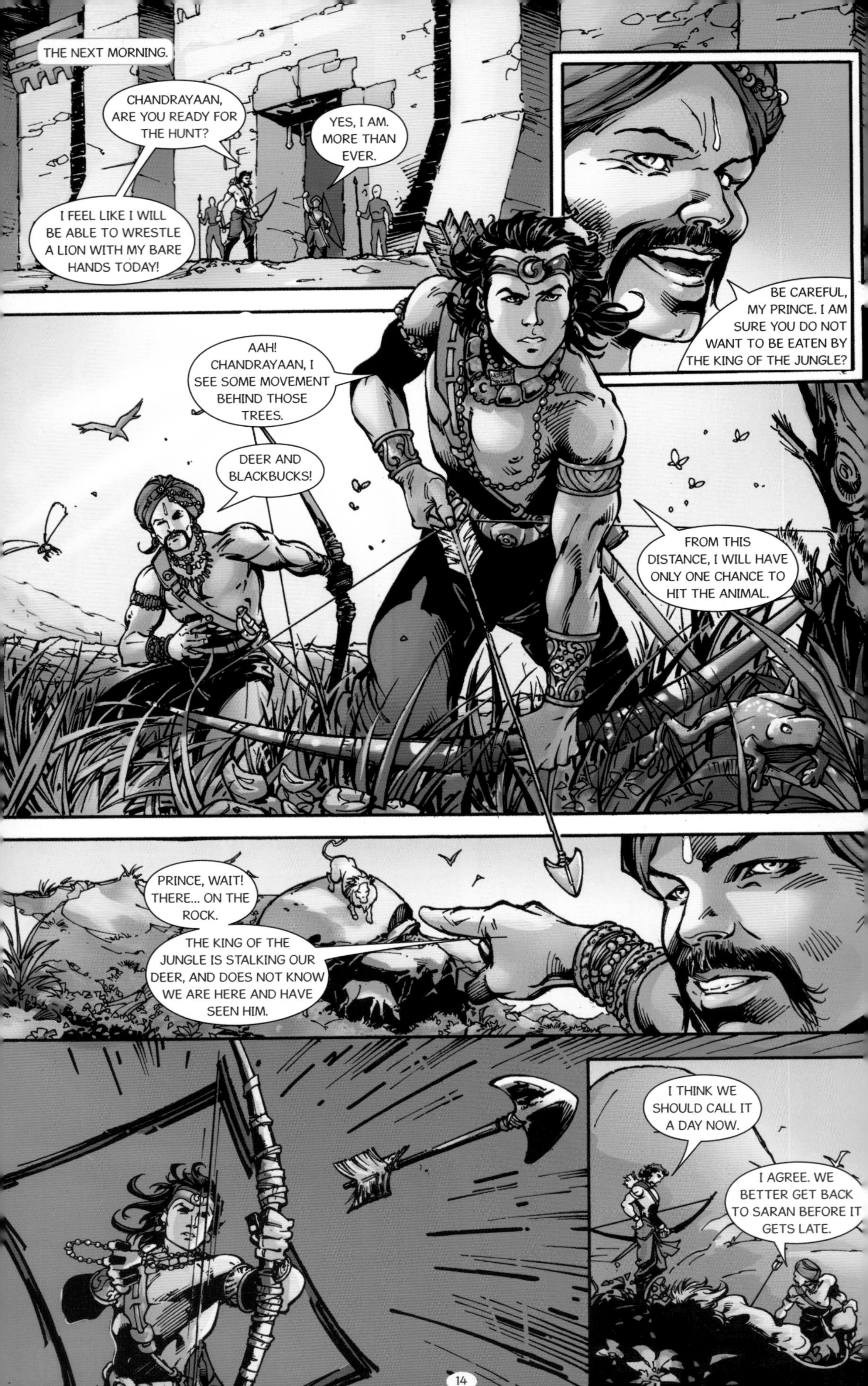
THE NEXT MORNING.
CHANDRAYAAN, ARE YOU READY FOR THE HUNT?
I FEEL LIKE I WILL BE ABLE TO WRESTLE A LION WITH MY BARE HANDS TODAY!
YES, I AM. MORE THAN EVER.
BE CAREFUL, MY PRINCE. I AM SURE YOU DO NOT WANT TO BE EATEN BY THE KING OF THE JUNGLE?
AAH! CHANDRAYAAN, I SEE SOME MOVEMENT BEHIND THOSE TREES.
DEER AND BLACKBUCKS!
FROM THIS DISTANCE, I WILL HAVE ONLY ONE CHANCE TO HIT THE ANIMAL.
PRINCE, WAIT! THERE... ON THE ROCK.
THE KING OF THE JUNGLE IS STALKING OUR DEER, AND DOES NOT KNOW WE ARE HERE AND HAVE SEEN HIM.
I THINK WE SHOULD CALL IT A DAY NOW.
I AGREE. WE BETTER GET BACK TO SARAN BEFORE IT GETS LATE.

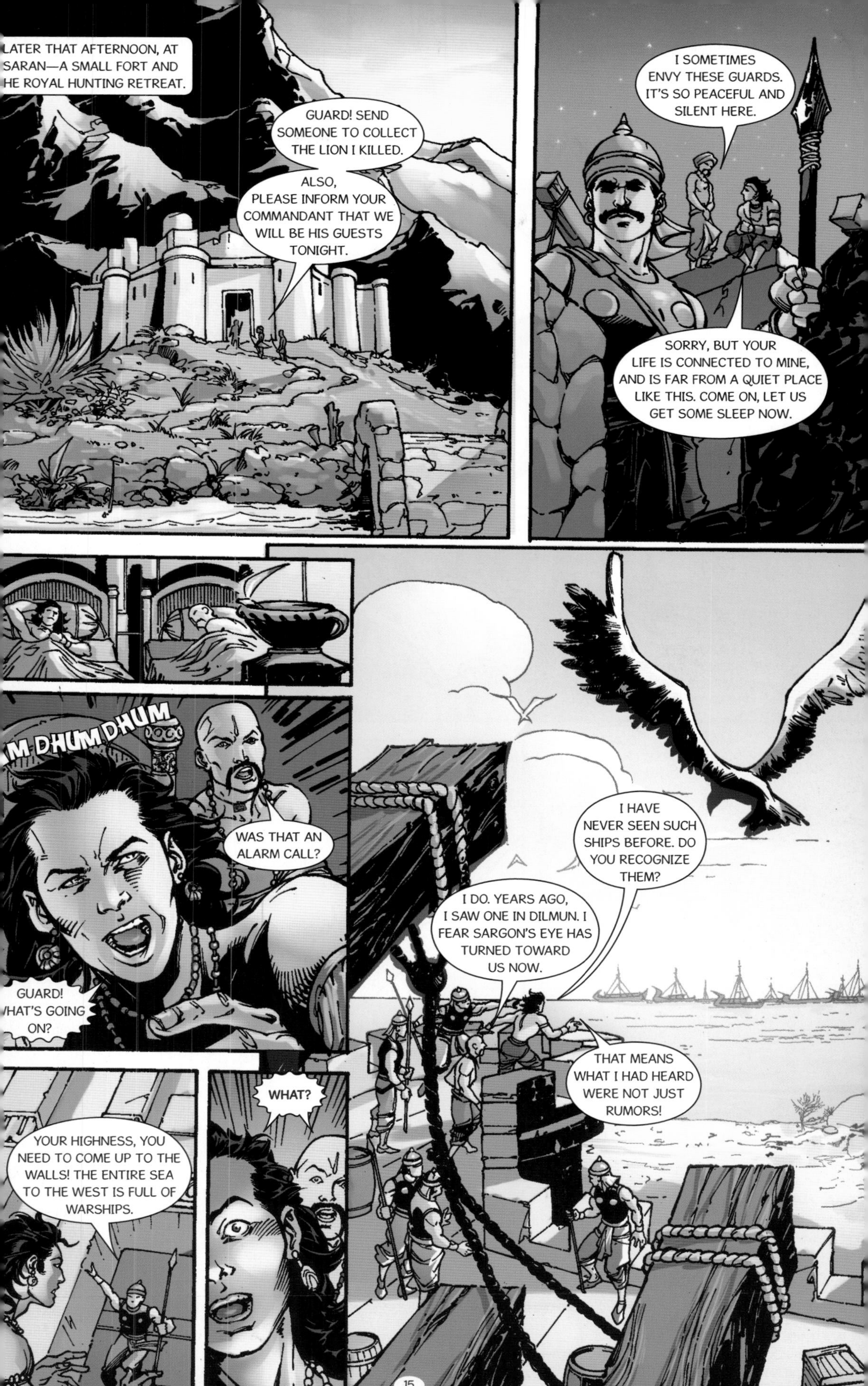
LATER THAT AFTERNOON, AT SARAN—A SMALL FORT AND HE ROYAL HUNTING RETREAT.
GUARD! SEND SOMEONE TO COLLECT THE LION I KILLED.
ALSO, PLEASE INFORM YOUR COMMANDANT THAT WE WILL BE HIS GUESTS TONIGHT.
I SOMETIMES ENVY THESE GUARDS. IT'S SO PEACEFUL AND SILENT HERE.
SORRY, BUT YOUR LIFE IS CONNECTED TO MINE, AND IS FAR FROM A QUIET PLACE LIKE THIS. COME ON, LET US GET SOME SLEEP NOW.
M DHUM DHUM
WAS THAT AN ALARM CALL?
GUARD! HAT'S GOING ON?
YOUR HIGHNESS, YOU NEED TO COME UP TO THE WALLS! THE ENTIRE SEA TO THE WEST IS FULL OF WARSHIPS.
WHAT?
I HAVE NEVER SEEN SUCH SHIPS BEFORE. DO YOU RECOGNIZE THEM?
I DO. YEARS AGO, I SAW ONE IN DILMUN. I FEAR SARGON'S EYE HAS TURNED TOWARD US NOW.
THAT MEANS WHAT I HAD HEARD WERE NOT JUST RUMORS!

WE NEED TO GET BACK TO DHOLAVIRA. THEY WILL NEED ALL THE HELP THEY CAN GET.

GUARDS, REMAIN ON ALERT TILL WE RETURN WITH HELP.

LET US FOLLOW THIS DRY RIVERBED. IT LEADS RIGHT TO THE CITY WALLS. IF WE FOLLOW THIS PATH, WE SHOULD BE THERE IN TIME TO SAVE OUR PEOPLE.

WE HAVE TO LEAVE IMMEDIATELY THEN, BEFORE THE AKKADIANS SURROUND THE CITY.

I JUST HOPE WE ARE NOT TOO LATE, AND CAN SLIP PAST THE ENEMY GUARDS.

CAMELS AND SOLDIERS! THIS IS AN OUTRIGHT INVASION!

DON'T WORRY, CHANDRAYAAN. DHOLAVIRA HAS STRONG WALLS! THEY WILL NOT BE ABLE TO BREAK IN THAT EASILY.

I THINK IT WOUL' BE BEST IF WE (BACK TO SARA? AND COME UP V ANOTHER PLAN BEFORE MORE TROOPS ARRIVE WE ARE CUT OF

I FEAR THE CITY IS SURROUNDED AND WE WILL NOT BE ABLE TO GET IN.

WE CAN TRY AND SEE IF THERE IS ANOTHER WAY IN, BUT I THINK YOU WILL BE PROVEN RIGHT.

EVEN IF WE CAN GET THROUGH BY SOME MIRACLE OF THE GODS, THEY WILL NEVER BE ABLE TO OPEN THE GATES FOR US BEFORE WE ARE SPOTTED AND KILLED.

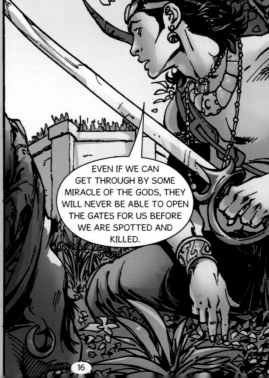

YOU ARE RIGHT. LET'S GO.

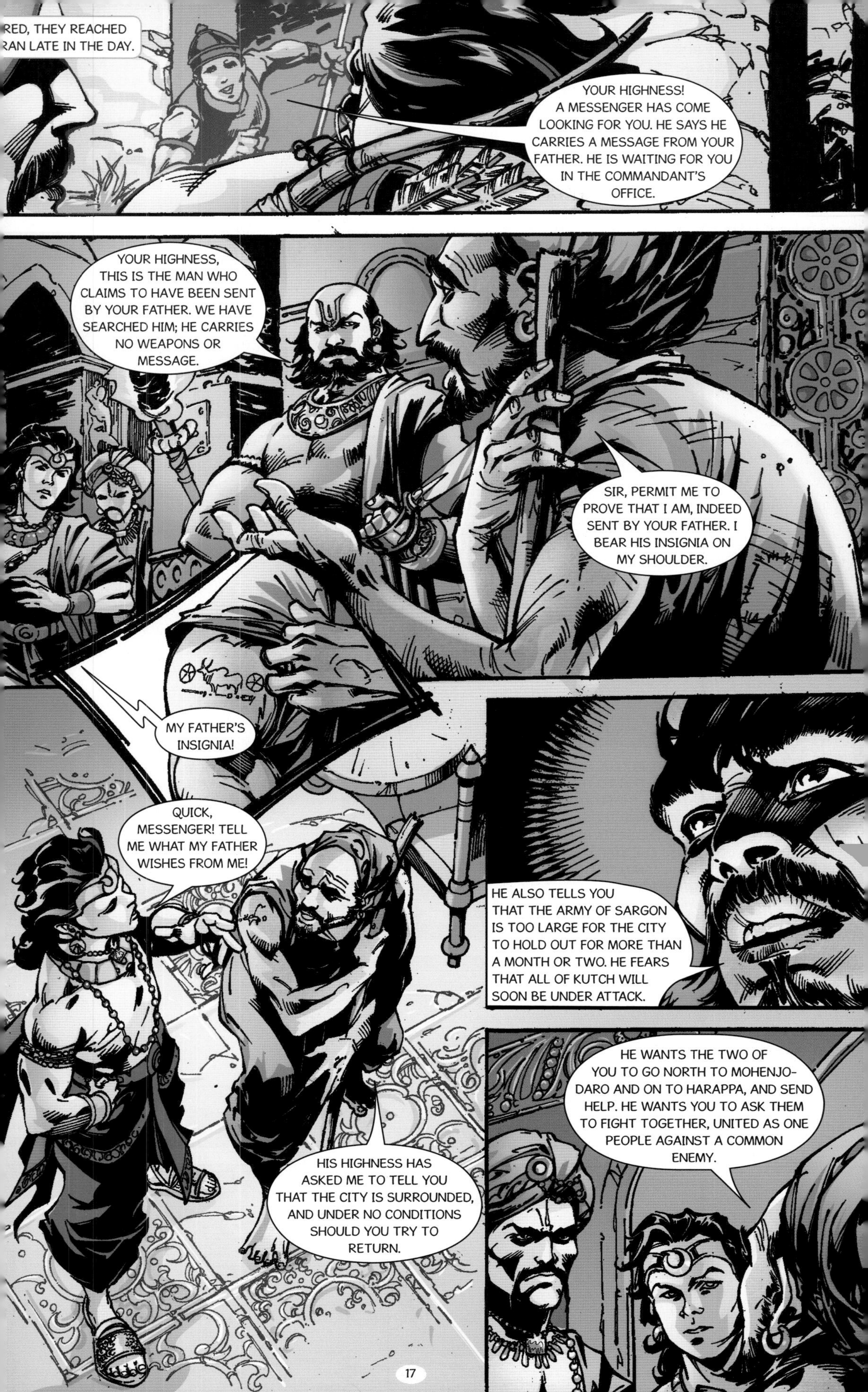

RED, THEY REACHED
RAN LATE IN THE DAY.
YOUR HIGHNESS! A MESSENGER HAS COME LOOKING FOR YOU. HE SAYS HE CARRIES A MESSAGE FROM YOUR FATHER. HE IS WAITING FOR YOU IN THE COMMANDANT'S OFFICE.
YOUR HIGHNESS, THIS IS THE MAN WHO CLAIMS TO HAVE BEEN SENT BY YOUR FATHER. WE HAVE SEARCHED HIM; HE CARRIES NO WEAPONS OR MESSAGE.
SIR, PERMIT ME TO PROVE THAT I AM, INDEED SENT BY YOUR FATHER. I BEAR HIS INSIGNIA ON MY SHOULDER.
MY FATHER'S INSIGNIA!
QUICK, MESSENGER! TELL ME WHAT MY FATHER WISHES FROM ME!
HIS HIGHNESS HAS ASKED ME TO TELL YOU THAT THE CITY IS SURROUNDED, AND UNDER NO CONDITIONS SHOULD YOU TRY TO RETURN.
HE ALSO TELLS YOU THAT THE ARMY OF SARGON IS TOO LARGE FOR THE CITY TO HOLD OUT FOR MORE THAN A MONTH OR TWO. HE FEARS THAT ALL OF KUTCH WILL SOON BE UNDER ATTACK.
HE WANTS THE TWO OF YOU TO GO NORTH TO MOHENJO-DARO AND ON TO HARAPPA, AND SEND HELP. HE WANTS YOU TO ASK THEM TO FIGHT TOGETHER, UNITED AS ONE PEOPLE AGAINST A COMMON ENEMY.

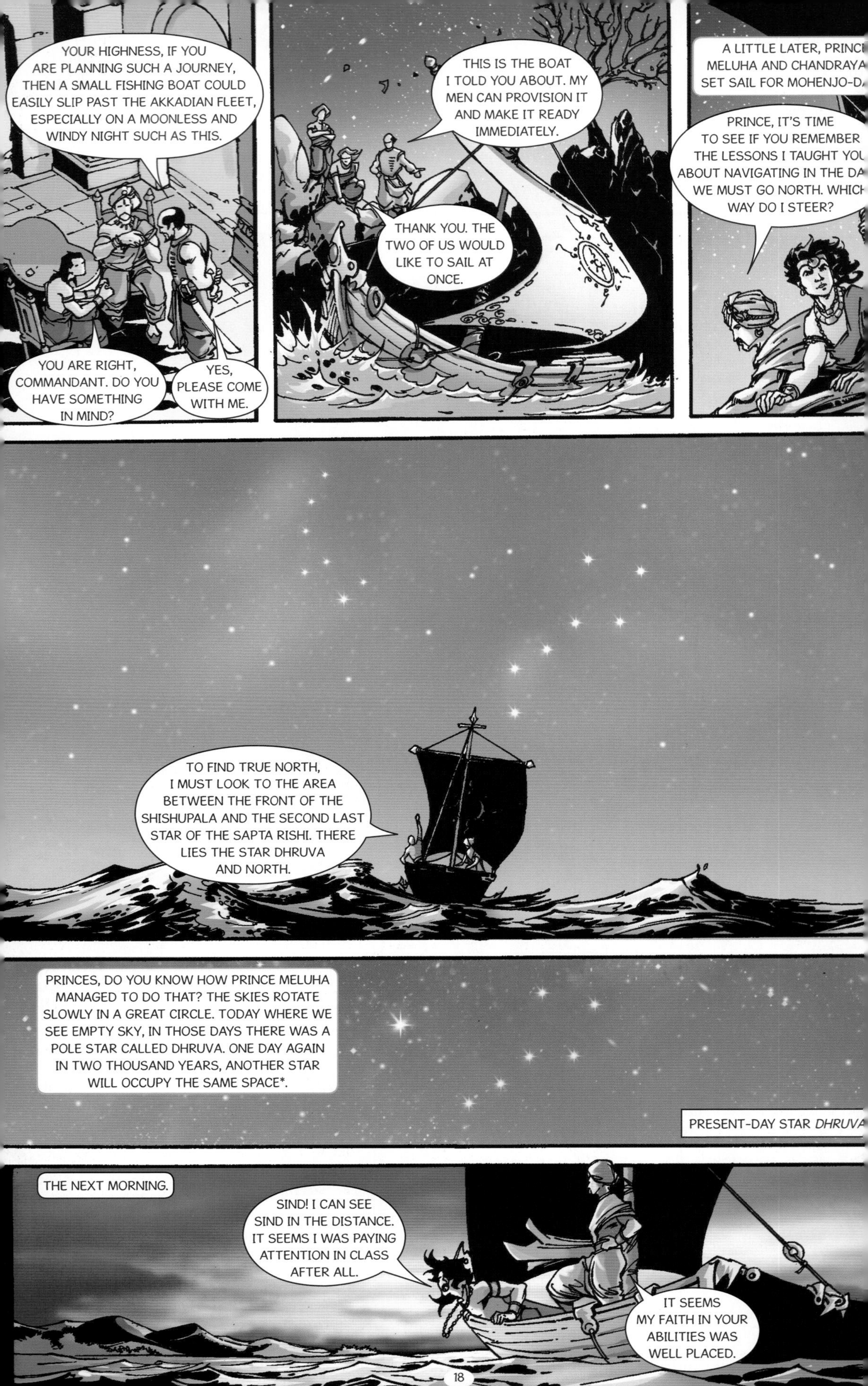
YOUR HIGHNESS, IF YOU ARE PLANNING SUCH A JOURNEY, THEN A SMALL FISHING BOAT COULD EASILY SLIP PAST THE AKKADIAN FLEET, ESPECIALLY ON A MOONLESS AND WINDY NIGHT SUCH AS THIS.
YOU ARE RIGHT, COMMANDANT. DO YOU HAVE SOMETHING IN MIND?
YES, PLEASE COME WITH ME.
THIS IS THE BOAT I TOLD YOU ABOUT. MY MEN CAN PROVISION IT AND MAKE IT READY IMMEDIATELY.
THANK YOU. THE TWO OF US WOULD LIKE TO SAIL AT ONCE.
PRINCE, IT'S TIME TO SEE IF YOU REMEMBER THE LESSONS I TAUGHT YOU ABOUT NAVIGATING IN THE DA WE MUST GO NORTH. WHICH WAY DO I STEER?
TO FIND TRUE NORTH, I MUST LOOK TO THE AREA BETWEEN THE FRONT OF THE SHISHUPALA AND THE SECOND LAST STAR OF THE SAPTA RISHI. THERE LIES THE STAR DHRUVA AND NORTH.
PRINCES, DO YOU KNOW HOW PRINCE MELUHA MANAGED TO DO THAT? THE SKIES ROTATE SLOWLY IN A GREAT CIRCLE. TODAY WHERE WE SEE EMPTY SKY, IN THOSE DAYS THERE WAS A POLE STAR CALLED DHRUVA. ONE DAY AGAIN IN TWO THOUSAND YEARS, ANOTHER STAR WILL OCCUPY THE SAME SPACE*.
PRESENT-DAY STAR *DHRUVA*
THE NEXT MORNING.
SIND! I CAN SEE SIND IN THE DISTANCE. IT SEEMS I WAS PAYING ATTENTION IN CLASS AFTER ALL.
IT SEEMS MY FAITH IN YOUR ABILITIES WAS WELL PLACED.

THERE, PRINCE, IS THE ~~TERNMOST~~ BRANCH OF THE ~~OHU'S~~ DELTA. WE WILL SAIL ~~UP~~ THIS CHANNEL UNTIL WE ~~E~~ TO THE MAIN RIVER. THEN ~~WE~~ WILL MOVE TO LAL DARO, THE FORT THAT CONTROLS ACCESS TO SIND.

LET US STOP HERE AND WALK THE REST OF THE WAY.

WHY? DO YOU SUSPECT TROUBLE?

LAL DARO'S IMPORTANCE IS WELL KNOWN. WHO KNOWS WHAT LIES AHEAD? OUR ENEMY IS BOUND TO HAVE PEOPLE WATCHING THIS AREA.

BE ON YOUR GUARD. ~~THE~~ LAST TIME I WAS HERE, ~~THIS~~ AREA WAS TEEMING WITH ~~FISH~~ERMEN. TODAY THERE IS ~~N~~OBODY. SOMETHING IS DEFINITELY AMISS.

SMOKE! LOTS OF IT! YOUR CAUTION, IT SEEMS, WAS WELL WARRANTED!

~~L~~AL DARO HAS FALLEN TO ~~DRA~~GON'S FORCES. I FEAR THE ~~GAT~~ES OF OUR LAND ARE NOW ~~WI~~DE OPEN FOR THE ENEMY TO ENTER AT WILL.

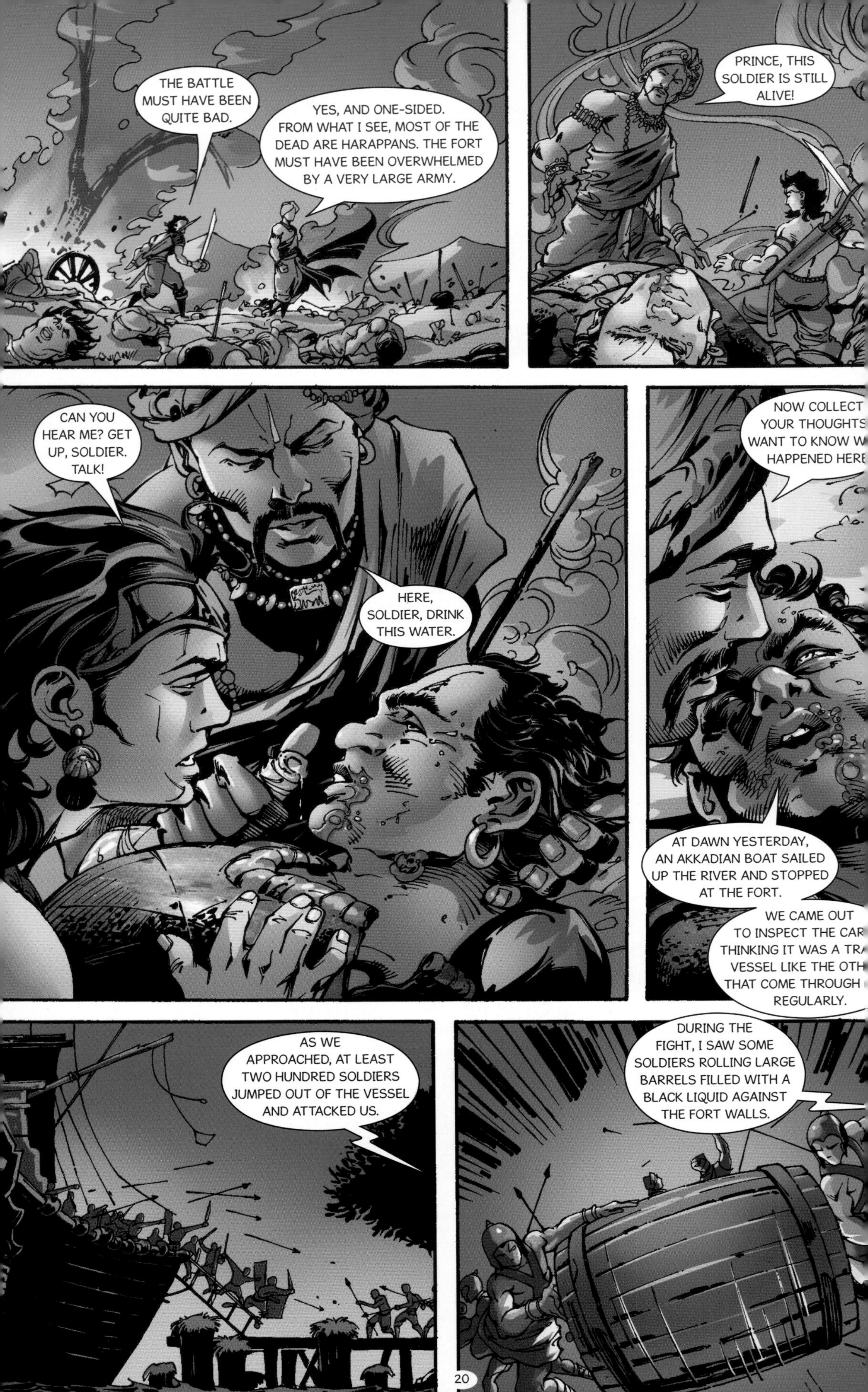
THE BATTLE MUST HAVE BEEN QUITE BAD.
YES, AND ONE-SIDED. FROM WHAT I SEE, MOST OF THE DEAD ARE HARAPPANS. THE FORT MUST HAVE BEEN OVERWHELMED BY A VERY LARGE ARMY.
PRINCE, THIS SOLDIER IS STILL ALIVE!
CAN YOU HEAR ME? GET UP, SOLDIER. TALK!
HERE, SOLDIER, DRINK THIS WATER.
NOW COLLECT YOUR THOUGHTS WANT TO KNOW W HAPPENED HERE
AT DAWN YESTERDAY, AN AKKADIAN BOAT SAILED UP THE RIVER AND STOPPED AT THE FORT.
WE CAME OUT TO INSPECT THE CAR THINKING IT WAS A TR VESSEL LIKE THE OTH THAT COME THROUGH REGULARLY.
AS WE APPROACHED, AT LEAST TWO HUNDRED SOLDIERS JUMPED OUT OF THE VESSEL AND ATTACKED US.
DURING THE FIGHT, I SAW SOME SOLDIERS ROLLING LARGE BARRELS FILLED WITH A BLACK LIQUID AGAINST THE FORT WALLS.

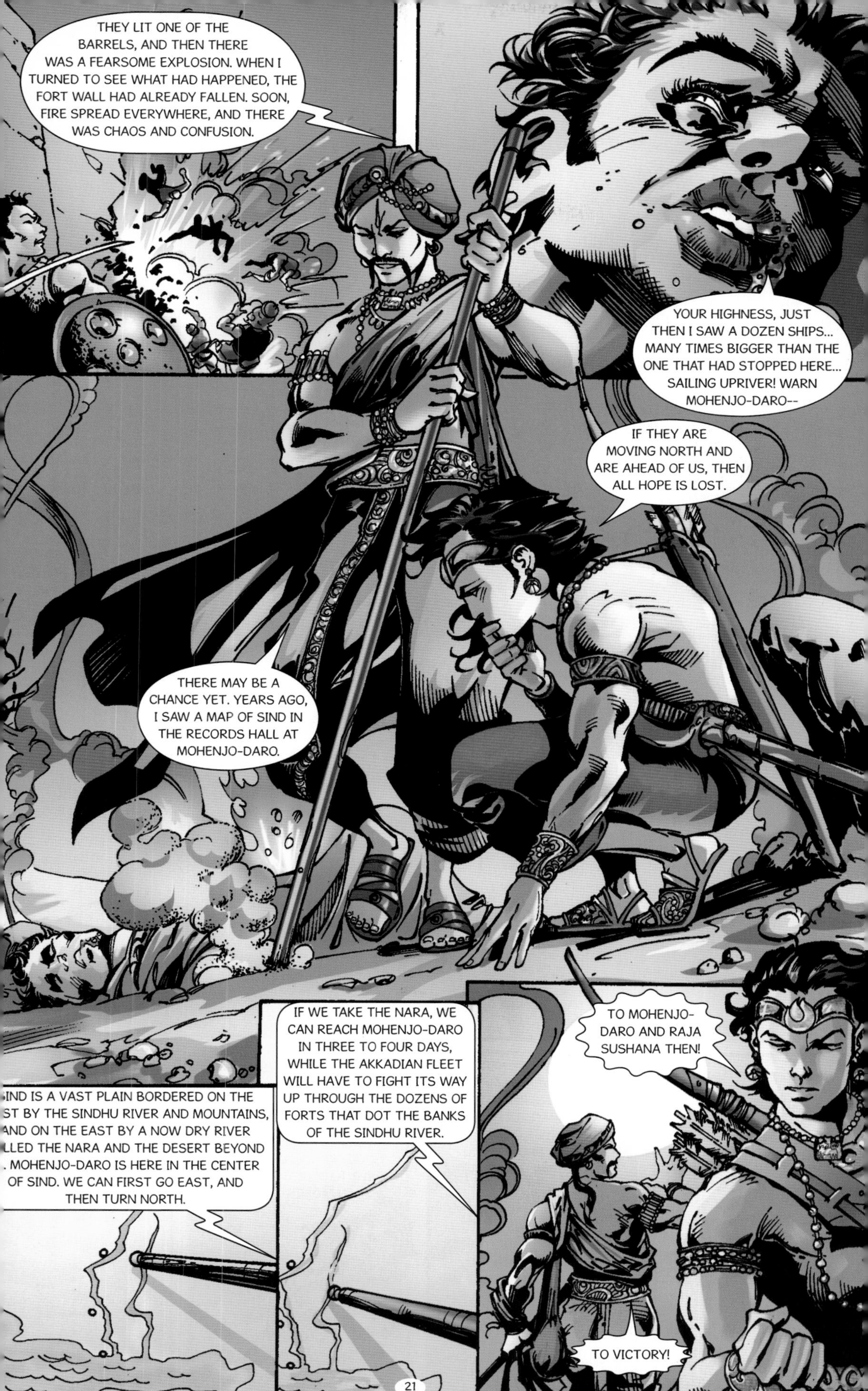
THEY LIT ONE OF THE BARRELS, AND THEN THERE WAS A FEARSOME EXPLOSION. WHEN I TURNED TO SEE WHAT HAD HAPPENED, THE FORT WALL HAD ALREADY FALLEN. SOON, FIRE SPREAD EVERYWHERE, AND THERE WAS CHAOS AND CONFUSION.
YOUR HIGHNESS, JUST THEN I SAW A DOZEN SHIPS... MANY TIMES BIGGER THAN THE ONE THAT HAD STOPPED HERE... SAILING UPRIVER! WARN MOHENJO-DARO--
IF THEY ARE MOVING NORTH AND ARE AHEAD OF US, THEN ALL HOPE IS LOST.
THERE MAY BE A CHANCE YET. YEARS AGO, I SAW A MAP OF SIND IN THE RECORDS HALL AT MOHENJO-DARO.
IND IS A VAST PLAIN BORDERED ON THE ST BY THE SINDHU RIVER AND MOUNTAINS, AND ON THE EAST BY A NOW DRY RIVER LLED THE NARA AND THE DESERT BEYOND . MOHENJO-DARO IS HERE IN THE CENTER OF SIND. WE CAN FIRST GO EAST, AND THEN TURN NORTH.
IF WE TAKE THE NARA, WE CAN REACH MOHENJO-DARO IN THREE TO FOUR DAYS, WHILE THE AKKADIAN FLEET WILL HAVE TO FIGHT ITS WAY UP THROUGH THE DOZENS OF FORTS THAT DOT THE BANKS OF THE SINDHU RIVER.
TO MOHENJO-DARO AND RAJA SUSHANA THEN!
TO VICTORY!

LOOK! THERE IS SOMEONE OVER THERE WITH A BULLOCK CART!

IT LOOKS LIKE A TRADER'S CART. LET US SEE IF THE TRADER CAN HELP US.

WHO ARE YOU? IF YOU WANT ANYTHING, YOU ARE TOO LATE. THE AKKADIANS TOOK EVERYTHING OF VALUE I HAD. ALL I HAVE NOW IS MY LIFE... TAKE IT IF YOU WANT!

WHEN DID THIS HAPPEN, AND IN WHICH DIRECTION DID THEY GO?

THIS HAPPENED YESTERDAY. THEY WENT UPRIVER AFTER LOOTING THE FORT AND SETTING IT ON FIRE. I CURSE THE DAY I DECIDED TO STOP AT LAL DARO FOR THE NIGHT INSTEAD OF GOING ON AS I HAD PLANNED!

NOW I AM STUCK HERE. THE ROAD UPRIVER TO MY HOME WILL LEAD ME RIGHT TO THE AKKADIAN FLEET. WORSE STILL, I HAVE NO GOLD LEFT TO BUY PROVISIONS.

PERHAPS THIS WILL SOOTHE YOUR PAIN...

...BUT THIS IS ONLY IN RETURN FOR YOUR TRANSPORT. WE NEED TO GO NORTH TO GET HELP TO DEFEAT THE INVADERS.

AND SO, OUR ADVENTUR[ERS] RODE AWAY, WITH THE S[UN] SHINING DOWN BRIGHT[LY] UPON THEM WITH HOP[E]

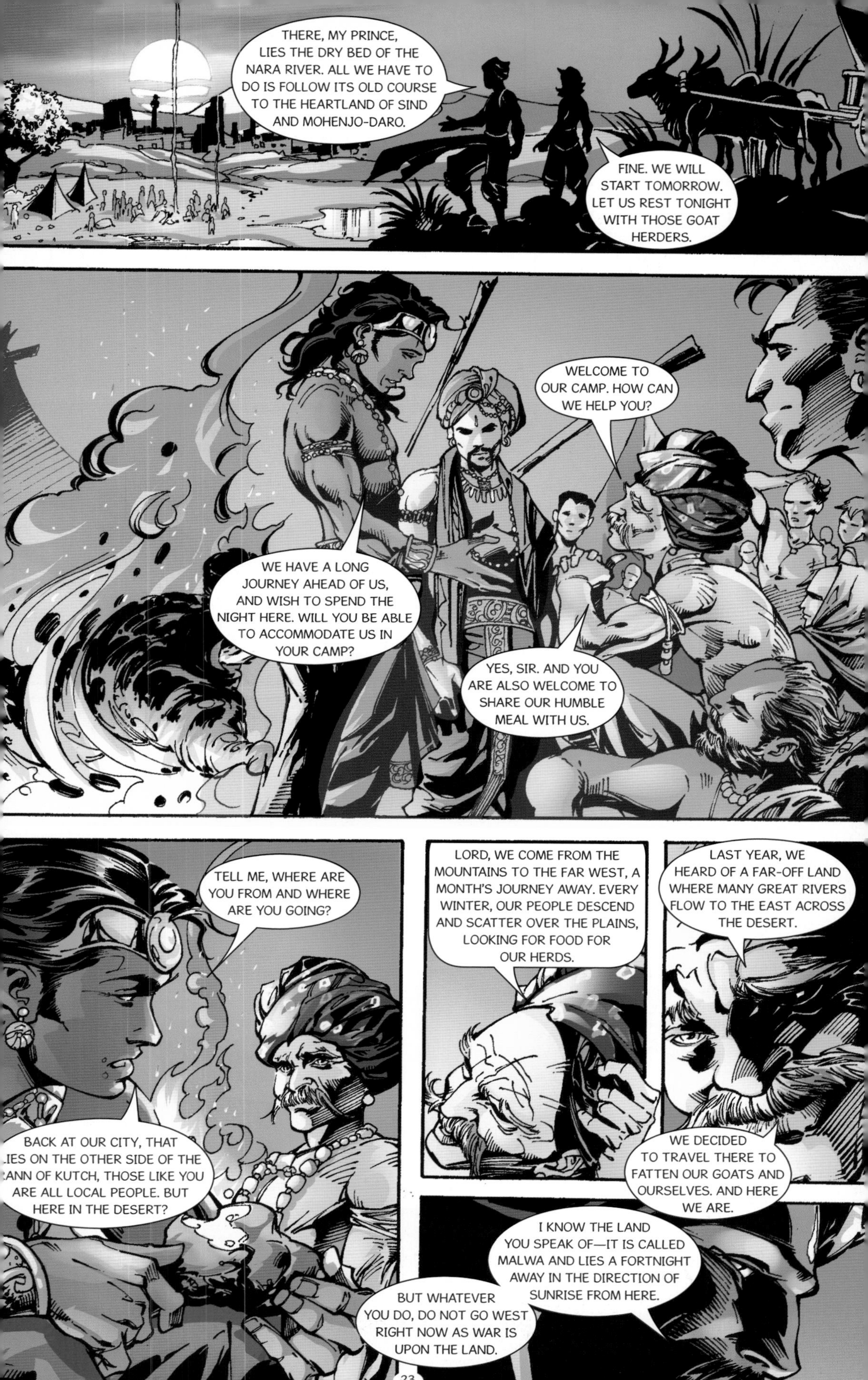
THERE, MY PRINCE, LIES THE DRY BED OF THE NARA RIVER. ALL WE HAVE TO DO IS FOLLOW ITS OLD COURSE TO THE HEARTLAND OF SIND AND MOHENJO-DARO.
FINE. WE WILL START TOMORROW. LET US REST TONIGHT WITH THOSE GOAT HERDERS.
WELCOME TO OUR CAMP. HOW CAN WE HELP YOU?
WE HAVE A LONG JOURNEY AHEAD OF US, AND WISH TO SPEND THE NIGHT HERE. WILL YOU BE ABLE TO ACCOMMODATE US IN YOUR CAMP?
YES, SIR. AND YOU ARE ALSO WELCOME TO SHARE OUR HUMBLE MEAL WITH US.
TELL ME, WHERE ARE YOU FROM AND WHERE ARE YOU GOING?
BACK AT OUR CITY, THAT LIES ON THE OTHER SIDE OF THE RANN OF KUTCH, THOSE LIKE YOU ARE ALL LOCAL PEOPLE. BUT HERE IN THE DESERT?
LORD, WE COME FROM THE MOUNTAINS TO THE FAR WEST, A MONTH'S JOURNEY AWAY. EVERY WINTER, OUR PEOPLE DESCEND AND SCATTER OVER THE PLAINS, LOOKING FOR FOOD FOR OUR HERDS.
LAST YEAR, WE HEARD OF A FAR-OFF LAND WHERE MANY GREAT RIVERS FLOW TO THE EAST ACROSS THE DESERT.
WE DECIDED TO TRAVEL THERE TO FATTEN OUR GOATS AND OURSELVES. AND HERE WE ARE.
I KNOW THE LAND YOU SPEAK OF—IT IS CALLED MALWA AND LIES A FORTNIGHT AWAY IN THE DIRECTION OF SUNRISE FROM HERE.
BUT WHATEVER YOU DO, DO NOT GO WEST RIGHT NOW AS WAR IS UPON THE LAND.

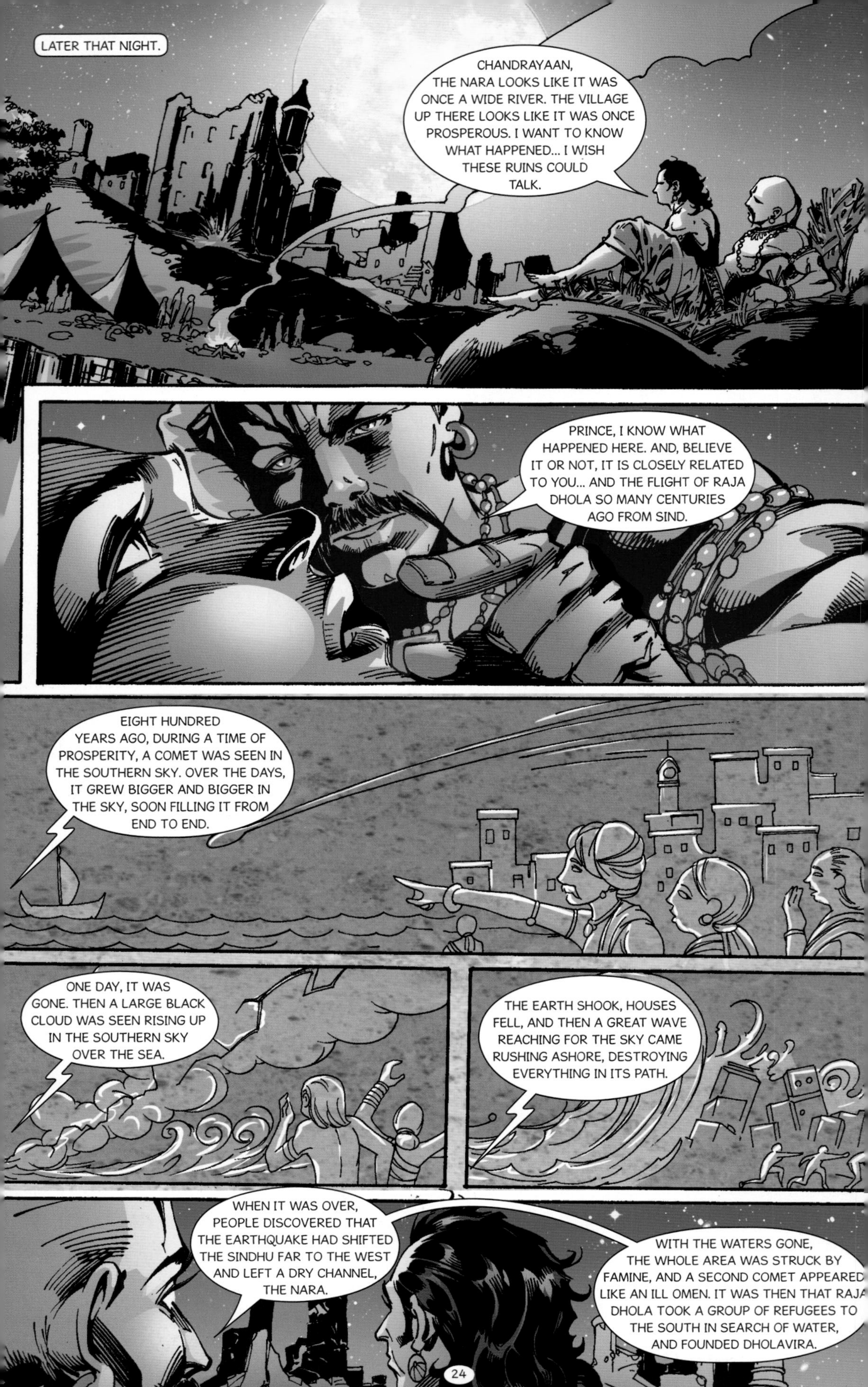
LATER THAT NIGHT.
CHANDRAYAAN, THE NARA LOOKS LIKE IT WAS ONCE A WIDE RIVER. THE VILLAGE UP THERE LOOKS LIKE IT WAS ONCE PROSPEROUS. I WANT TO KNOW WHAT HAPPENED... I WISH THESE RUINS COULD TALK.
PRINCE, I KNOW WHAT HAPPENED HERE. AND, BELIEVE IT OR NOT, IT IS CLOSELY RELATED TO YOU... AND THE FLIGHT OF RAJA DHOLA SO MANY CENTURIES AGO FROM SIND.
EIGHT HUNDRED YEARS AGO, DURING A TIME OF PROSPERITY, A COMET WAS SEEN IN THE SOUTHERN SKY. OVER THE DAYS, IT GREW BIGGER AND BIGGER IN THE SKY, SOON FILLING IT FROM END TO END.
ONE DAY, IT WAS GONE. THEN A LARGE BLACK CLOUD WAS SEEN RISING UP IN THE SOUTHERN SKY OVER THE SEA.
THE EARTH SHOOK, HOUSES FELL, AND THEN A GREAT WAVE REACHING FOR THE SKY CAME RUSHING ASHORE, DESTROYING EVERYTHING IN ITS PATH.
WHEN IT WAS OVER, PEOPLE DISCOVERED THAT THE EARTHQUAKE HAD SHIFTED THE SINDHU FAR TO THE WEST AND LEFT A DRY CHANNEL, THE NARA.
WITH THE WATERS GONE, THE WHOLE AREA WAS STRUCK BY FAMINE, AND A SECOND COMET APPEARED LIKE AN ILL OMEN. IT WAS THEN THAT RAJA DHOLA TOOK A GROUP OF REFUGEES TO THE SOUTH IN SEARCH OF WATER, AND FOUNDED DHOLAVIRA.

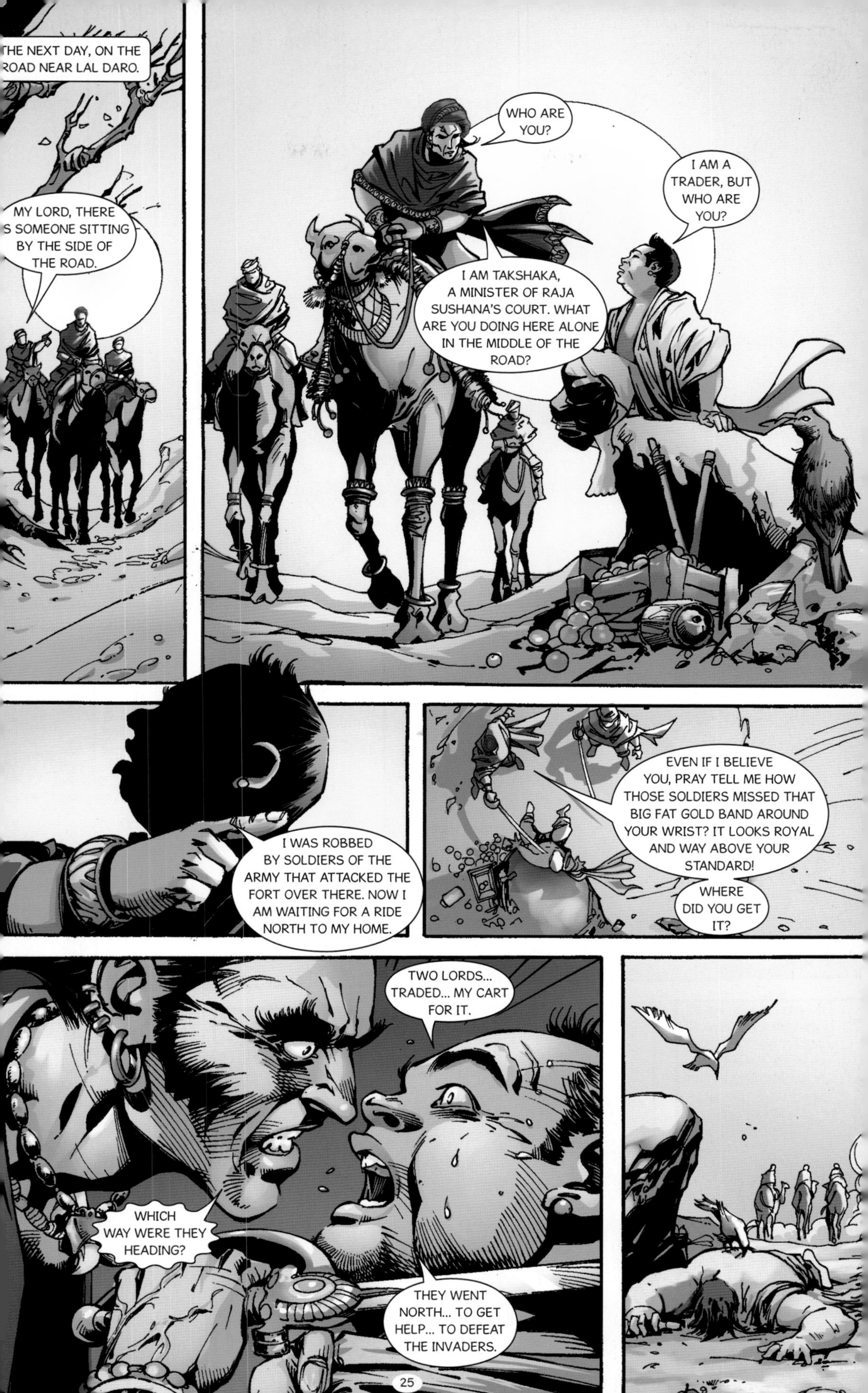
THE NEXT DAY, ON THE ROAD NEAR LAL DARO.
MY LORD, THERE IS SOMEONE SITTING BY THE SIDE OF THE ROAD.
WHO ARE YOU?
I AM A TRADER, BUT WHO ARE YOU?
I AM TAKSHAKA, A MINISTER OF RAJA SUSHANA'S COURT. WHAT ARE YOU DOING HERE ALONE IN THE MIDDLE OF THE ROAD?
I WAS ROBBED BY SOLDIERS OF THE ARMY THAT ATTACKED THE FORT OVER THERE. NOW I AM WAITING FOR A RIDE NORTH TO MY HOME.
EVEN IF I BELIEVE YOU, PRAY TELL ME HOW THOSE SOLDIERS MISSED THAT BIG FAT GOLD BAND AROUND YOUR WRIST? IT LOOKS ROYAL AND WAY ABOVE YOUR STANDARD!
WHERE DID YOU GET IT?
TWO LORDS... TRADED... MY CART FOR IT.
WHICH WAY WERE THEY HEADING?
THEY WENT NORTH... TO GET HELP... TO DEFEAT THE INVADERS.

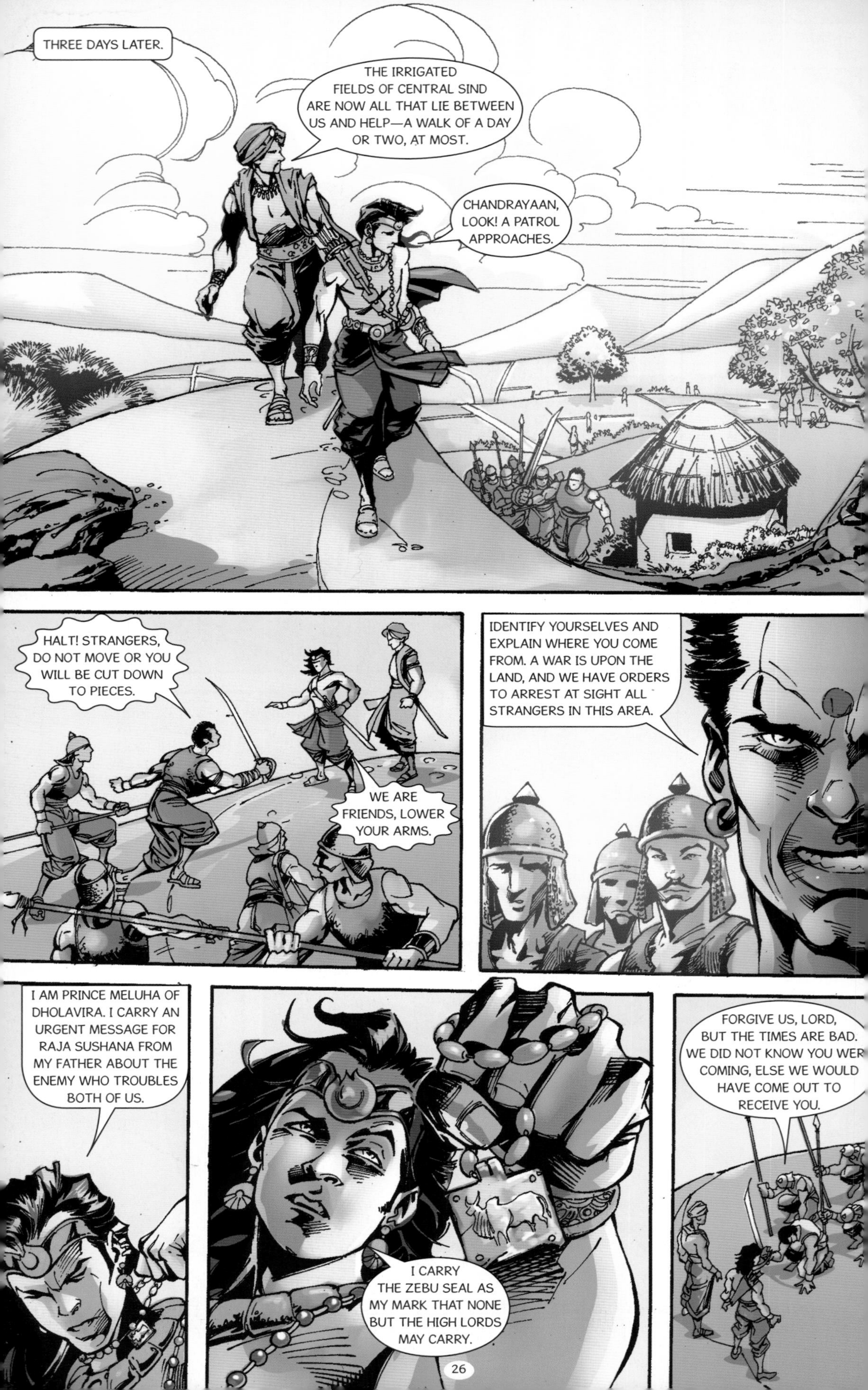

THREE DAYS LATER.
THE IRRIGATED FIELDS OF CENTRAL SIND ARE NOW ALL THAT LIE BETWEEN US AND HELP—A WALK OF A DAY OR TWO, AT MOST.
CHANDRAYAAN, LOOK! A PATROL APPROACHES.
HALT! STRANGERS, DO NOT MOVE OR YOU WILL BE CUT DOWN TO PIECES.
WE ARE FRIENDS, LOWER YOUR ARMS.
IDENTIFY YOURSELVES AND EXPLAIN WHERE YOU COME FROM. A WAR IS UPON THE LAND, AND WE HAVE ORDERS TO ARREST AT SIGHT ALL STRANGERS IN THIS AREA.
I AM PRINCE MELUHA OF DHOLAVIRA. I CARRY AN URGENT MESSAGE FOR RAJA SUSHANA FROM MY FATHER ABOUT THE ENEMY WHO TROUBLES BOTH OF US.
I CARRY THE ZEBU SEAL AS MY MARK THAT NONE BUT THE HIGH LORDS MAY CARRY.
FORGIVE US, LORD, BUT THE TIMES ARE BAD. WE DID NOT KNOW YOU WER COMING, ELSE WE WOULD HAVE COME OUT TO RECEIVE YOU.

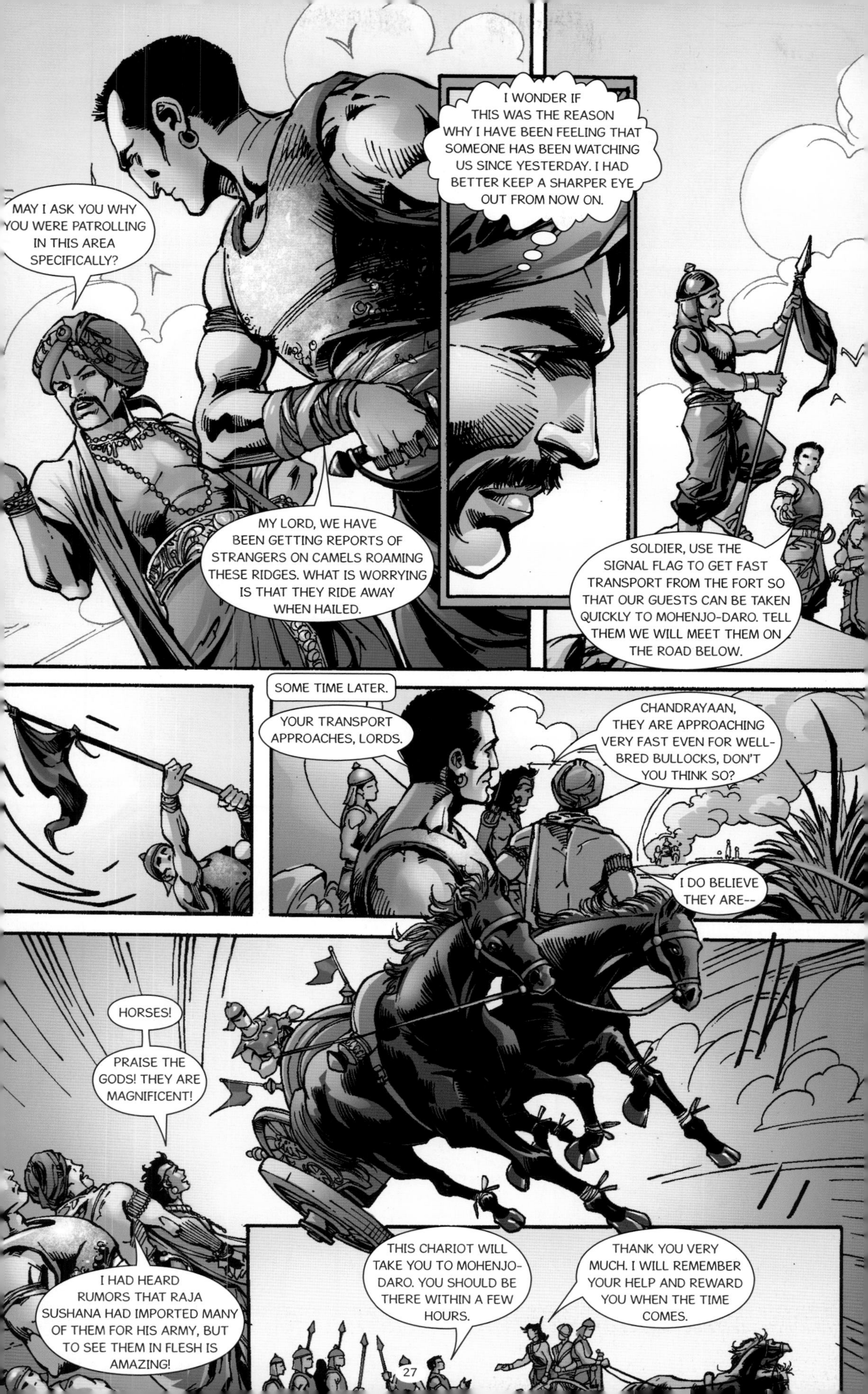
MAY I ASK YOU WHY YOU WERE PATROLLING IN THIS AREA SPECIFICALLY?
MY LORD, WE HAVE BEEN GETTING REPORTS OF STRANGERS ON CAMELS ROAMING THESE RIDGES. WHAT IS WORRYING IS THAT THEY RIDE AWAY WHEN HAILED.
I WONDER IF THIS WAS THE REASON WHY I HAVE BEEN FEELING THAT SOMEONE HAS BEEN WATCHING US SINCE YESTERDAY. I HAD BETTER KEEP A SHARPER EYE OUT FROM NOW ON.
SOLDIER, USE THE SIGNAL FLAG TO GET FAST TRANSPORT FROM THE FORT SO THAT OUR GUESTS CAN BE TAKEN QUICKLY TO MOHENJO-DARO. TELL THEM WE WILL MEET THEM ON THE ROAD BELOW.
SOME TIME LATER.
YOUR TRANSPORT APPROACHES, LORDS.
CHANDRAYAAN, THEY ARE APPROACHING VERY FAST EVEN FOR WELL-BRED BULLOCKS, DON'T YOU THINK SO?
I DO BELIEVE THEY ARE--
HORSES!
PRAISE THE GODS! THEY ARE MAGNIFICENT!
I HAD HEARD RUMORS THAT RAJA SUSHANA HAD IMPORTED MANY OF THEM FOR HIS ARMY, BUT TO SEE THEM IN FLESH IS AMAZING!
THIS CHARIOT WILL TAKE YOU TO MOHENJO-DARO. YOU SHOULD BE THERE WITHIN A FEW HOURS.
THANK YOU VERY MUCH. I WILL REMEMBER YOUR HELP AND REWARD YOU WHEN THE TIME COMES.

CHARIOTEER, TELL ME WHERE DO THESE HORSES COME FROM?

MY LORD, THEY HAVE BEEN COMING TO MOHENJO-DARO FOR THE LAST SIX MONTHS, AND ARE NOW BEING DISTRIBUTED ALL OVER OUR LAND TO BE USED AS A MEANS FOR FAST COMMUNICATION.

FROM THE LITTLE I KNOW, THEY ARE BEING BROUGHT TO US BY TRADERS, WHO WERE SENT OUT BY OUR KING TO THE LANDS THAT LIE NORTH OF ARIA.

IMAGINE AN ARMY OF THESE; THEY WOULD SWEEP OVER THE LAND! THE AKKADIANS WOULD BE SWEPT AWAY!

CHANDRAYAAN, THESE LANDS MUST BE FABULOUSLY RICH AND POWERFUL.

OUR LANDS ARE NOTHING LIKE THESE... WILL THEY EVEN LISTEN TO OUR PLEA FOR HELP?

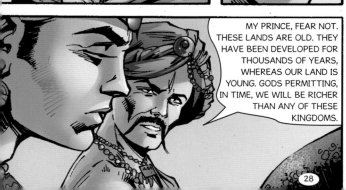

MY PRINCE, FEAR NOT. THESE LANDS ARE OLD. THEY HAVE BEEN DEVELOPED FOR THOUSANDS OF YEARS, WHEREAS OUR LAND IS YOUNG. GODS PERMITTING, IN TIME, WE WILL BE RICHER THAN ANY OF THESE KINGDOMS.

LOOK AROUND AND LEARN A LESSON TODAY...

EMPIRES BECOME RICH OVERNIGHT ONLY BY LOOTING OTHERS. RICH LANDS DEVELOP SLOWLY THROUGH HARD WORK AND PLANNING UNDER THE GUIDANCE OF GENERATIONS OF GREAT LEADERS.

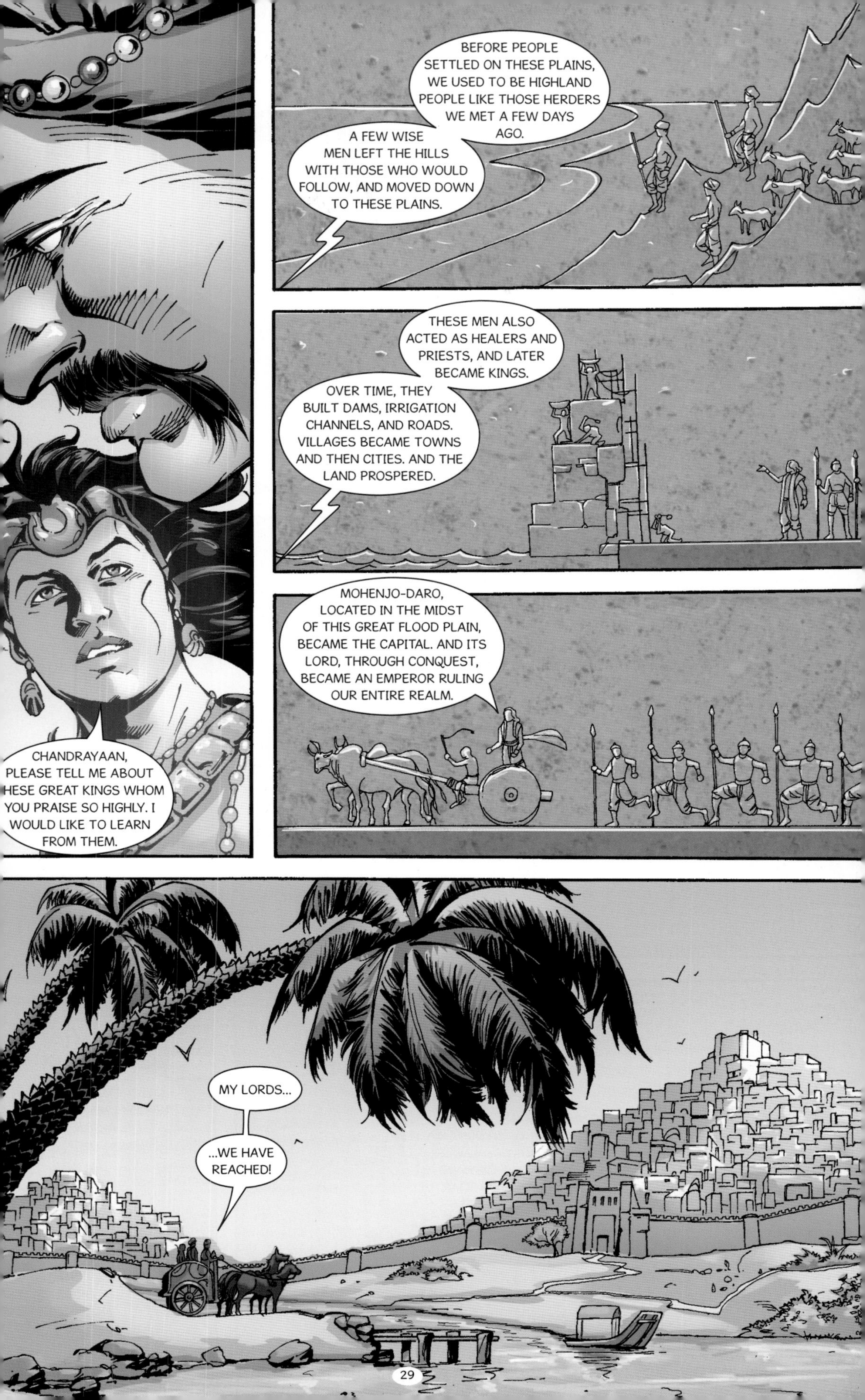
CHANDRAYAAN, PLEASE TELL ME ABOUT HESE GREAT KINGS WHOM YOU PRAISE SO HIGHLY. I WOULD LIKE TO LEARN FROM THEM.
BEFORE PEOPLE SETTLED ON THESE PLAINS, WE USED TO BE HIGHLAND PEOPLE LIKE THOSE HERDERS WE MET A FEW DAYS AGO.
A FEW WISE MEN LEFT THE HILLS WITH THOSE WHO WOULD FOLLOW, AND MOVED DOWN TO THESE PLAINS.
THESE MEN ALSO ACTED AS HEALERS AND PRIESTS, AND LATER BECAME KINGS.
OVER TIME, THEY BUILT DAMS, IRRIGATION CHANNELS, AND ROADS. VILLAGES BECAME TOWNS AND THEN CITIES. AND THE LAND PROSPERED.
MOHENJO-DARO, LOCATED IN THE MIDST OF THIS GREAT FLOOD PLAIN, BECAME THE CAPITAL. AND ITS LORD, THROUGH CONQUEST, BECAME AN EMPEROR RULING OUR ENTIRE REALM.
MY LORDS...
...WE HAVE REACHED!

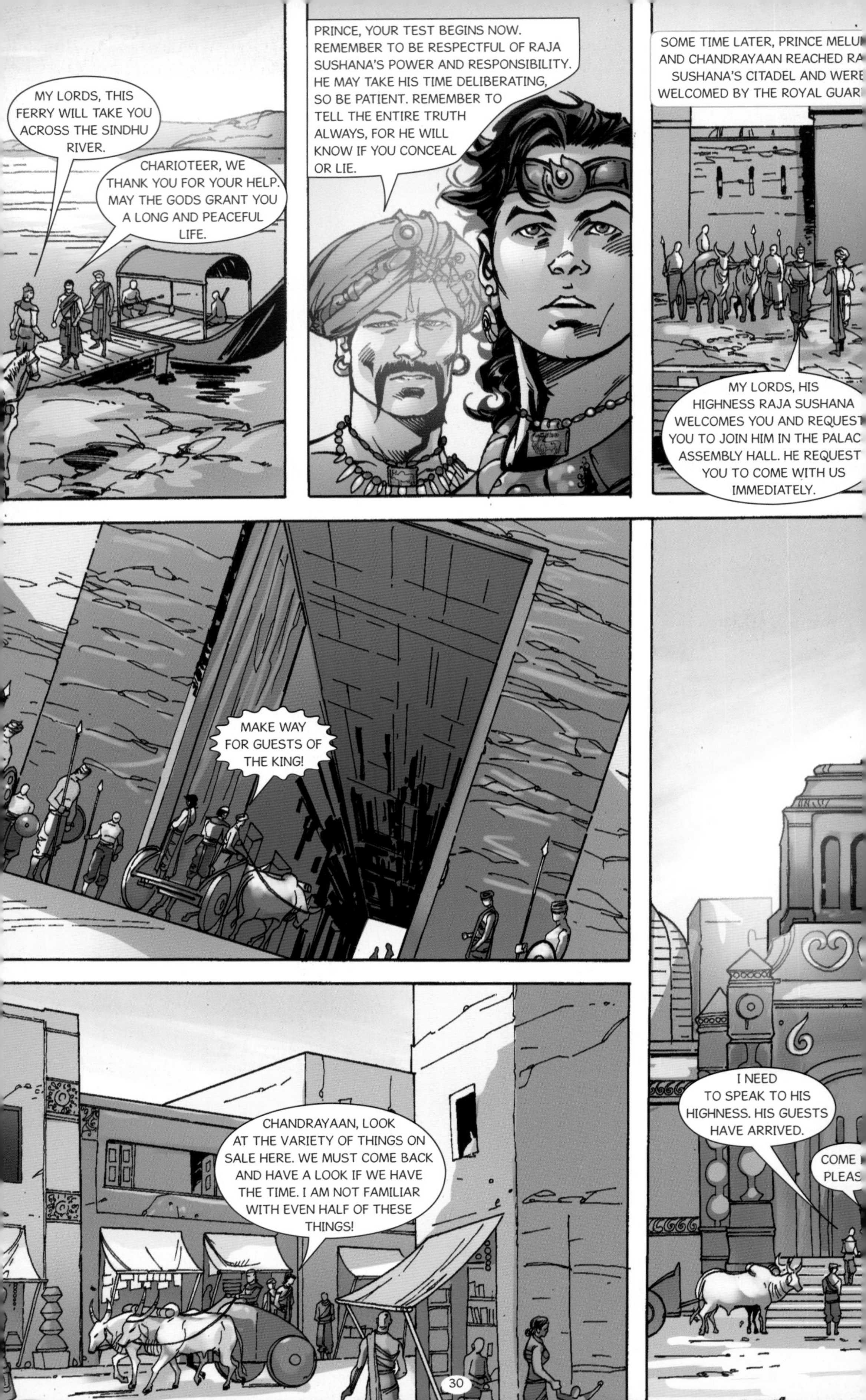
MY LORDS, THIS FERRY WILL TAKE YOU ACROSS THE SINDHU RIVER.
CHARIOTEER, WE THANK YOU FOR YOUR HELP. MAY THE GODS GRANT YOU A LONG AND PEACEFUL LIFE.
PRINCE, YOUR TEST BEGINS NOW. REMEMBER TO BE RESPECTFUL OF RAJA SUSHANA'S POWER AND RESPONSIBILITY. HE MAY TAKE HIS TIME DELIBERATING, SO BE PATIENT. REMEMBER TO TELL THE ENTIRE TRUTH ALWAYS, FOR HE WILL KNOW IF YOU CONCEAL OR LIE.
SOME TIME LATER, PRINCE MELU AND CHANDRAYAAN REACHED RA SUSHANA'S CITADEL AND WERE WELCOMED BY THE ROYAL GUAR
MY LORDS, HIS HIGHNESS RAJA SUSHANA WELCOMES YOU AND REQUEST YOU TO JOIN HIM IN THE PALAC ASSEMBLY HALL. HE REQUEST YOU TO COME WITH US IMMEDIATELY.
MAKE WAY FOR GUESTS OF THE KING!
CHANDRAYAAN, LOOK AT THE VARIETY OF THINGS ON SALE HERE. WE MUST COME BACK AND HAVE A LOOK IF WE HAVE THE TIME. I AM NOT FAMILIAR WITH EVEN HALF OF THESE THINGS!
I NEED TO SPEAK TO HIS HIGHNESS. HIS GUESTS HAVE ARRIVED.
COME PLEAS

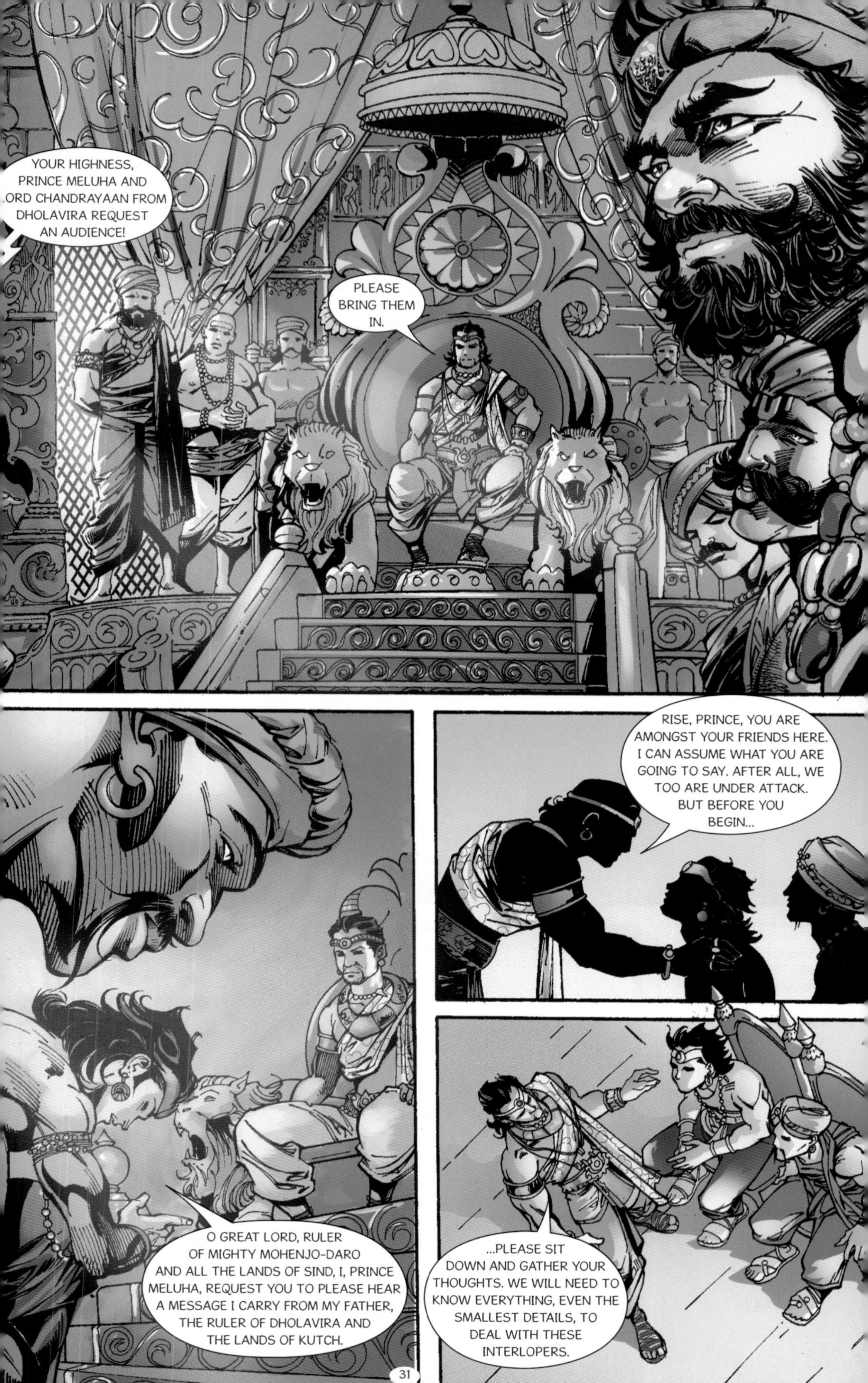
YOUR HIGHNESS, PRINCE MELUHA AND ORD CHANDRAYAAN FROM DHOLAVIRA REQUEST AN AUDIENCE!
PLEASE BRING THEM IN.
O GREAT LORD, RULER OF MIGHTY MOHENJO-DARO AND ALL THE LANDS OF SIND, I, PRINCE MELUHA, REQUEST YOU TO PLEASE HEAR A MESSAGE I CARRY FROM MY FATHER, THE RULER OF DHOLAVIRA AND THE LANDS OF KUTCH.
RISE, PRINCE, YOU ARE AMONGST YOUR FRIENDS HERE. I CAN ASSUME WHAT YOU ARE GOING TO SAY. AFTER ALL, WE TOO ARE UNDER ATTACK. BUT BEFORE YOU BEGIN...
...PLEASE SIT DOWN AND GATHER YOUR THOUGHTS. WE WILL NEED TO KNOW EVERYTHING, EVEN THE SMALLEST DETAILS, TO DEAL WITH THESE INTERLOPERS.

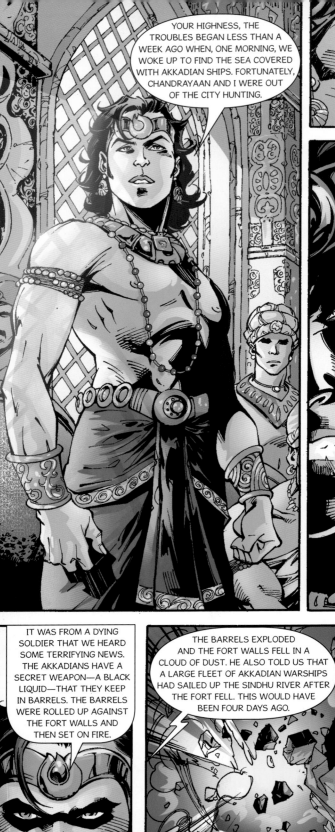

YOUR HIGHNESS, THE TROUBLES BEGAN LESS THAN A WEEK AGO WHEN, ONE MORNING, WE WOKE UP TO FIND THE SEA COVERED WITH AKKADIAN SHIPS. FORTUNATELY, CHANDRAYAAN AND I WERE OUT OF THE CITY HUNTING.

WE TRIED TO RETURN, BUT THE CITY WAS ALREADY UNDER SIEGE. A MESSENGER REAC[H]ED US THAT EVENING SAYING THAT M[Y] FATHER WANTED US TO GO NOR[TH] TO THE OTHER KINGDOMS AND GET HELP.

WE SET SAIL SECRETLY THAT NIGHT ACROSS THE RANN TO LAL DARO, YOUR GATEWAY FORT, ONLY TO FIND IT BURNING... ITS GARRISO[N] DEAD OR DYING... THE AKKADIAN FLEET HAVING REACHED THERE BEFORE WE COULD.

IT WAS FROM A DYING SOLDIER THAT WE HEARD SOME TERRIFYING NEWS. THE AKKADIANS HAVE A SECRET WEAPON—A BLACK LIQUID—THAT THEY KEEP IN BARRELS. THE BARRELS WERE ROLLED UP AGAINST THE FORT WALLS AND THEN SET ON FIRE.

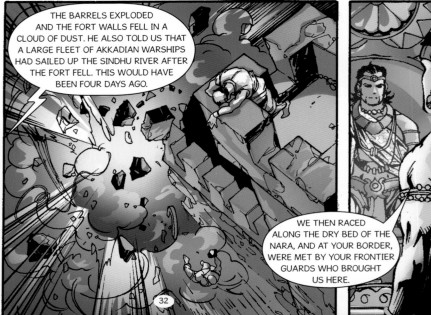

THE BARRELS EXPLODED AND THE FORT WALLS FELL IN A CLOUD OF DUST. HE ALSO TOLD US THAT A LARGE FLEET OF AKKADIAN WARSHIPS HAD SAILED UP THE SINDHU RIVER AFTER THE FORT FELL. THIS WOULD HAVE BEEN FOUR DAYS AGO.

WE THEN RACED ALONG THE DRY BED OF THE NARA, AND AT YOUR BORDER, WERE MET BY YOUR FRONTIER GUARDS WHO BROUGHT US HERE.

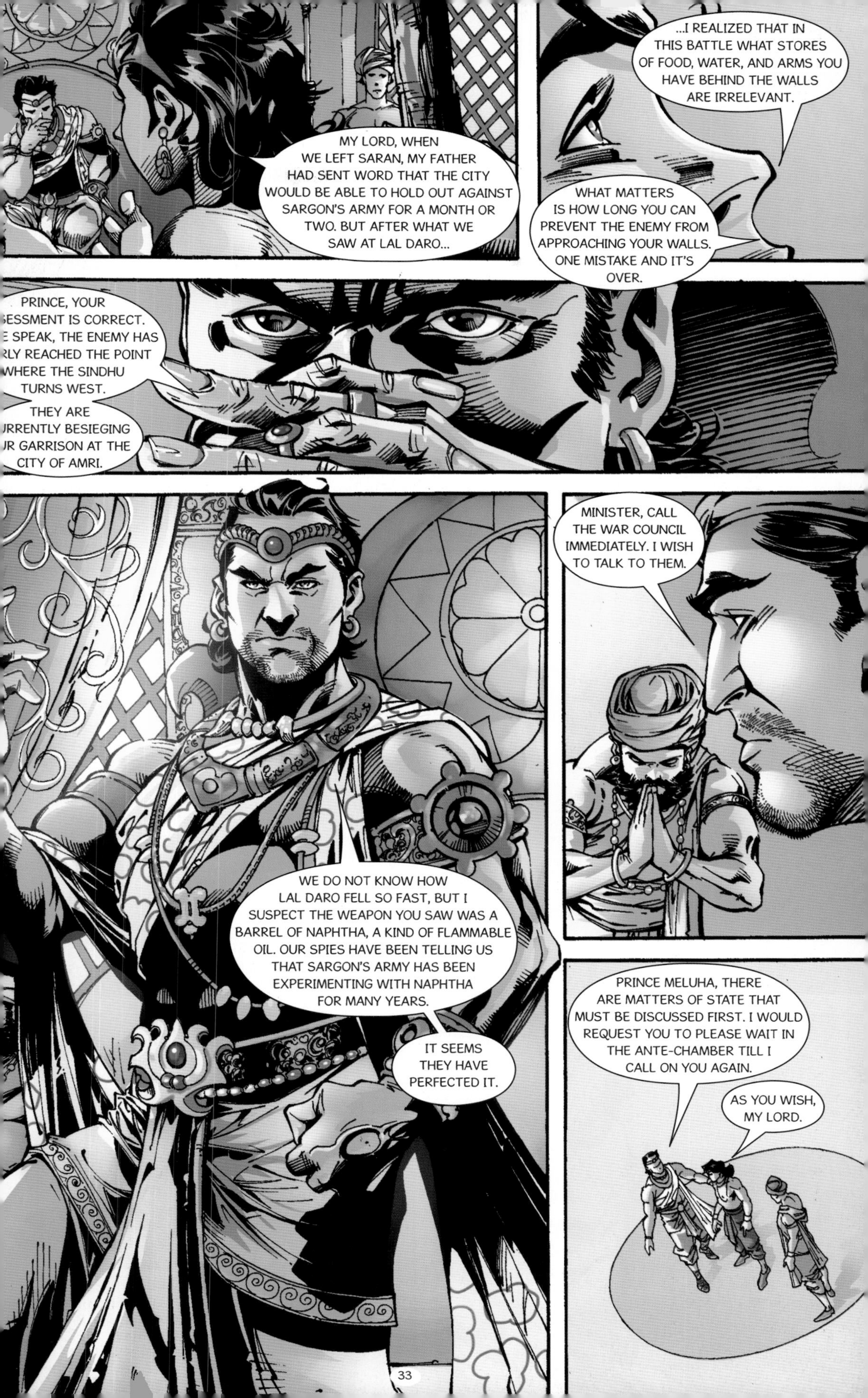
MY LORD, WHEN WE LEFT SARAN, MY FATHER HAD SENT WORD THAT THE CITY WOULD BE ABLE TO HOLD OUT AGAINST SARGON'S ARMY FOR A MONTH OR TWO. BUT AFTER WHAT WE SAW AT LAL DARO...
...I REALIZED THAT IN THIS BATTLE WHAT STORES OF FOOD, WATER, AND ARMS YOU HAVE BEHIND THE WALLS ARE IRRELEVANT.
WHAT MATTERS IS HOW LONG YOU CAN PREVENT THE ENEMY FROM APPROACHING YOUR WALLS. ONE MISTAKE AND IT'S OVER.
PRINCE, YOUR SESSMENT IS CORRECT. E SPEAK, THE ENEMY HAS RLY REACHED THE POINT WHERE THE SINDHU TURNS WEST.
THEY ARE URRENTLY BESIEGING UR GARRISON AT THE CITY OF AMRI.
WE DO NOT KNOW HOW LAL DARO FELL SO FAST, BUT I SUSPECT THE WEAPON YOU SAW WAS A BARREL OF NAPHTHA, A KIND OF FLAMMABLE OIL. OUR SPIES HAVE BEEN TELLING US THAT SARGON'S ARMY HAS BEEN EXPERIMENTING WITH NAPHTHA FOR MANY YEARS.
IT SEEMS THEY HAVE PERFECTED IT.
MINISTER, CALL THE WAR COUNCIL IMMEDIATELY. I WISH TO TALK TO THEM.
PRINCE MELUHA, THERE ARE MATTERS OF STATE THAT MUST BE DISCUSSED FIRST. I WOULD REQUEST YOU TO PLEASE WAIT IN THE ANTE-CHAMBER TILL I CALL ON YOU AGAIN.
AS YOU WISH, MY LORD.

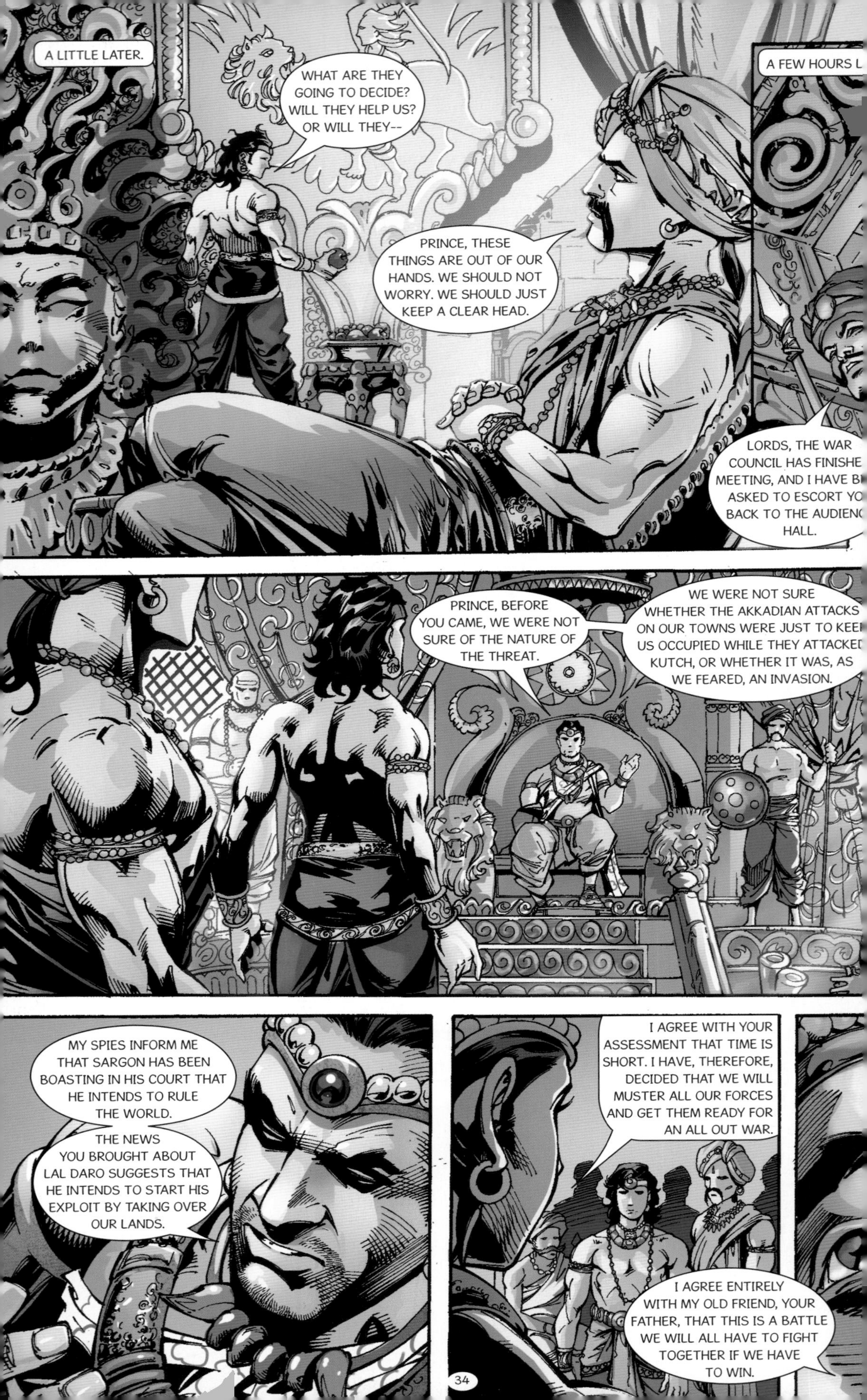
A LITTLE LATER.
WHAT ARE THEY GOING TO DECIDE? WILL THEY HELP US? OR WILL THEY--
PRINCE, THESE THINGS ARE OUT OF OUR HANDS. WE SHOULD NOT WORRY. WE SHOULD JUST KEEP A CLEAR HEAD.
A FEW HOURS L
LORDS, THE WAR COUNCIL HAS FINISHE MEETING, AND I HAVE B ASKED TO ESCORT YO BACK TO THE AUDIEN HALL.
PRINCE, BEFORE YOU CAME, WE WERE NOT SURE OF THE NATURE OF THE THREAT.
WE WERE NOT SURE WHETHER THE AKKADIAN ATTACKS ON OUR TOWNS WERE JUST TO KEE US OCCUPIED WHILE THEY ATTACKE KUTCH, OR WHETHER IT WAS, AS WE FEARED, AN INVASION.
MY SPIES INFORM ME THAT SARGON HAS BEEN BOASTING IN HIS COURT THAT HE INTENDS TO RULE THE WORLD.
THE NEWS YOU BROUGHT ABOUT LAL DARO SUGGESTS THAT HE INTENDS TO START HIS EXPLOIT BY TAKING OVER OUR LANDS.
I AGREE WITH YOUR ASSESSMENT THAT TIME IS SHORT. I HAVE, THEREFORE, DECIDED THAT WE WILL MUSTER ALL OUR FORCES AND GET THEM READY FOR AN ALL OUT WAR.
I AGREE ENTIRELY WITH MY OLD FRIEND, YOUR FATHER, THAT THIS IS A BATTLE WE WILL ALL HAVE TO FIGHT TOGETHER IF WE HAVE TO WIN.

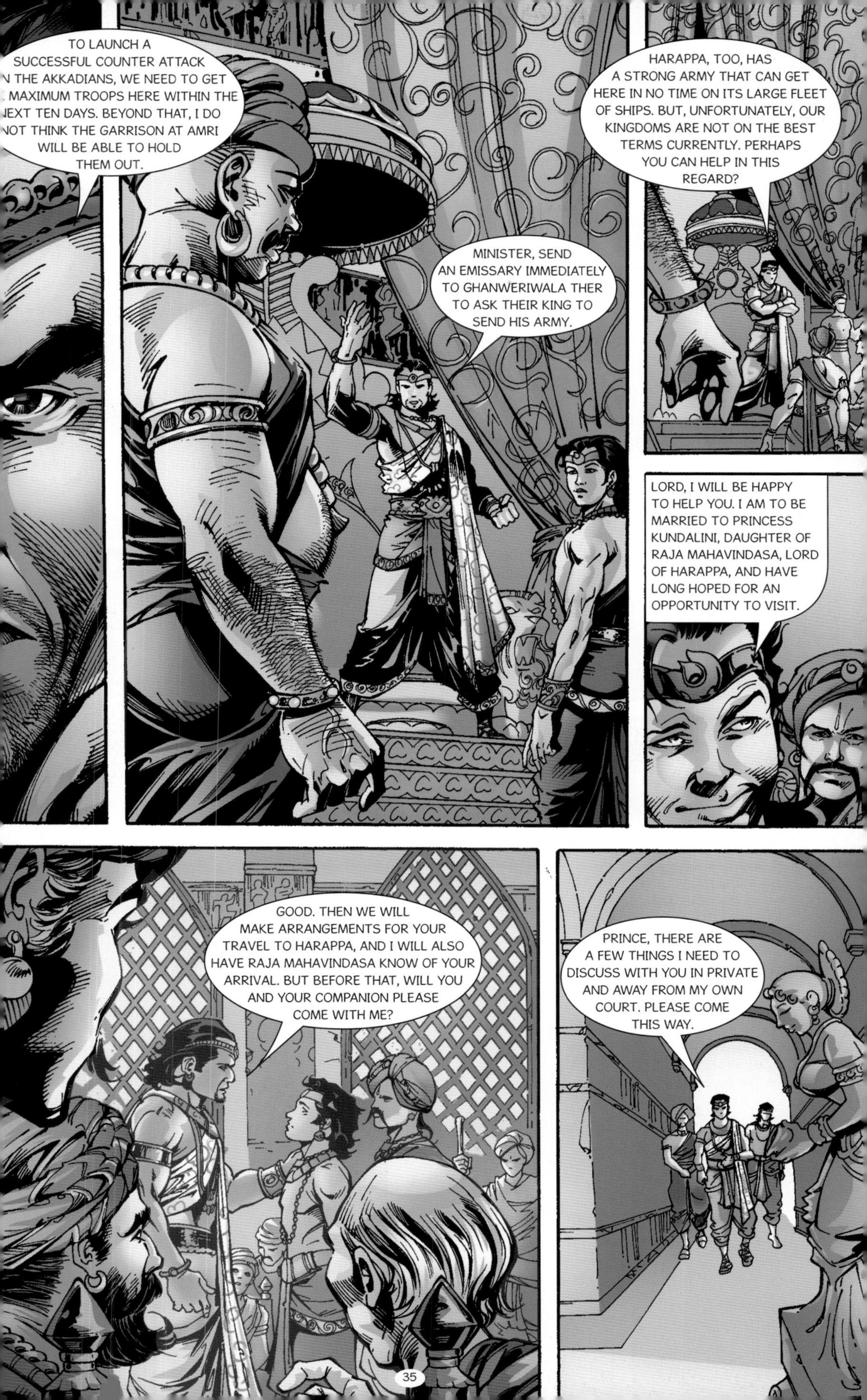
TO LAUNCH A SUCCESSFUL COUNTER ATTACK N THE AKKADIANS, WE NEED TO GET MAXIMUM TROOPS HERE WITHIN THE NEXT TEN DAYS. BEYOND THAT, I DO NOT THINK THE GARRISON AT AMRI WILL BE ABLE TO HOLD THEM OUT.
MINISTER, SEND AN EMISSARY IMMEDIATELY TO GHANWERIWALA THER TO ASK THEIR KING TO SEND HIS ARMY.
HARAPPA, TOO, HAS A STRONG ARMY THAT CAN GET HERE IN NO TIME ON ITS LARGE FLEET OF SHIPS. BUT, UNFORTUNATELY, OUR KINGDOMS ARE NOT ON THE BEST TERMS CURRENTLY. PERHAPS YOU CAN HELP IN THIS REGARD?
LORD, I WILL BE HAPPY TO HELP YOU. I AM TO BE MARRIED TO PRINCESS KUNDALINI, DAUGHTER OF RAJA MAHAVINDASA, LORD OF HARAPPA, AND HAVE LONG HOPED FOR AN OPPORTUNITY TO VISIT.
GOOD. THEN WE WILL MAKE ARRANGEMENTS FOR YOUR TRAVEL TO HARAPPA, AND I WILL ALSO HAVE RAJA MAHAVINDASA KNOW OF YOUR ARRIVAL. BUT BEFORE THAT, WILL YOU AND YOUR COMPANION PLEASE COME WITH ME?
PRINCE, THERE ARE A FEW THINGS I NEED TO DISCUSS WITH YOU IN PRIVATE AND AWAY FROM MY OWN COURT. PLEASE COME THIS WAY.

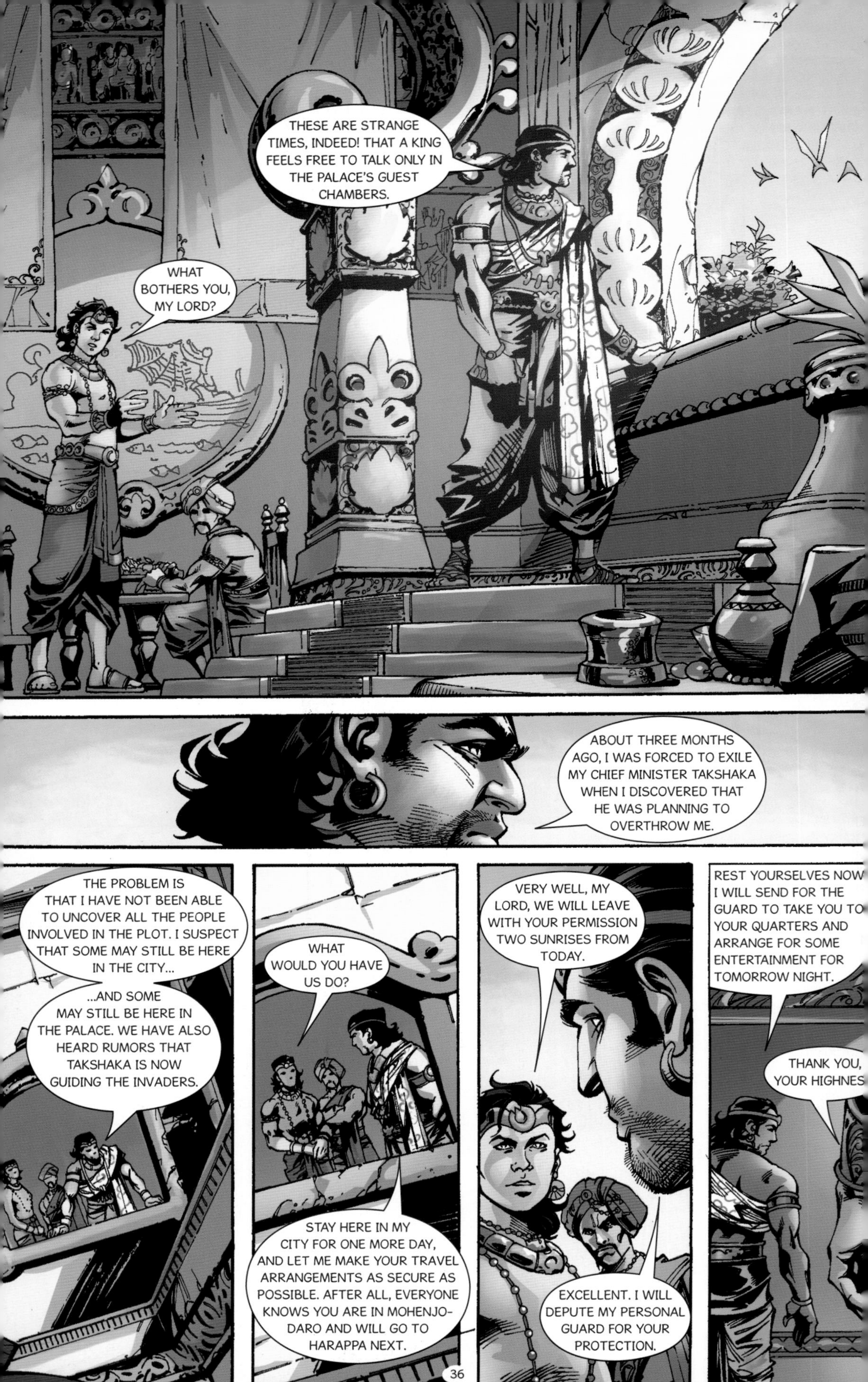
THESE ARE STRANGE TIMES, INDEED! THAT A KING FEELS FREE TO TALK ONLY IN THE PALACE'S GUEST CHAMBERS.
WHAT BOTHERS YOU, MY LORD?
ABOUT THREE MONTHS AGO, I WAS FORCED TO EXILE MY CHIEF MINISTER TAKSHAKA WHEN I DISCOVERED THAT HE WAS PLANNING TO OVERTHROW ME.
THE PROBLEM IS THAT I HAVE NOT BEEN ABLE TO UNCOVER ALL THE PEOPLE INVOLVED IN THE PLOT. I SUSPECT THAT SOME MAY STILL BE HERE IN THE CITY...
...AND SOME MAY STILL BE HERE IN THE PALACE. WE HAVE ALSO HEARD RUMORS THAT TAKSHAKA IS NOW GUIDING THE INVADERS.
WHAT WOULD YOU HAVE US DO?
STAY HERE IN MY CITY FOR ONE MORE DAY, AND LET ME MAKE YOUR TRAVEL ARRANGEMENTS AS SECURE AS POSSIBLE. AFTER ALL, EVERYONE KNOWS YOU ARE IN MOHENJO-DARO AND WILL GO TO HARAPPA NEXT.
VERY WELL, MY LORD, WE WILL LEAVE WITH YOUR PERMISSION TWO SUNRISES FROM TODAY.
EXCELLENT. I WILL DEPUTE MY PERSONAL GUARD FOR YOUR PROTECTION.
REST YOURSELVES NOW I WILL SEND FOR THE GUARD TO TAKE YOU TO YOUR QUARTERS AND ARRANGE FOR SOME ENTERTAINMENT FOR TOMORROW NIGHT.
THANK YOU, YOUR HIGHNES

THE NEXT MORNING.

CHANDRAYAAN, [L]US GO AND SEE THIS [THA]T YOU HAVE TOLD [S]O MUCH ABOUT OVER THE YEARS.

VERY WELL, BUT PLEASE REMEMBER TO STAY NEAR ME AND THE GUARDS. I REMEMBER TAKSHAKA WELL, AND HE IS VERY DANGEROUS.

AFTER BREAKFAST, PRINCE MELUHA AND [CH]ANDRAYAAN, WITH THE KING'S PERMISSION [A]ND TWO GUARDS, WENT TO SEE THE CITY.

LOOK AROUND AND LEARN, PRINCE. THIS CHAOS OF SO MANY THOUSANDS OF PEOPLE BUYING AND SELLING GOODS IS ACTUALLY MADE POSSIBLE BY A VERY EFFICIENT SYSTEM OF REGULATIONS.

YOU WILL NOT SEE ANY [ ]DELIVERY CARTS HERE. [TH]ERE ARE SPECIFIC TIMES [SE]T FOR THE PICK UP AND [DELI]VERY OF GOODS, SO THE [ST]REETS STAY CLEAR FOR [SHO]PPERS THE REST OF THE [T]IME. THE GARBAGE HAS TO BE CLEARED MANY [ ]TIMES A DAY BY A TEAM OF SWEEPERS.

LAPIZ BEADS!

YES, MY PRINCE. THEY ARE BROUGHT ALL THE WAY FROM ARIA. IMAGINE THE LONG TRADE NETWORKS THAT HAVE TO BE MADE AND CONTROLLED TO BRING THESE BEADS HERE, AFTER OVER A MONTH'S JOURNEY.

SEE THE SHELL BANGLES—THEY ARE FROM KUTCH. THEY PROBABLY PASSED THROUGH DHOLAVIRA ON THEIR WAY HERE.

LOOK AT THE VARIETY OF VEGETABLES. HAVE YOU EVER SEEN SO MANY TYPES OF GREEN LEAVES?

ARE THESE VEGETABLES LOCALLY PRODUCED IN THE FIELDS WE PASSED?

YES, WITHIN A DAY OR TWO'S WALK, AT THE MOST.

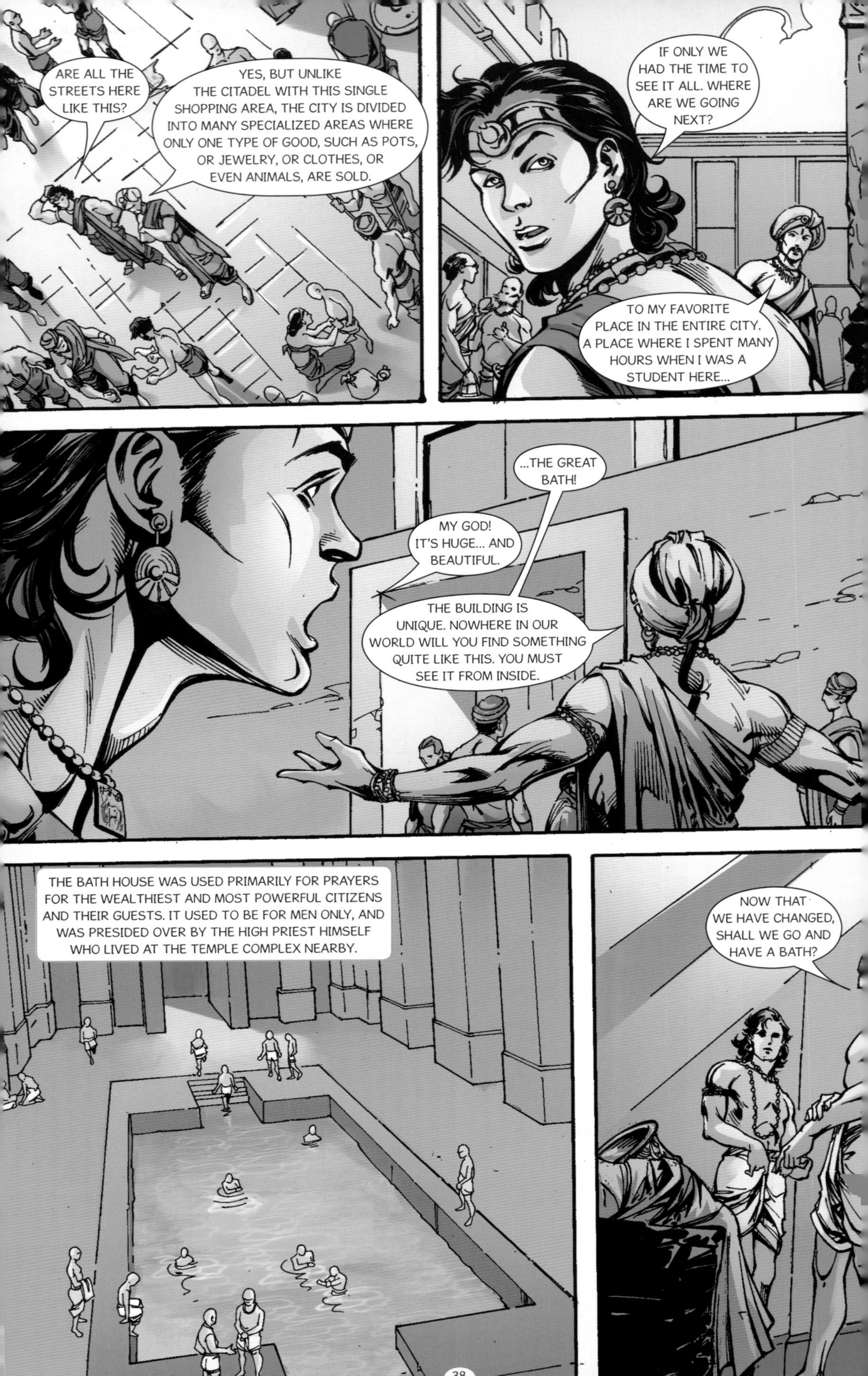
ARE ALL THE STREETS HERE LIKE THIS?
YES, BUT UNLIKE THE CITADEL WITH THIS SINGLE SHOPPING AREA, THE CITY IS DIVIDED INTO MANY SPECIALIZED AREAS WHERE ONLY ONE TYPE OF GOOD, SUCH AS POTS, OR JEWELRY, OR CLOTHES, OR EVEN ANIMALS, ARE SOLD.
IF ONLY WE HAD THE TIME TO SEE IT ALL. WHERE ARE WE GOING NEXT?
TO MY FAVORITE PLACE IN THE ENTIRE CITY. A PLACE WHERE I SPENT MANY HOURS WHEN I WAS A STUDENT HERE...
...THE GREAT BATH!
MY GOD! IT'S HUGE... AND BEAUTIFUL.
THE BUILDING IS UNIQUE. NOWHERE IN OUR WORLD WILL YOU FIND SOMETHING QUITE LIKE THIS. YOU MUST SEE IT FROM INSIDE.
THE BATH HOUSE WAS USED PRIMARILY FOR PRAYERS FOR THE WEALTHIEST AND MOST POWERFUL CITIZENS AND THEIR GUESTS. IT USED TO BE FOR MEN ONLY, AND WAS PRESIDED OVER BY THE HIGH PRIEST HIMSELF WHO LIVED AT THE TEMPLE COMPLEX NEARBY.
NOW THAT WE HAVE CHANGED, SHALL WE GO AND HAVE A BATH?

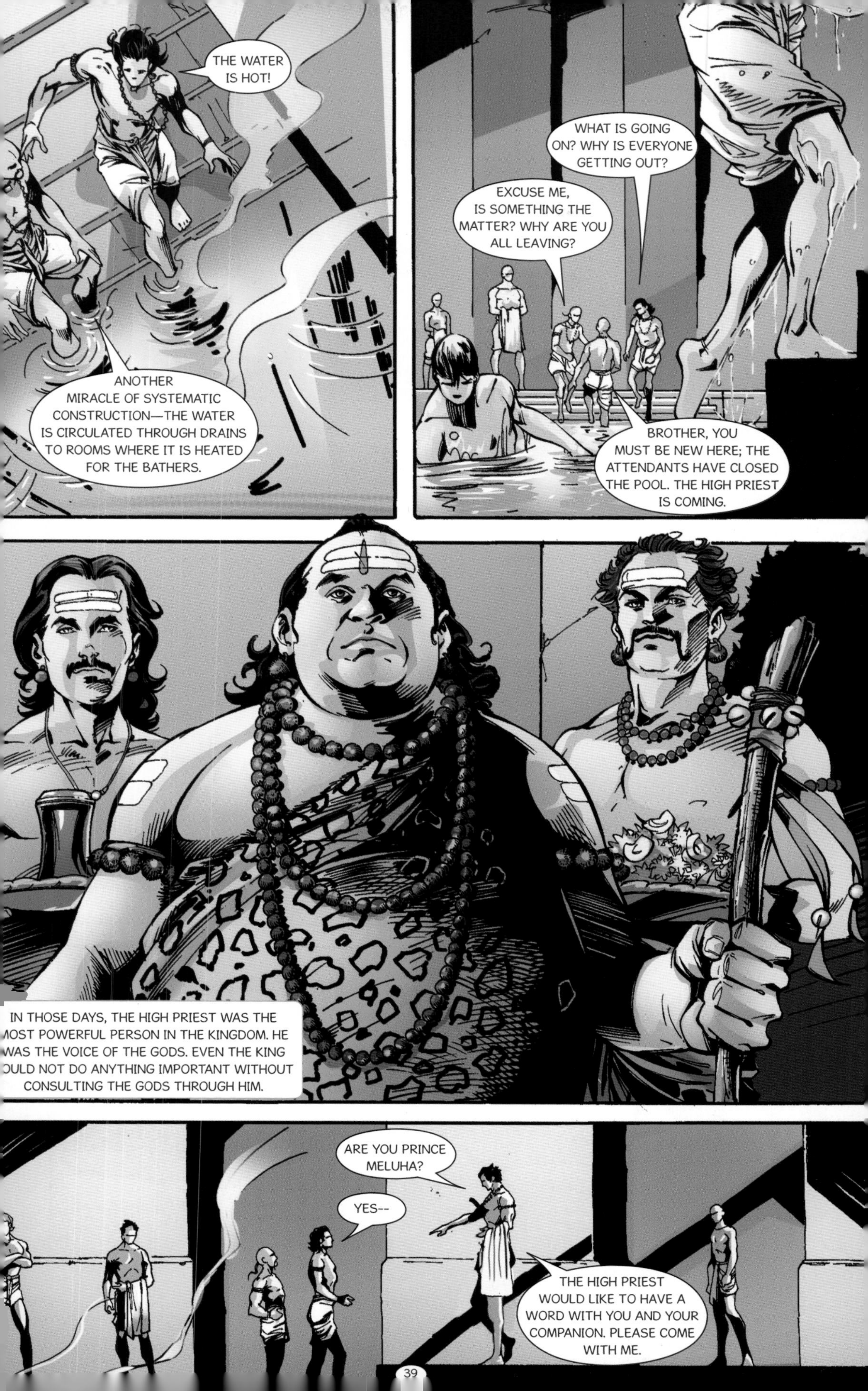
THE WATER IS HOT!
ANOTHER MIRACLE OF SYSTEMATIC CONSTRUCTION—THE WATER IS CIRCULATED THROUGH DRAINS TO ROOMS WHERE IT IS HEATED FOR THE BATHERS.
WHAT IS GOING ON? WHY IS EVERYONE GETTING OUT?
EXCUSE ME, IS SOMETHING THE MATTER? WHY ARE YOU ALL LEAVING?
BROTHER, YOU MUST BE NEW HERE; THE ATTENDANTS HAVE CLOSED THE POOL. THE HIGH PRIEST IS COMING.
IN THOSE DAYS, THE HIGH PRIEST WAS THE MOST POWERFUL PERSON IN THE KINGDOM. HE WAS THE VOICE OF THE GODS. EVEN THE KING COULD NOT DO ANYTHING IMPORTANT WITHOUT CONSULTING THE GODS THROUGH HIM.
ARE YOU PRINCE MELUHA?
YES--
THE HIGH PRIEST WOULD LIKE TO HAVE A WORD WITH YOU AND YOUR COMPANION. PLEASE COME WITH ME.

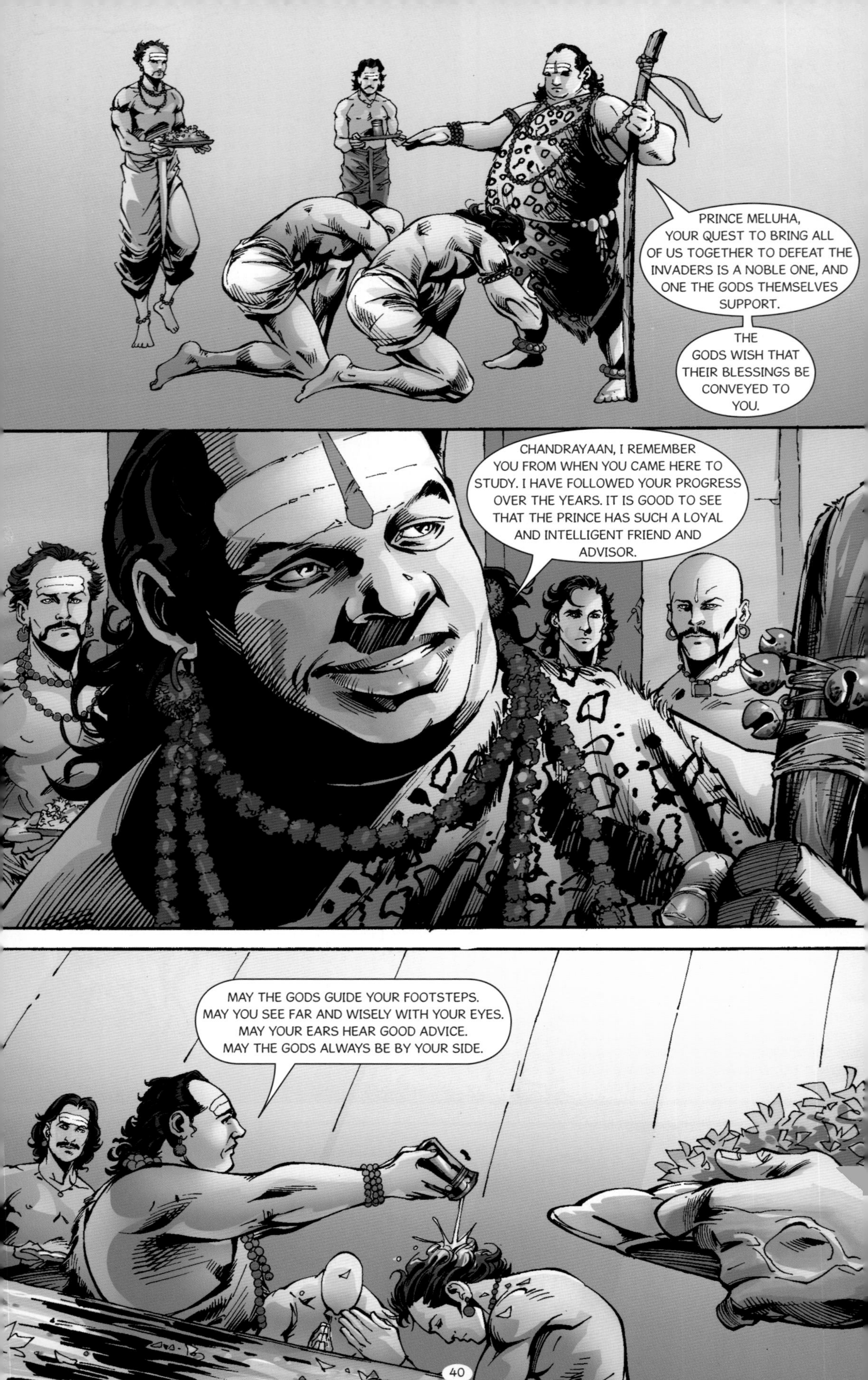
PRINCE MELUHA, YOUR QUEST TO BRING ALL OF US TOGETHER TO DEFEAT THE INVADERS IS A NOBLE ONE, AND ONE THE GODS THEMSELVES SUPPORT.
THE GODS WISH THAT THEIR BLESSINGS BE CONVEYED TO YOU.
CHANDRAYAAN, I REMEMBER YOU FROM WHEN YOU CAME HERE TO STUDY. I HAVE FOLLOWED YOUR PROGRESS OVER THE YEARS. IT IS GOOD TO SEE THAT THE PRINCE HAS SUCH A LOYAL AND INTELLIGENT FRIEND AND ADVISOR.
MAY THE GODS GUIDE YOUR FOOTSTEPS. MAY YOU SEE FAR AND WISELY WITH YOUR EYES. MAY YOUR EARS HEAR GOOD ADVICE. MAY THE GODS ALWAYS BE BY YOUR SIDE.

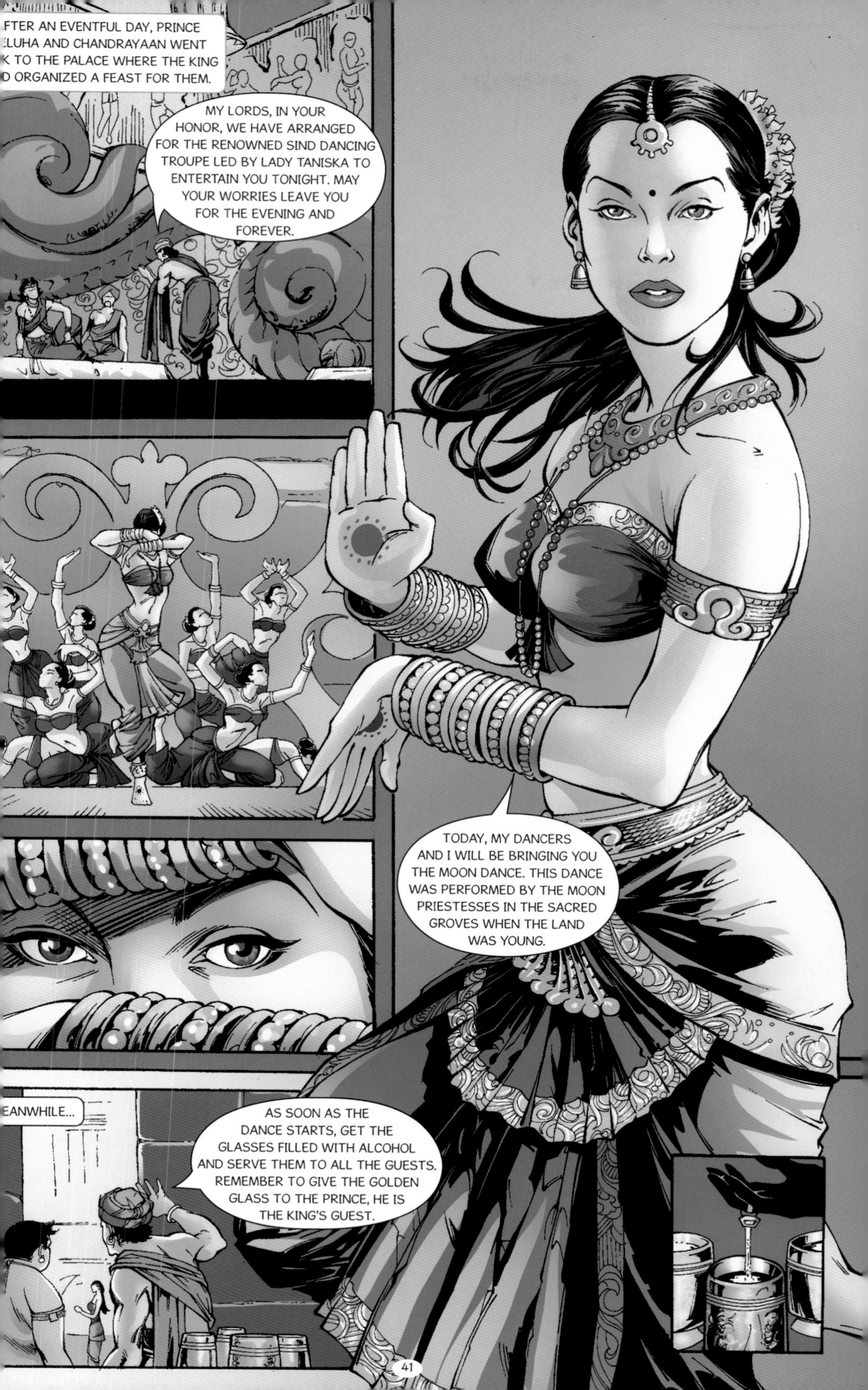

FTER AN EVENTFUL DAY, PRINCE ELUHA AND CHANDRAYAAN WENT K TO THE PALACE WHERE THE KING D ORGANIZED A FEAST FOR THEM.
MY LORDS, IN YOUR HONOR, WE HAVE ARRANGED FOR THE RENOWNED SIND DANCING TROUPE LED BY LADY TANISKA TO ENTERTAIN YOU TONIGHT. MAY YOUR WORRIES LEAVE YOU FOR THE EVENING AND FOREVER.
TODAY, MY DANCERS AND I WILL BE BRINGING YOU THE MOON DANCE. THIS DANCE WAS PERFORMED BY THE MOON PRIESTESSES IN THE SACRED GROVES WHEN THE LAND WAS YOUNG.
EANWHILE...
AS SOON AS THE DANCE STARTS, GET THE GLASSES FILLED WITH ALCOHOL AND SERVE THEM TO ALL THE GUESTS. REMEMBER TO GIVE THE GOLDEN GLASS TO THE PRINCE, HE IS THE KING'S GUEST.

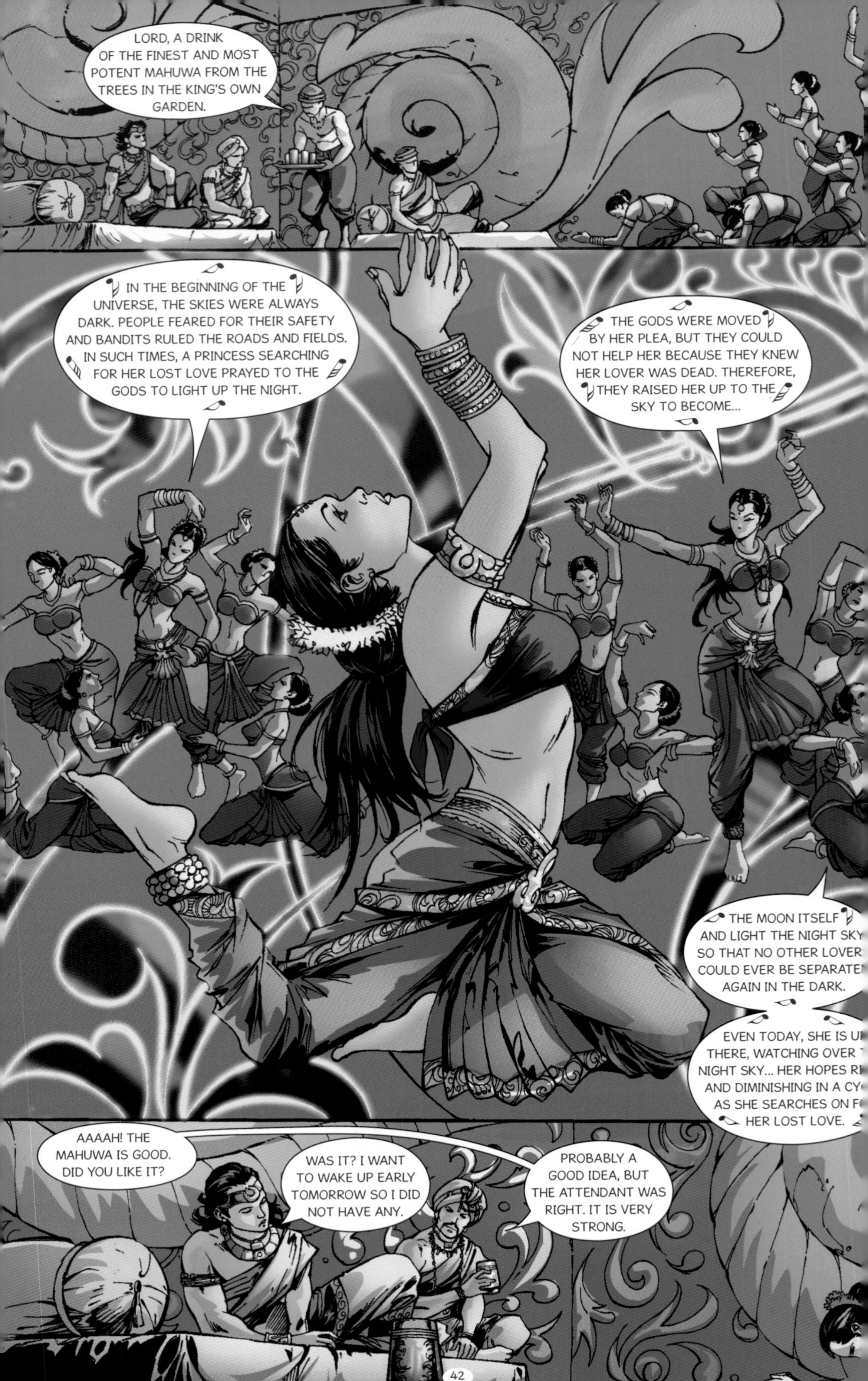
LORD, A DRINK OF THE FINEST AND MOST POTENT MAHUWA FROM THE TREES IN THE KING'S OWN GARDEN.
IN THE BEGINNING OF THE UNIVERSE, THE SKIES WERE ALWAYS DARK. PEOPLE FEARED FOR THEIR SAFETY AND BANDITS RULED THE ROADS AND FIELDS. IN SUCH TIMES, A PRINCESS SEARCHING FOR HER LOST LOVE PRAYED TO THE GODS TO LIGHT UP THE NIGHT.
THE GODS WERE MOVED BY HER PLEA, BUT THEY COULD NOT HELP HER BECAUSE THEY KNEW HER LOVER WAS DEAD. THEREFORE, THEY RAISED HER UP TO THE SKY TO BECOME...
THE MOON ITSELF AND LIGHT THE NIGHT SKY SO THAT NO OTHER LOVER COULD EVER BE SEPARATE AGAIN IN THE DARK.
EVEN TODAY, SHE IS U THERE, WATCHING OVER NIGHT SKY... HER HOPES R AND DIMINISHING IN A CY AS SHE SEARCHES ON F HER LOST LOVE.
AAAAH! THE MAHUWA IS GOOD. DID YOU LIKE IT?
WAS IT? I WANT TO WAKE UP EARLY TOMORROW SO I DID NOT HAVE ANY.
PROBABLY A GOOD IDEA, BUT THE ATTENDANT WAS RIGHT. IT IS VERY STRONG.

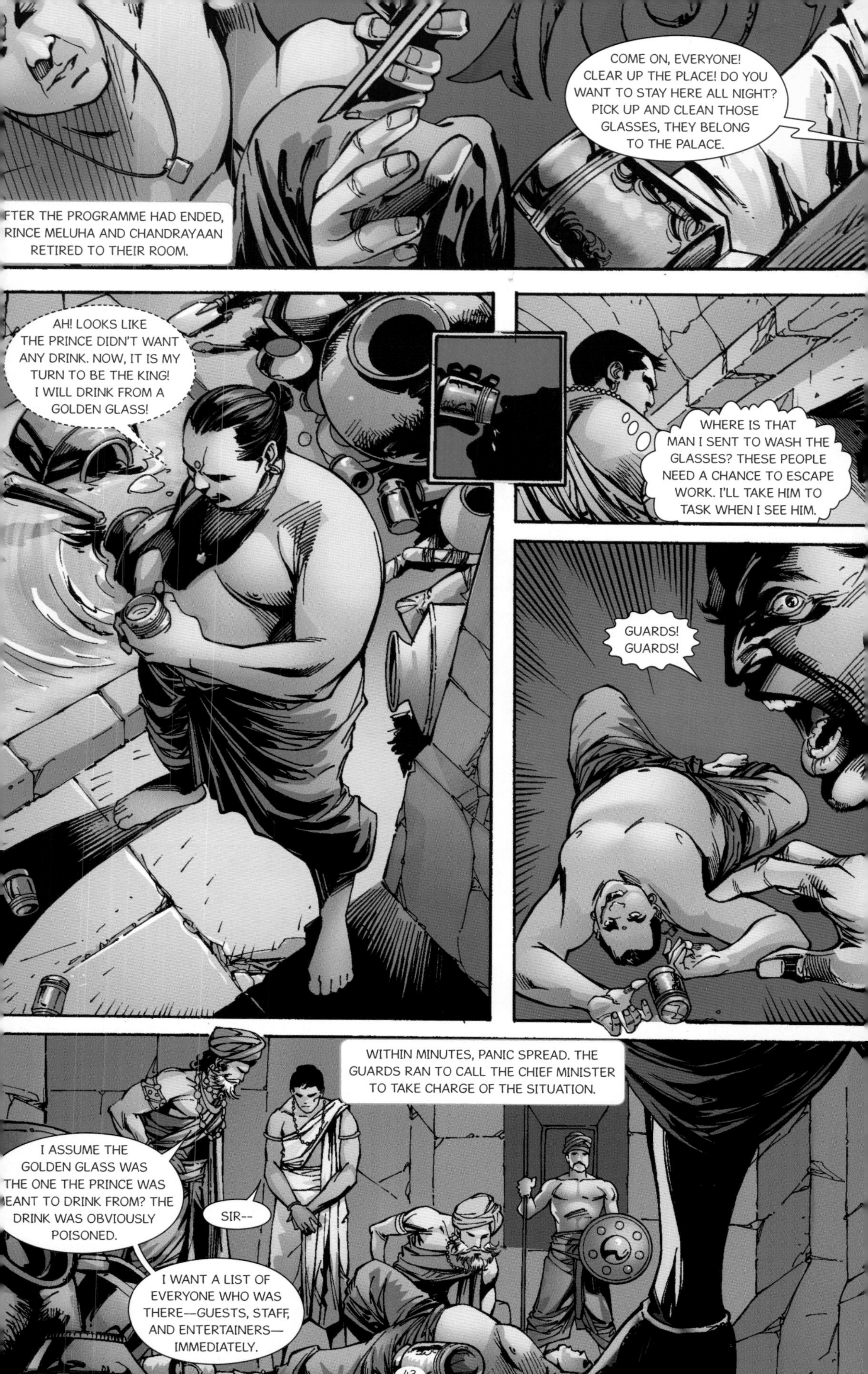
COME ON, EVERYONE! CLEAR UP THE PLACE! DO YOU WANT TO STAY HERE ALL NIGHT? PICK UP AND CLEAN THOSE GLASSES, THEY BELONG TO THE PALACE.
FTER THE PROGRAMME HAD ENDED, RINCE MELUHA AND CHANDRAYAAN RETIRED TO THEIR ROOM.
AH! LOOKS LIKE THE PRINCE DIDN'T WANT ANY DRINK. NOW, IT IS MY TURN TO BE THE KING! I WILL DRINK FROM A GOLDEN GLASS!
WHERE IS THAT MAN I SENT TO WASH THE GLASSES? THESE PEOPLE NEED A CHANCE TO ESCAPE WORK. I'LL TAKE HIM TO TASK WHEN I SEE HIM.
GUARDS! GUARDS!
WITHIN MINUTES, PANIC SPREAD. THE GUARDS RAN TO CALL THE CHIEF MINISTER TO TAKE CHARGE OF THE SITUATION.
I ASSUME THE GOLDEN GLASS WAS THE ONE THE PRINCE WAS EANT TO DRINK FROM? THE DRINK WAS OBVIOUSLY POISONED.
SIR--
I WANT A LIST OF EVERYONE WHO WAS THERE--GUESTS, STAFF, AND ENTERTAINERS--IMMEDIATELY.

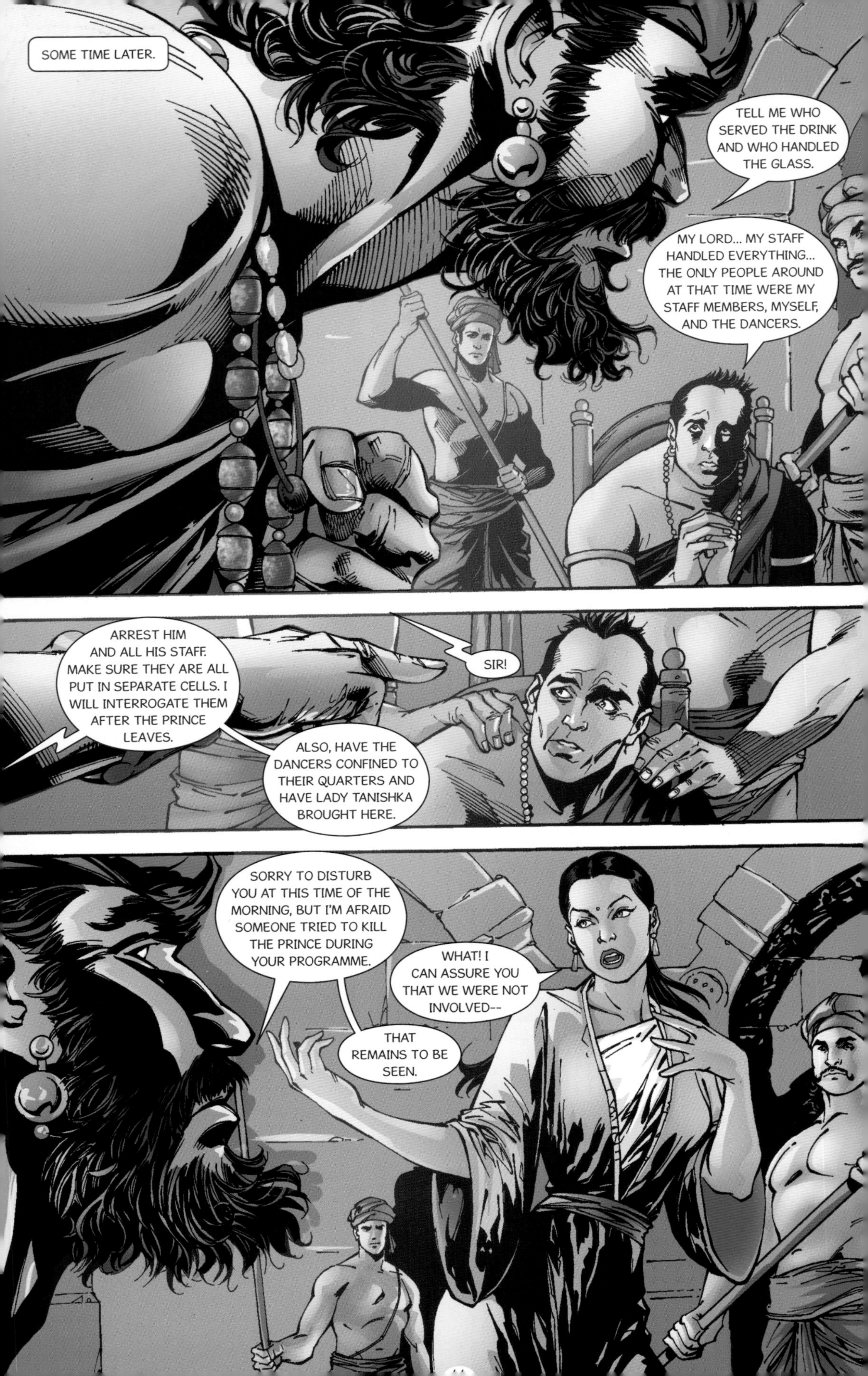
SOME TIME LATER.
TELL ME WHO SERVED THE DRINK AND WHO HANDLED THE GLASS.
MY LORD... MY STAFF HANDLED EVERYTHING... THE ONLY PEOPLE AROUND AT THAT TIME WERE MY STAFF MEMBERS, MYSELF, AND THE DANCERS.
ARREST HIM AND ALL HIS STAFF. MAKE SURE THEY ARE ALL PUT IN SEPARATE CELLS. I WILL INTERROGATE THEM AFTER THE PRINCE LEAVES.
SIR!
ALSO, HAVE THE DANCERS CONFINED TO THEIR QUARTERS AND HAVE LADY TANISHKA BROUGHT HERE.
SORRY TO DISTURB YOU AT THIS TIME OF THE MORNING, BUT I'M AFRAID SOMEONE TRIED TO KILL THE PRINCE DURING YOUR PROGRAMME.
WHAT! I CAN ASSURE YOU THAT WE WERE NOT INVOLVED--
THAT REMAINS TO BE SEEN.

THE NEXT DAY.

A LOVELY [MO]RNING AND A [FINE] DAY TO START [THE] JOURNEY TO [H]ARAPPA.

YES, A LIGHT MEAL AND WE WILL BE READY TO LEAVE.

HIS HIGHNESS HAS SENT ME TO REQUEST YOU TO [R]EMAIN HERE AND NOT VENTURE OUT TILL HE COMES HIMSELF. HE WISHES TO SPEAK TO YOU IN PRIVATE.

AFTER SOME TIME, THE KING WALKED INTO PRINCE MELUHA'S ROOM WITHOUT ANY GUARD IN SIGHT.

SORRY FOR DETAINING YOU LIKE THIS, BUT SOMEONE TRIED TO KILL YOU LAST NIGHT.

WHAT?

THE GLASS OF MAHUWA THAT YOU WERE OFFERED DURING THE PROGRAMME WAS POISONED. THE CLEANER, WHO DRANK IT AFTERWARD, WAS FOUND DEAD EARLY THIS MORNING.

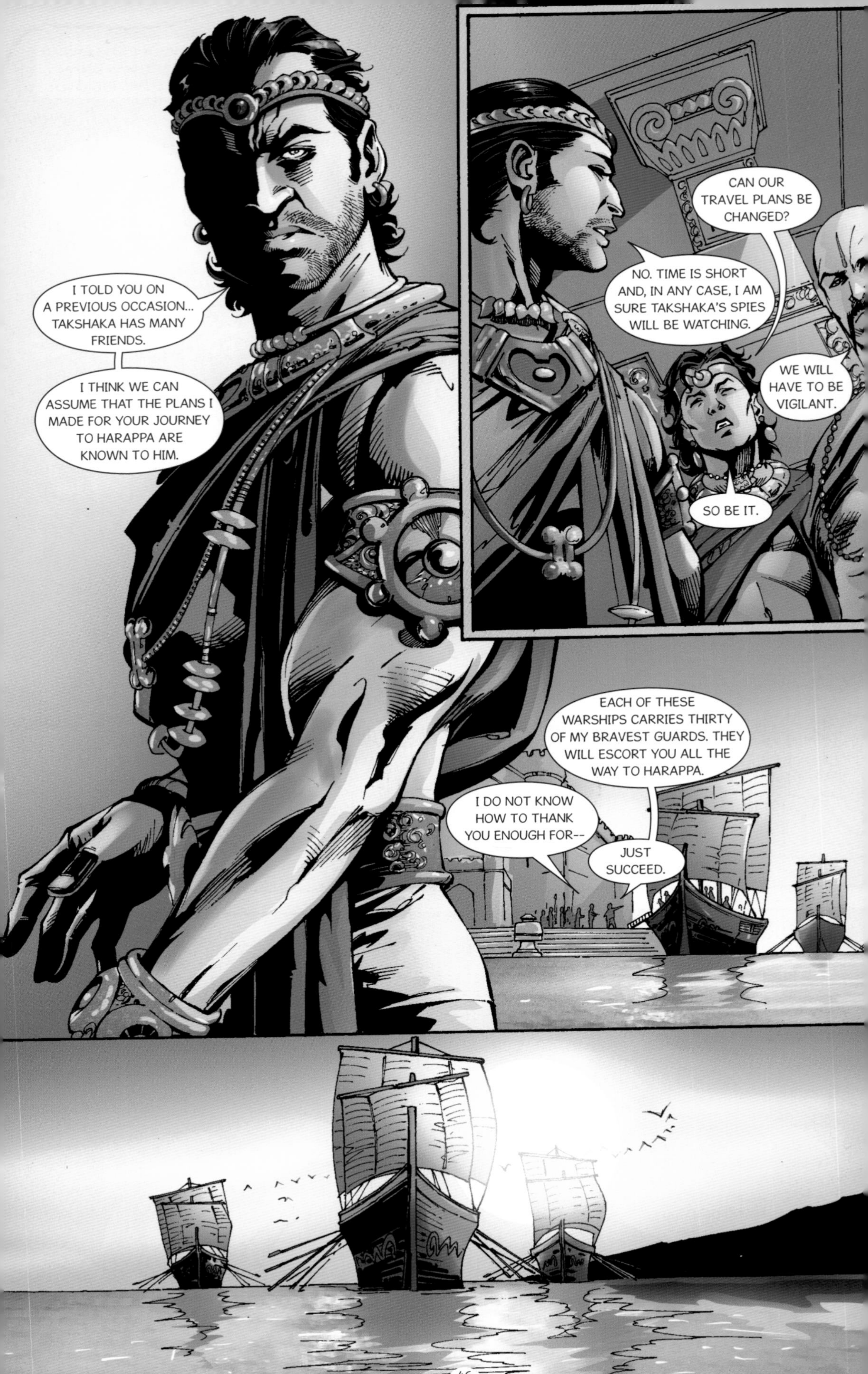
I TOLD YOU ON A PREVIOUS OCCASION... TAKSHAKA HAS MANY FRIENDS.
I THINK WE CAN ASSUME THAT THE PLANS I MADE FOR YOUR JOURNEY TO HARAPPA ARE KNOWN TO HIM.
CAN OUR TRAVEL PLANS BE CHANGED?
NO. TIME IS SHORT AND, IN ANY CASE, I AM SURE TAKSHAKA'S SPIES WILL BE WATCHING.
WE WILL HAVE TO BE VIGILANT.
SO BE IT.
EACH OF THESE WARSHIPS CARRIES THIRTY OF MY BRAVEST GUARDS. THEY WILL ESCORT YOU ALL THE WAY TO HARAPPA.
I DO NOT KNOW HOW TO THANK YOU ENOUGH FOR--
JUST SUCCEED.

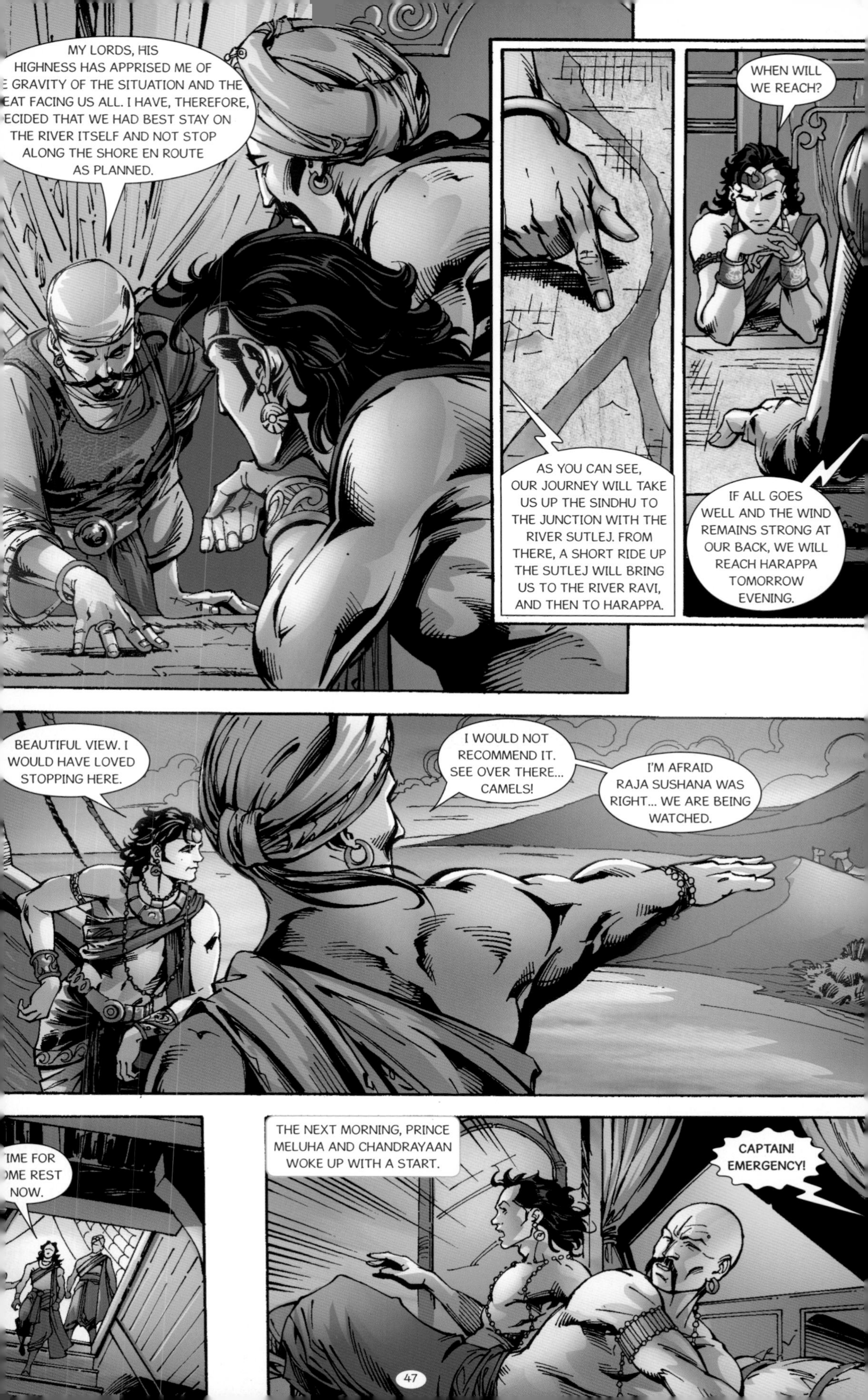
MY LORDS, HIS HIGHNESS HAS APPRISED ME OF E GRAVITY OF THE SITUATION AND THE EAT FACING US ALL. I HAVE, THEREFORE, ECIDED THAT WE HAD BEST STAY ON THE RIVER ITSELF AND NOT STOP ALONG THE SHORE EN ROUTE AS PLANNED.
AS YOU CAN SEE, OUR JOURNEY WILL TAKE US UP THE SINDHU TO THE JUNCTION WITH THE RIVER SUTLEJ. FROM THERE, A SHORT RIDE UP THE SUTLEJ WILL BRING US TO THE RIVER RAVI, AND THEN TO HARAPPA.
WHEN WILL WE REACH?
IF ALL GOES WELL AND THE WIND REMAINS STRONG AT OUR BACK, WE WILL REACH HARAPPA TOMORROW EVENING.
BEAUTIFUL VIEW. I WOULD HAVE LOVED STOPPING HERE.
I WOULD NOT RECOMMEND IT. SEE OVER THERE... CAMELS!
I'M AFRAID RAJA SUSHANA WAS RIGHT... WE ARE BEING WATCHED.
IME FOR OME REST NOW.
THE NEXT MORNING, PRINCE MELUHA AND CHANDRAYAAN WOKE UP WITH A START.
CAPTAIN! EMERGENCY!

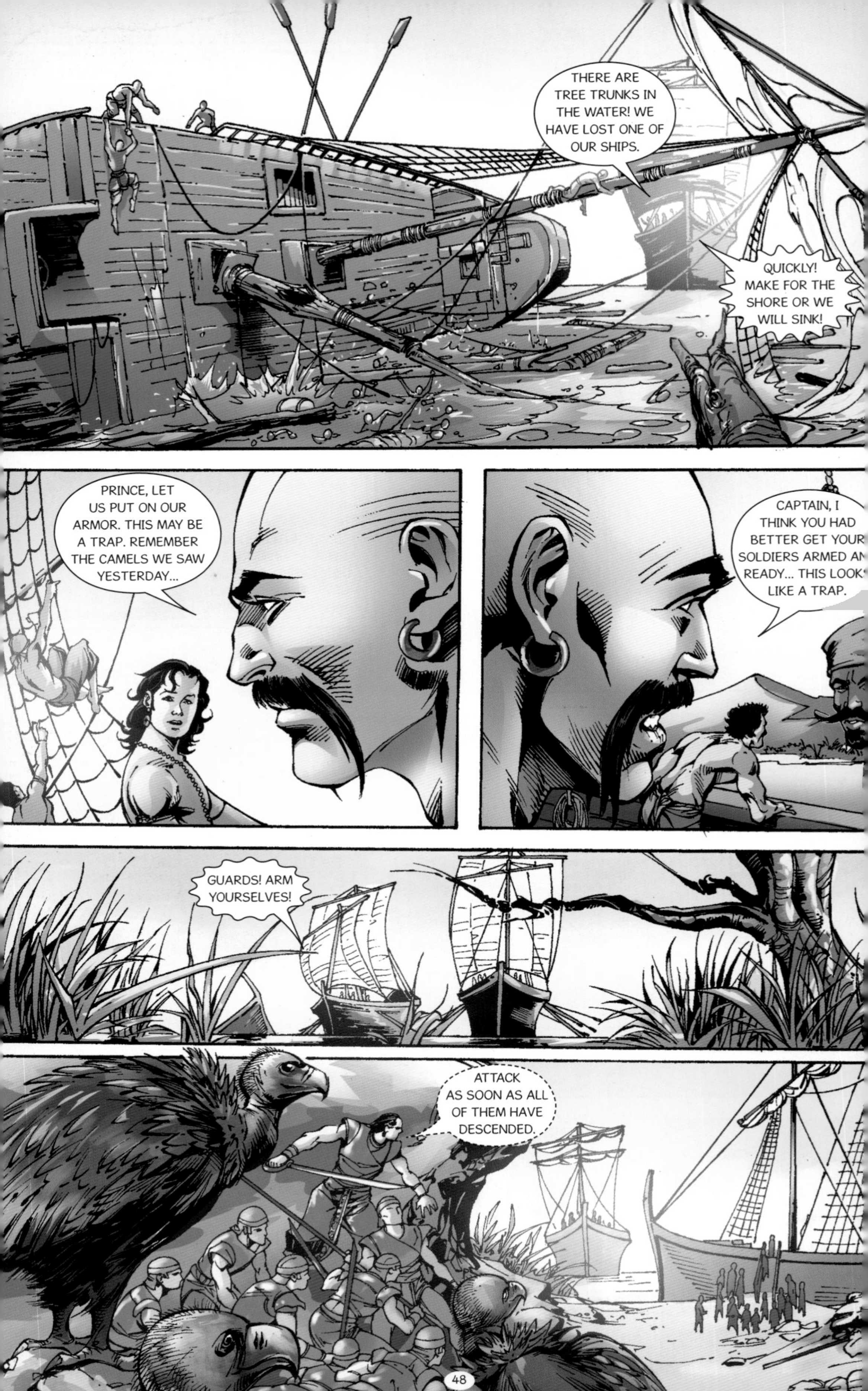
THERE ARE TREE TRUNKS IN THE WATER! WE HAVE LOST ONE OF OUR SHIPS.
QUICKLY! MAKE FOR THE SHORE OR WE WILL SINK!
PRINCE, LET US PUT ON OUR ARMOR. THIS MAY BE A TRAP. REMEMBER THE CAMELS WE SAW YESTERDAY...
CAPTAIN, I THINK YOU HAD BETTER GET YOUR SOLDIERS ARMED AN READY... THIS LOOK LIKE A TRAP.
GUARDS! ARM YOURSELVES!
ATTACK AS SOON AS ALL OF THEM HAVE DESCENDED.

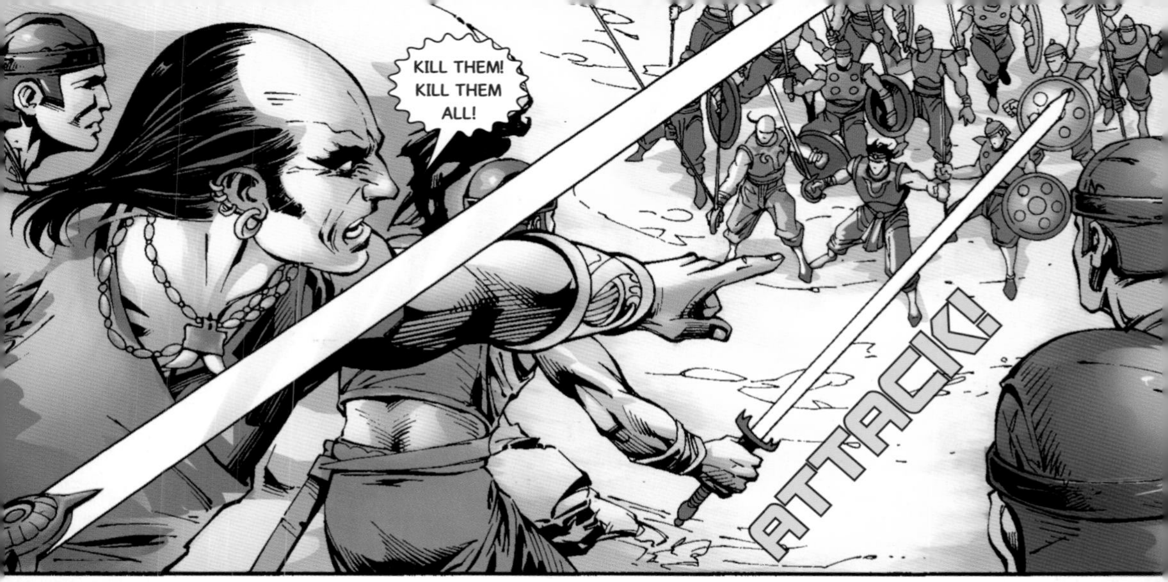
KILL THEM! KILL THEM ALL!
ATTACK!

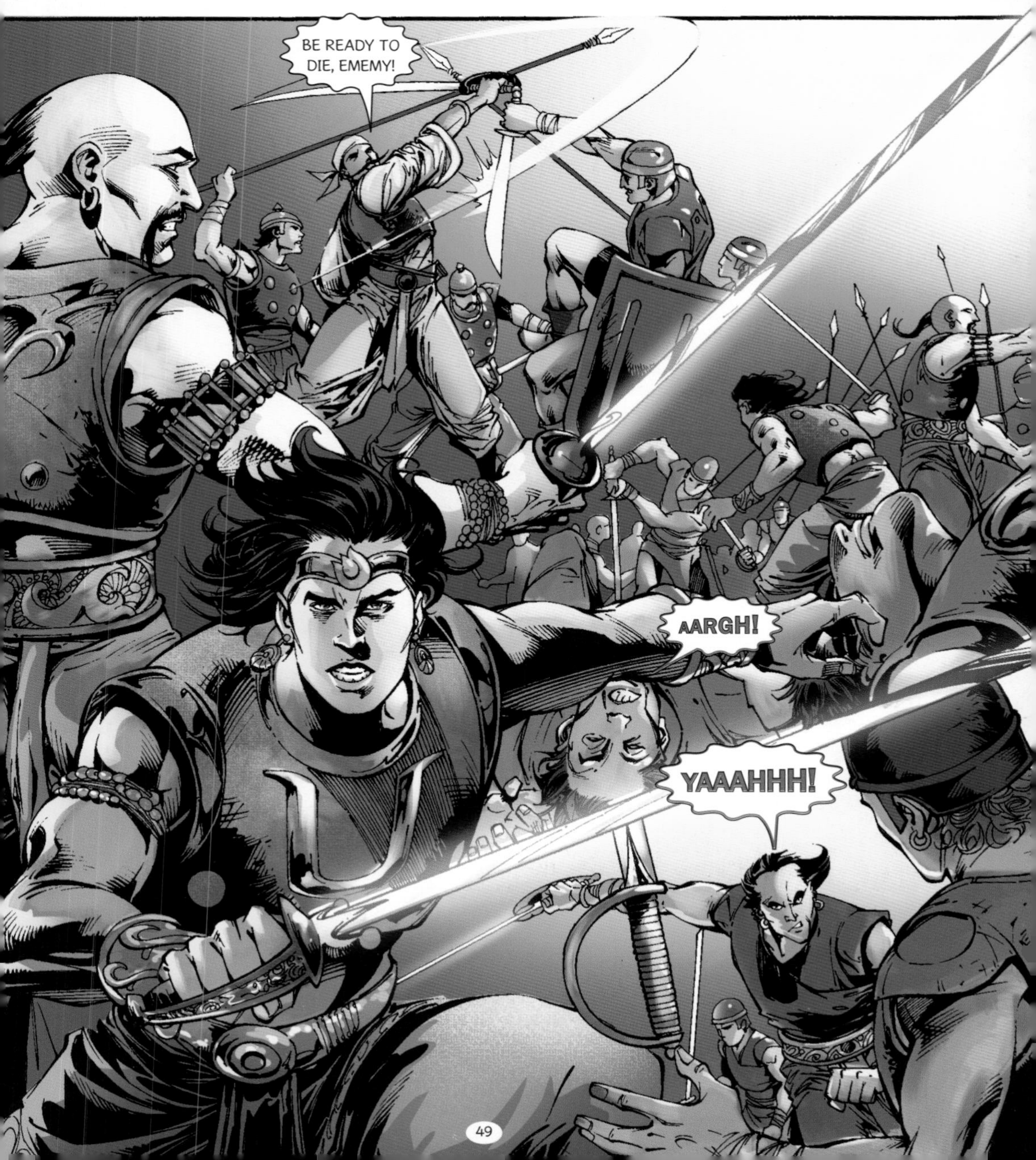
BE READY TO DIE, EMEMY!
AARGH!
YAAAHHH!

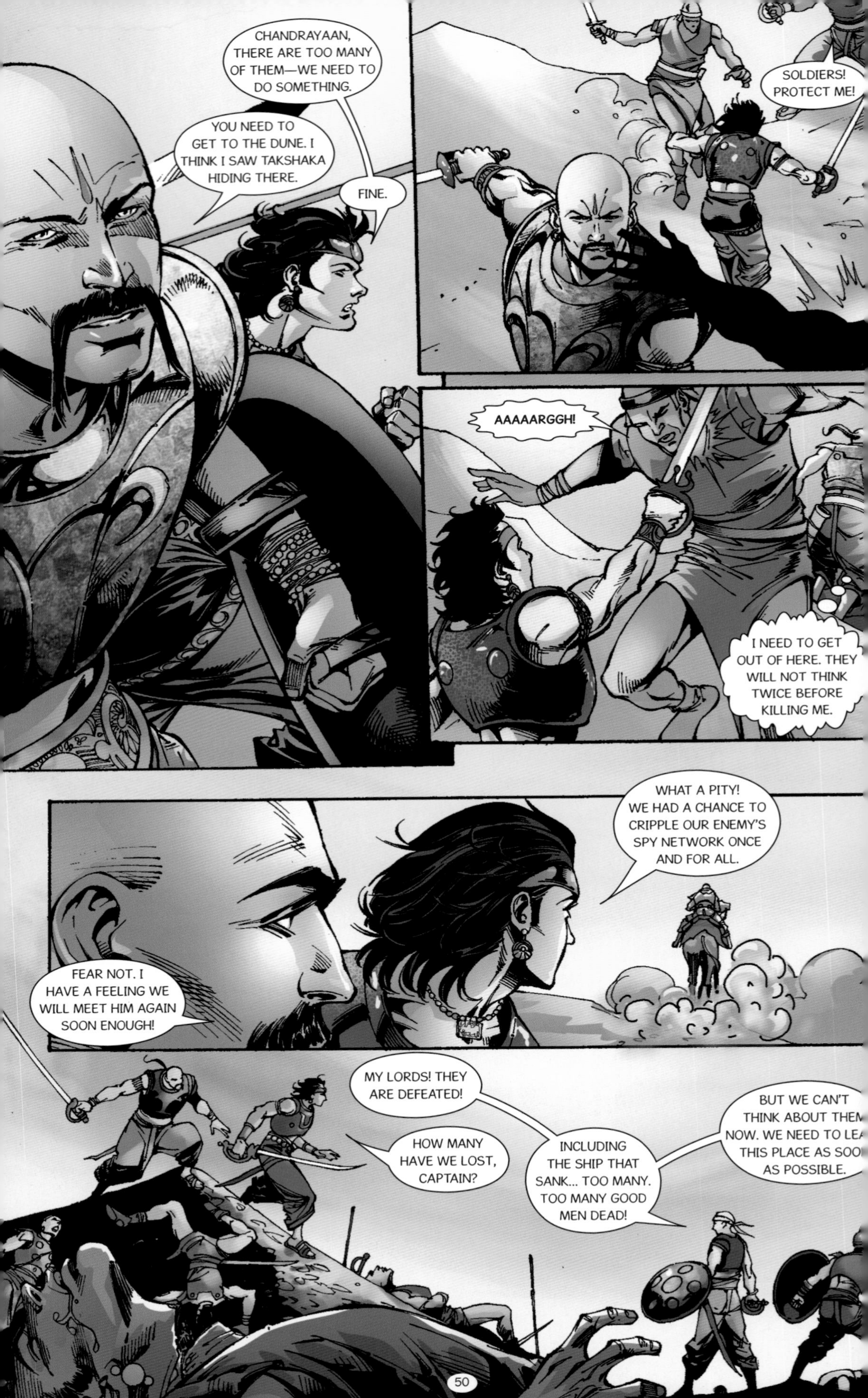
CHANDRAYAAN, THERE ARE TOO MANY OF THEM—WE NEED TO DO SOMETHING.
YOU NEED TO GET TO THE DUNE. I THINK I SAW TAKSHAKA HIDING THERE.
FINE.
SOLDIERS! PROTECT ME!
AAAAARGGH!
I NEED TO GET OUT OF HERE. THEY WILL NOT THINK TWICE BEFORE KILLING ME.
WHAT A PITY! WE HAD A CHANCE TO CRIPPLE OUR ENEMY'S SPY NETWORK ONCE AND FOR ALL.
FEAR NOT. I HAVE A FEELING WE WILL MEET HIM AGAIN SOON ENOUGH!
MY LORDS! THEY ARE DEFEATED!
HOW MANY HAVE WE LOST, CAPTAIN?
INCLUDING THE SHIP THAT SANK... TOO MANY. TOO MANY GOOD MEN DEAD!
BUT WE CAN'T THINK ABOUT THEM NOW. WE NEED TO LEA THIS PLACE AS SOO AS POSSIBLE.

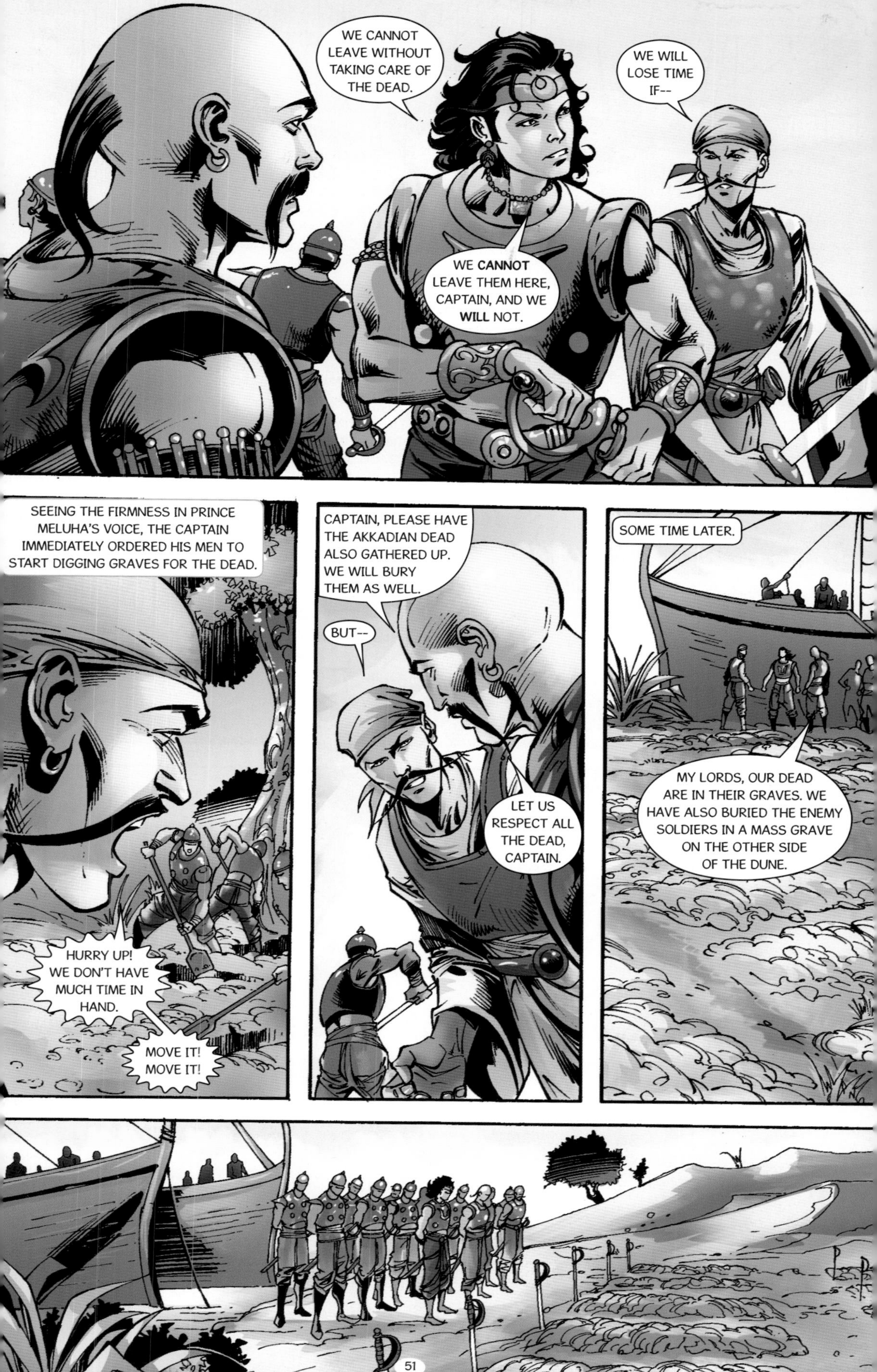
WE CANNOT LEAVE WITHOUT TAKING CARE OF THE DEAD.
WE WILL LOSE TIME IF--
WE CANNOT LEAVE THEM HERE, CAPTAIN, AND WE WILL NOT.
SEEING THE FIRMNESS IN PRINCE MELUHA'S VOICE, THE CAPTAIN IMMEDIATELY ORDERED HIS MEN TO START DIGGING GRAVES FOR THE DEAD.
HURRY UP! WE DON'T HAVE MUCH TIME IN HAND.
MOVE IT! MOVE IT!
CAPTAIN, PLEASE HAVE THE AKKADIAN DEAD ALSO GATHERED UP. WE WILL BURY THEM AS WELL.
BUT--
LET US RESPECT ALL THE DEAD, CAPTAIN.
SOME TIME LATER.
MY LORDS, OUR DEAD ARE IN THEIR GRAVES. WE HAVE ALSO BURIED THE ENEMY SOLDIERS IN A MASS GRAVE ON THE OTHER SIDE OF THE DUNE.

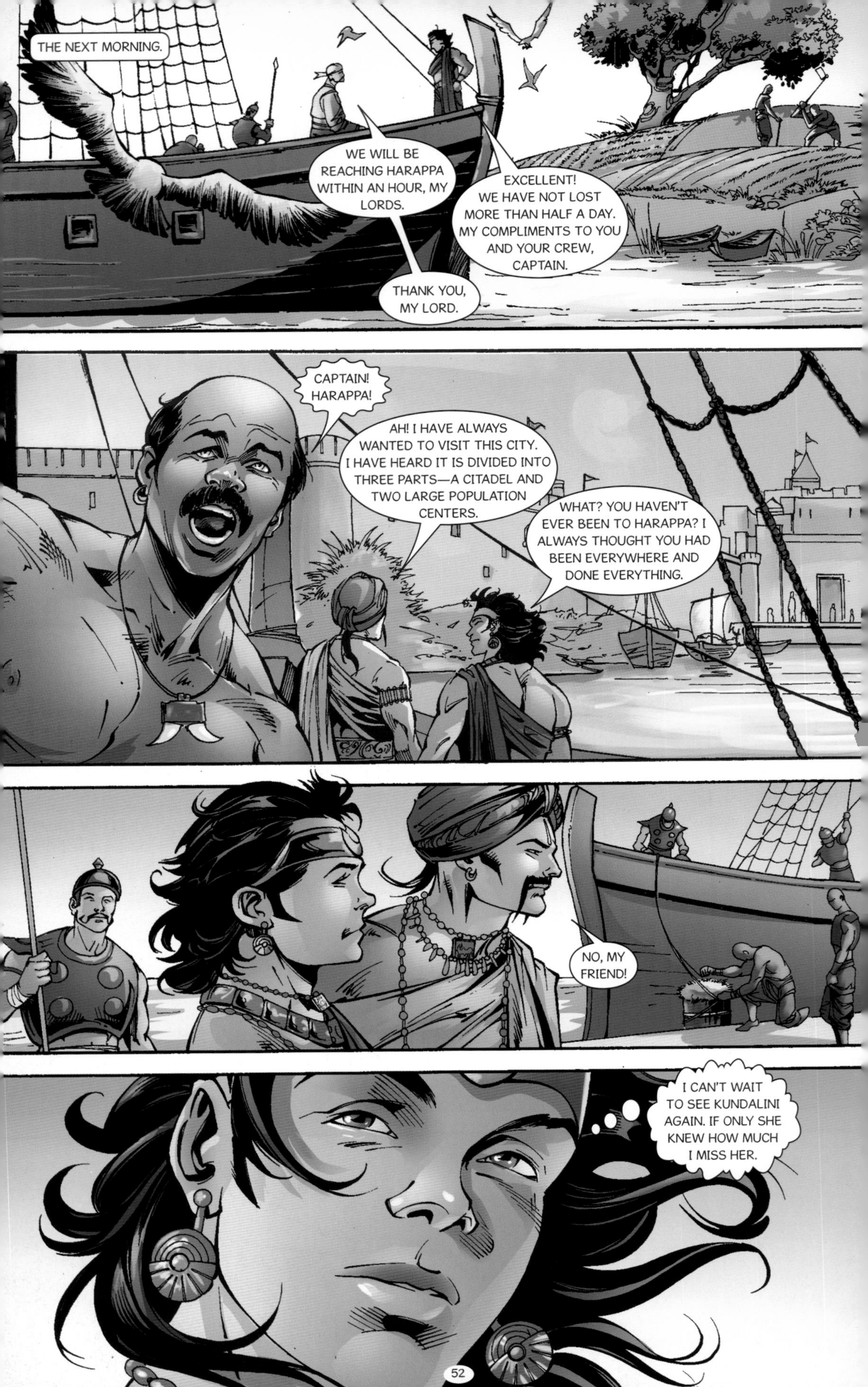
THE NEXT MORNING.
WE WILL BE REACHING HARAPPA WITHIN AN HOUR, MY LORDS.
EXCELLENT! WE HAVE NOT LOST MORE THAN HALF A DAY. MY COMPLIMENTS TO YOU AND YOUR CREW, CAPTAIN.
THANK YOU, MY LORD.
CAPTAIN! HARAPPA!
AH! I HAVE ALWAYS WANTED TO VISIT THIS CITY. I HAVE HEARD IT IS DIVIDED INTO THREE PARTS—A CITADEL AND TWO LARGE POPULATION CENTERS.
WHAT? YOU HAVEN'T EVER BEEN TO HARAPPA? I ALWAYS THOUGHT YOU HAD BEEN EVERYWHERE AND DONE EVERYTHING.
NO, MY FRIEND!
I CAN'T WAIT TO SEE KUNDALINI AGAIN. IF ONLY SHE KNEW HOW MUCH I MISS HER.

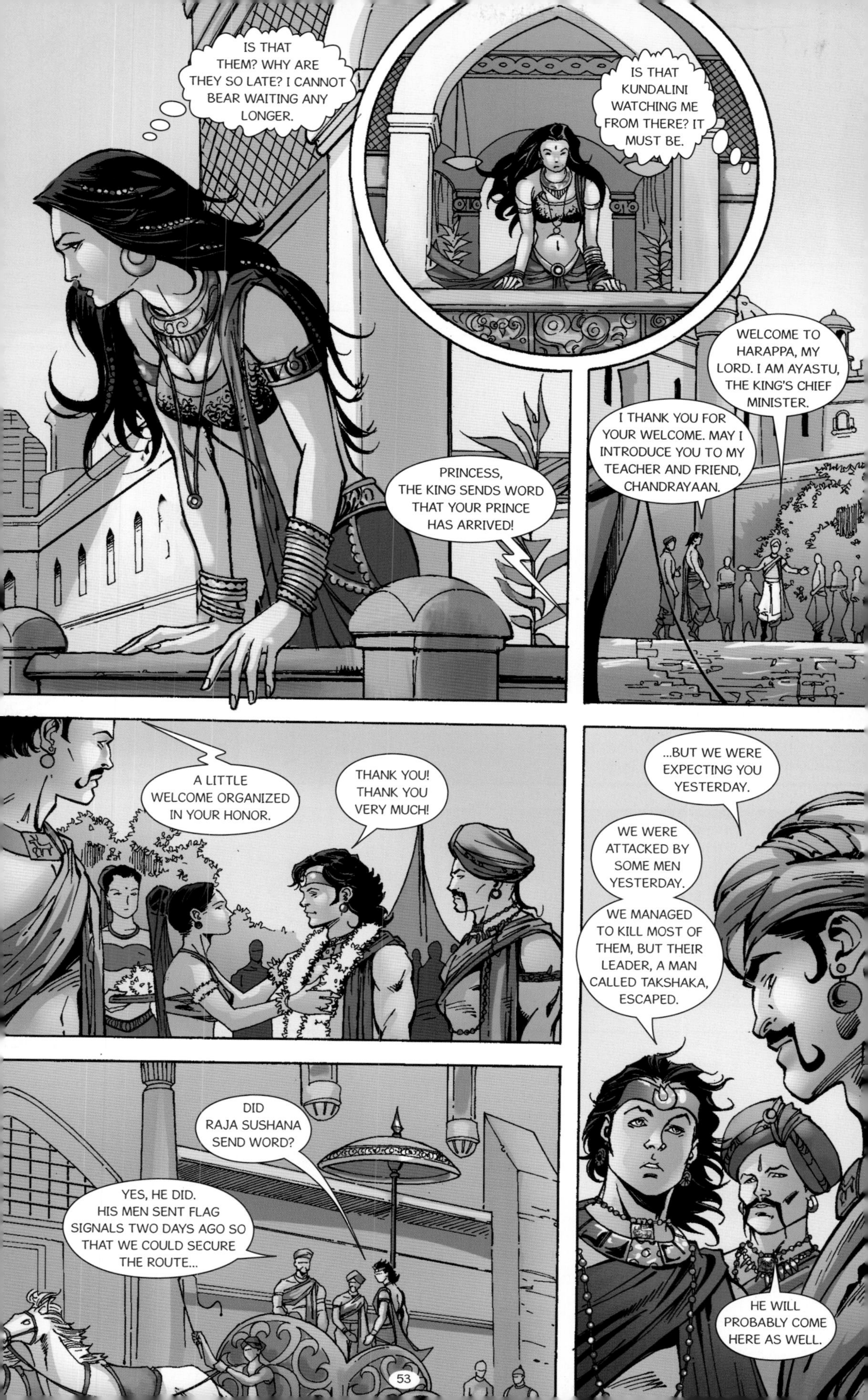
IS THAT THEM? WHY ARE THEY SO LATE? I CANNOT BEAR WAITING ANY LONGER.
IS THAT KUNDALINI WATCHING ME FROM THERE? IT MUST BE.
PRINCESS, THE KING SENDS WORD THAT YOUR PRINCE HAS ARRIVED!
WELCOME TO HARAPPA, MY LORD. I AM AYASTU, THE KING'S CHIEF MINISTER.
I THANK YOU FOR YOUR WELCOME. MAY I INTRODUCE YOU TO MY TEACHER AND FRIEND, CHANDRAYAAN.
A LITTLE WELCOME ORGANIZED IN YOUR HONOR.
THANK YOU! THANK YOU VERY MUCH!
DID RAJA SUSHANA SEND WORD?
YES, HE DID. HIS MEN SENT FLAG SIGNALS TWO DAYS AGO SO THAT WE COULD SECURE THE ROUTE...
...BUT WE WERE EXPECTING YOU YESTERDAY.
WE WERE ATTACKED BY SOME MEN YESTERDAY.
WE MANAGED TO KILL MOST OF THEM, BUT THEIR LEADER, A MAN CALLED TAKSHAKA, ESCAPED.
HE WILL PROBABLY COME HERE AS WELL.

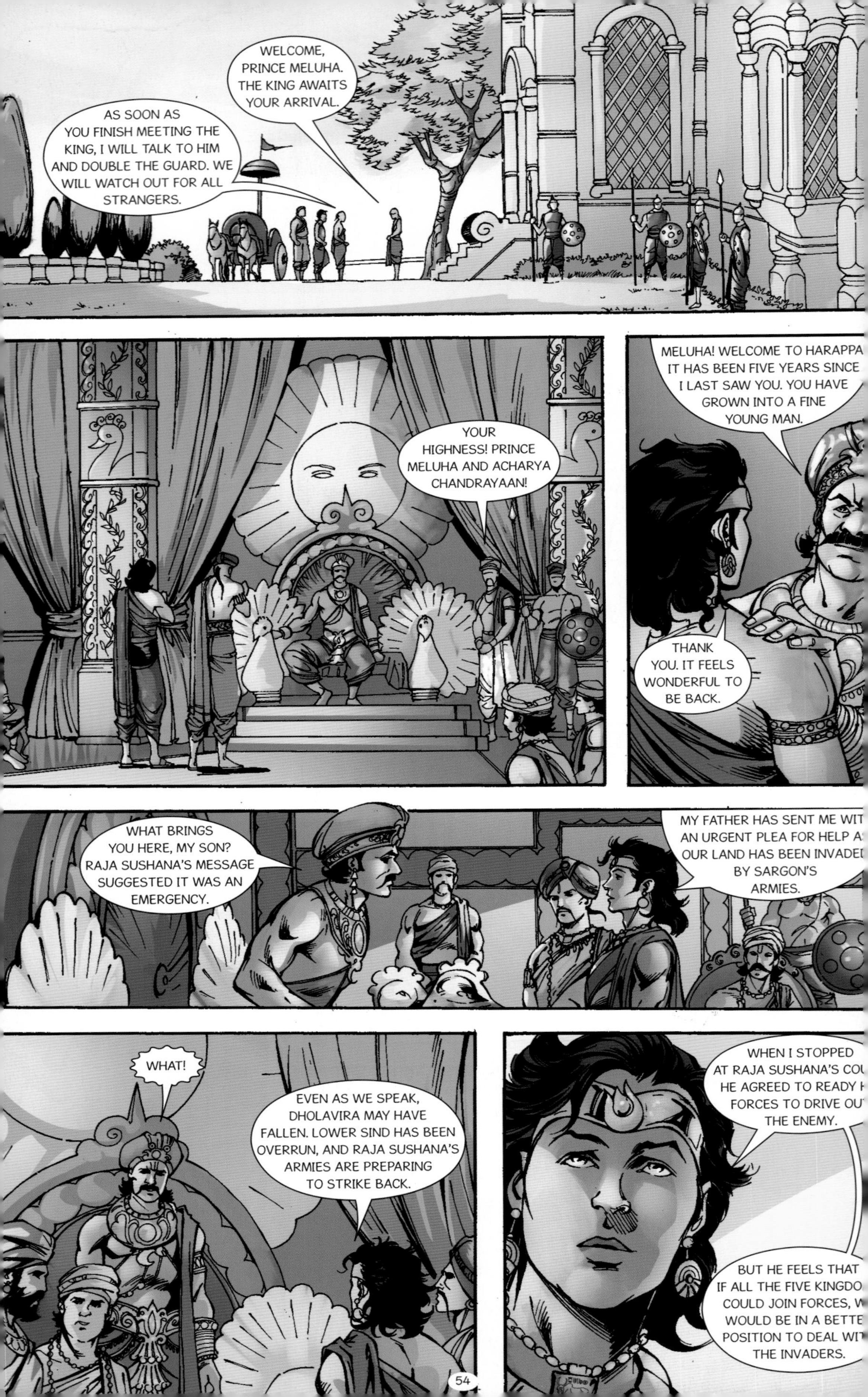

WELCOME, PRINCE MELUHA. THE KING AWAITS YOUR ARRIVAL.
AS SOON AS YOU FINISH MEETING THE KING, I WILL TALK TO HIM AND DOUBLE THE GUARD. WE WILL WATCH OUT FOR ALL STRANGERS.
YOUR HIGHNESS! PRINCE MELUHA AND ACHARYA CHANDRAYAAN!
MELUHA! WELCOME TO HARAPPA IT HAS BEEN FIVE YEARS SINCE I LAST SAW YOU. YOU HAVE GROWN INTO A FINE YOUNG MAN.
THANK YOU. IT FEELS WONDERFUL TO BE BACK.
WHAT BRINGS YOU HERE, MY SON? RAJA SUSHANA'S MESSAGE SUGGESTED IT WAS AN EMERGENCY.
MY FATHER HAS SENT ME WIT AN URGENT PLEA FOR HELP A OUR LAND HAS BEEN INVADE BY SARGON'S ARMIES.
WHAT!
EVEN AS WE SPEAK, DHOLAVIRA MAY HAVE FALLEN. LOWER SIND HAS BEEN OVERRUN, AND RAJA SUSHANA'S ARMIES ARE PREPARING TO STRIKE BACK.
WHEN I STOPPED AT RAJA SUSHANA'S CO HE AGREED TO READY FORCES TO DRIVE OU THE ENEMY.
BUT HE FEELS THAT IF ALL THE FIVE KINGDO COULD JOIN FORCES, WOULD BE IN A BETTE POSITION TO DEAL WI THE INVADERS.

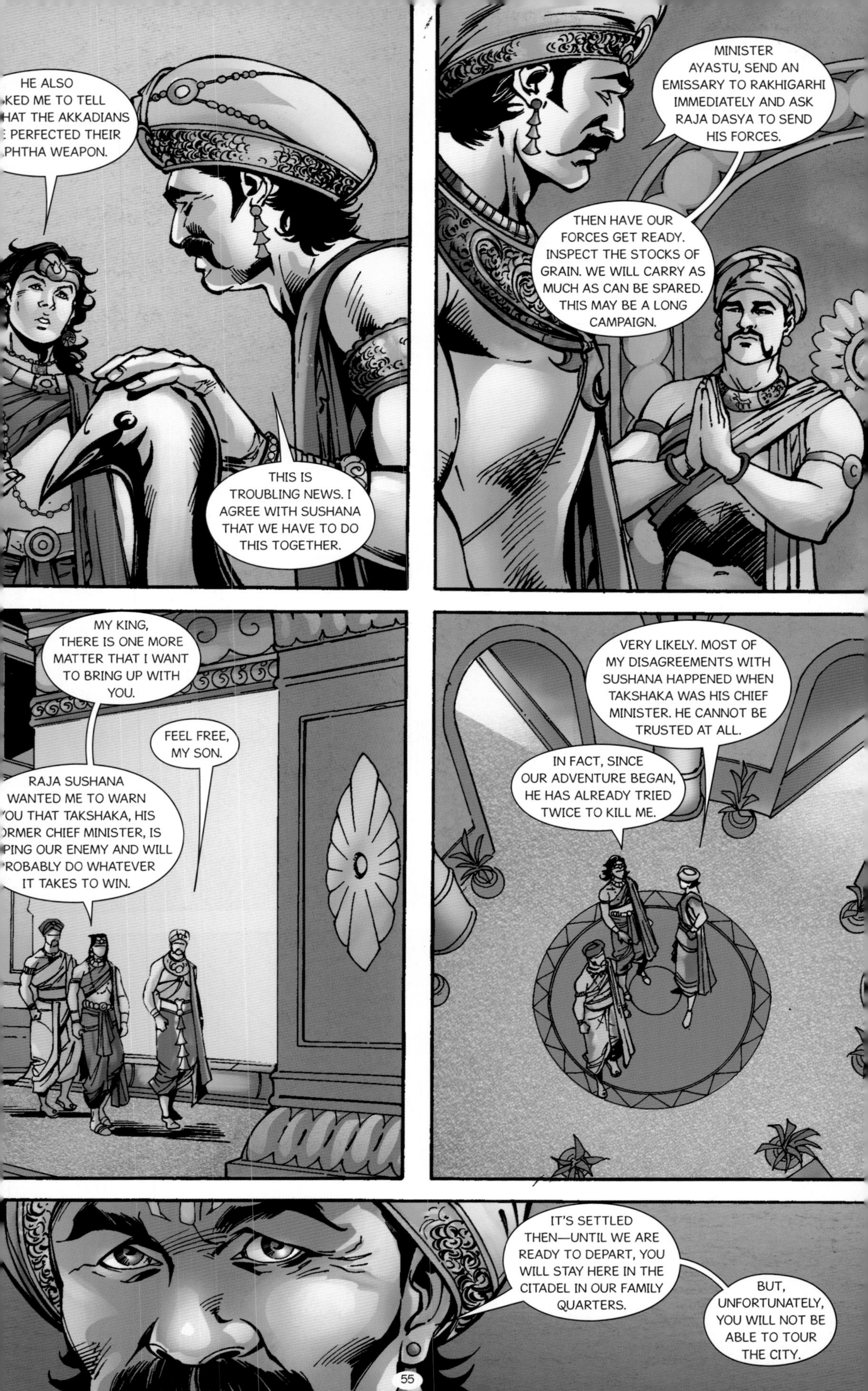

HE ALSO
KED ME TO TELL
HAT THE AKKADIANS
PERFECTED THEIR
PHTHA WEAPON.
THIS IS TROUBLING NEWS. I AGREE WITH SUSHANA THAT WE HAVE TO DO THIS TOGETHER.
MINISTER AYASTU, SEND AN EMISSARY TO RAKHIGARHI IMMEDIATELY AND ASK RAJA DASYA TO SEND HIS FORCES.
THEN HAVE OUR FORCES GET READY. INSPECT THE STOCKS OF GRAIN. WE WILL CARRY AS MUCH AS CAN BE SPARED. THIS MAY BE A LONG CAMPAIGN.
MY KING, THERE IS ONE MORE MATTER THAT I WANT TO BRING UP WITH YOU.
FEEL FREE, MY SON.
RAJA SUSHANA
WANTED ME TO WARN
OU THAT TAKSHAKA, HIS
RMER CHIEF MINISTER, IS
PING OUR ENEMY AND WILL
ROBABLY DO WHATEVER
IT TAKES TO WIN.
VERY LIKELY. MOST OF MY DISAGREEMENTS WITH SUSHANA HAPPENED WHEN TAKSHAKA WAS HIS CHIEF MINISTER. HE CANNOT BE TRUSTED AT ALL.
IN FACT, SINCE OUR ADVENTURE BEGAN, HE HAS ALREADY TRIED TWICE TO KILL ME.
IT'S SETTLED THEN—UNTIL WE ARE READY TO DEPART, YOU WILL STAY HERE IN THE CITADEL IN OUR FAMILY QUARTERS.
BUT, UNFORTUNATELY, YOU WILL NOT BE ABLE TO TOUR THE CITY.

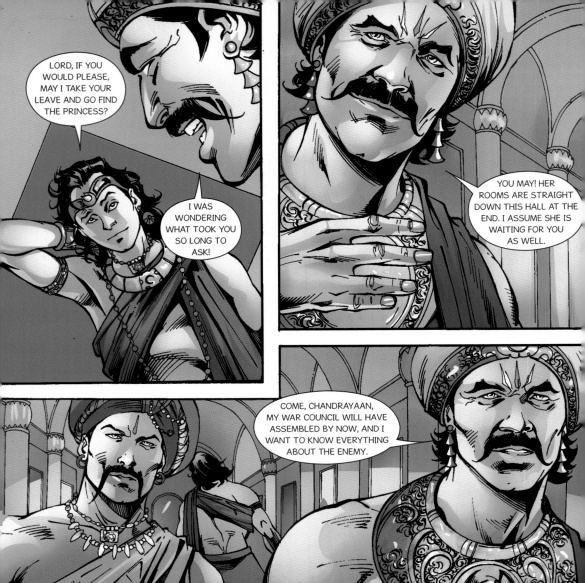

LORD, IF YOU WOULD PLEASE, MAY I TAKE YOUR LEAVE AND GO FIND THE PRINCESS?

I WAS WONDERING WHAT TOOK YOU SO LONG TO ASK!

YOU MAY! HER ROOMS ARE STRAIGHT DOWN THIS HALL AT THE END. I ASSUME SHE IS WAITING FOR YOU AS WELL.

COME, CHANDRAYAAN, MY WAR COUNCIL WILL HAVE ASSEMBLED BY NOW, AND I WANT TO KNOW EVERYTHING ABOUT THE ENEMY.

KUNDALINI!

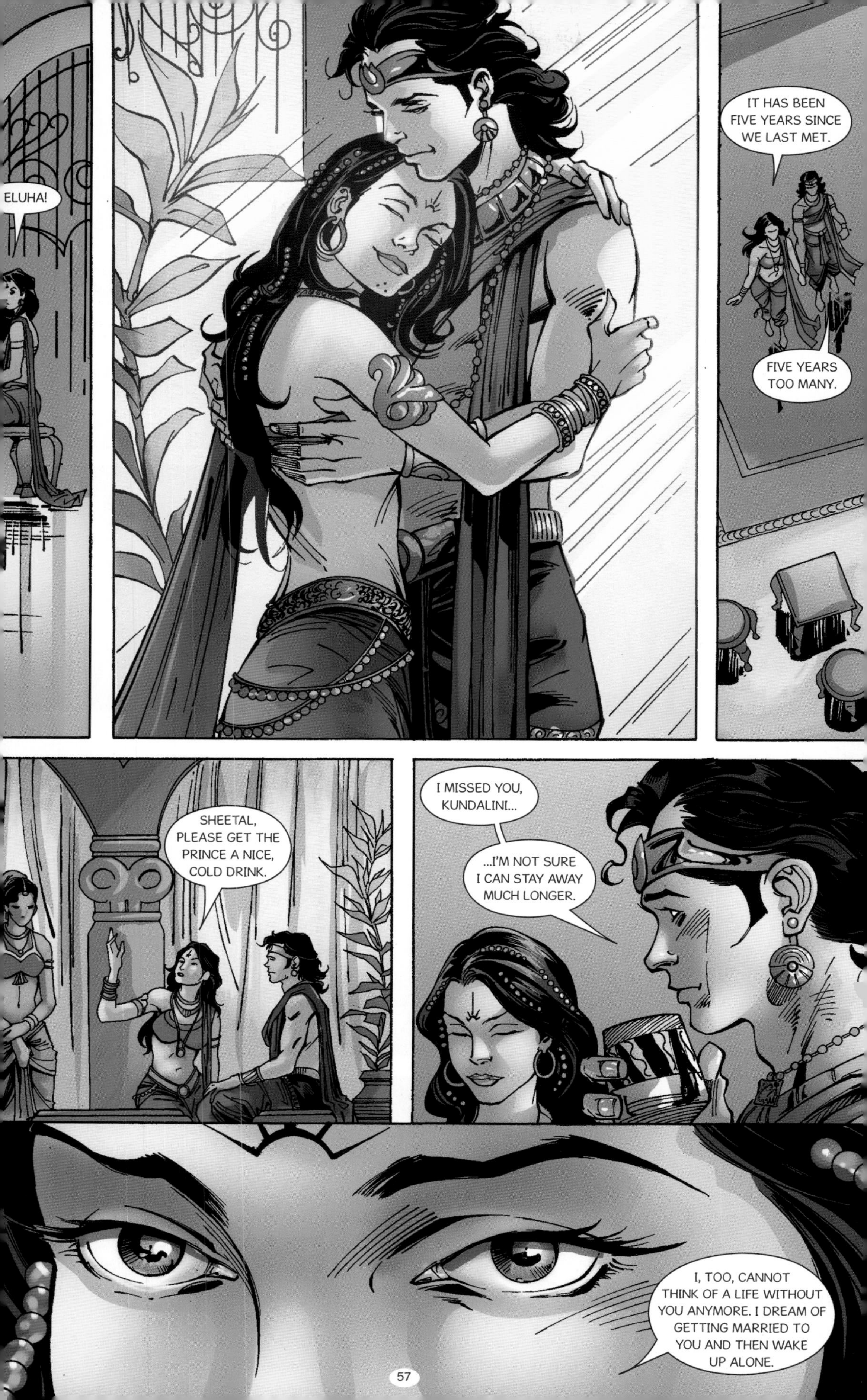

ELUHA!
IT HAS BEEN FIVE YEARS SINCE WE LAST MET.
FIVE YEARS TOO MANY.
SHEETAL, PLEASE GET THE PRINCE A NICE, COLD DRINK.
I MISSED YOU, KUNDALINI...
...I'M NOT SURE I CAN STAY AWAY MUCH LONGER.
I, TOO, CANNOT THINK OF A LIFE WITHOUT YOU ANYMORE. I DREAM OF GETTING MARRIED TO YOU AND THEN WAKE UP ALONE.

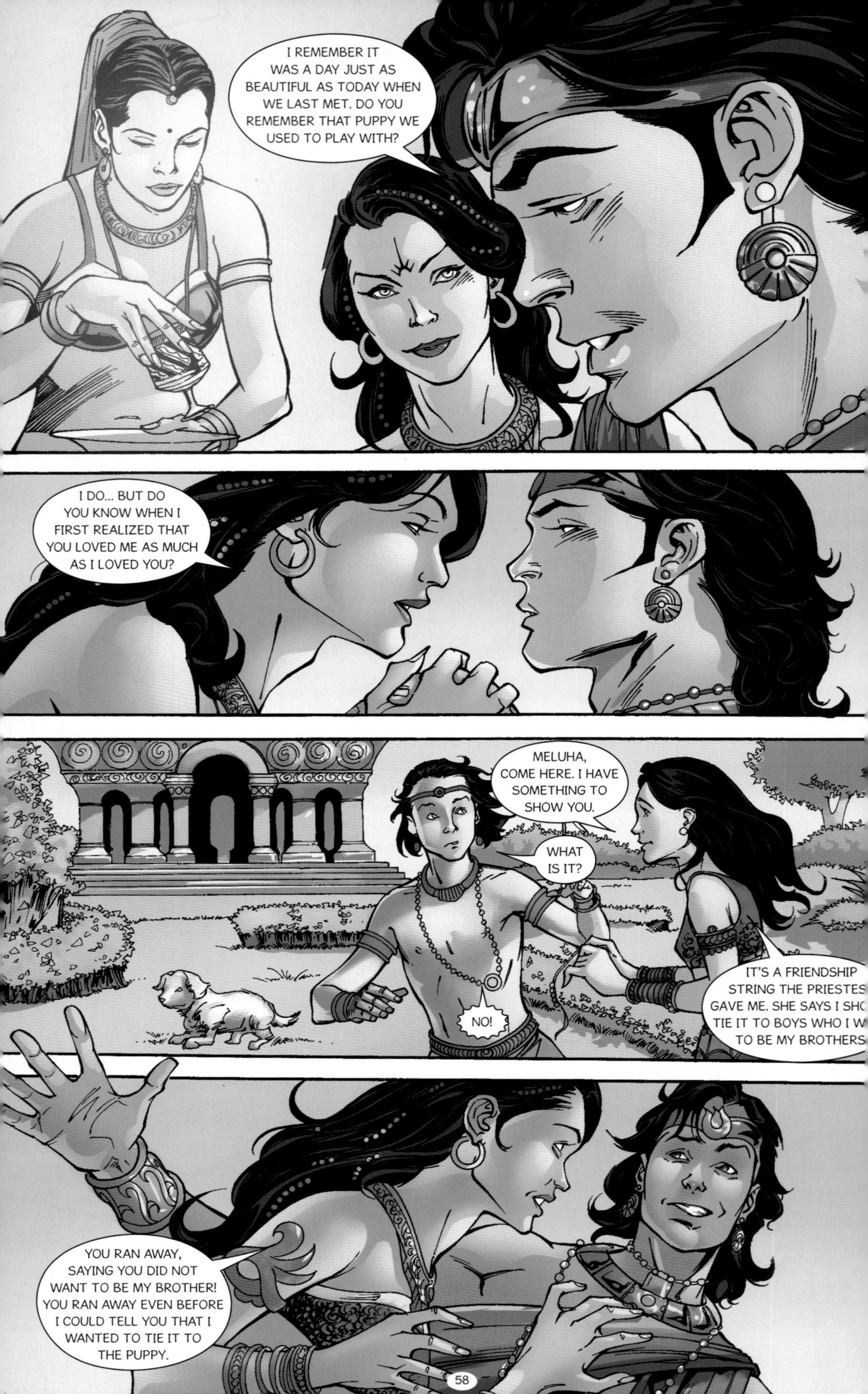

I REMEMBER IT WAS A DAY JUST AS BEAUTIFUL AS TODAY WHEN WE LAST MET. DO YOU REMEMBER THAT PUPPY WE USED TO PLAY WITH?
I DO... BUT DO YOU KNOW WHEN I FIRST REALIZED THAT YOU LOVED ME AS MUCH AS I LOVED YOU?
MELUHA, COME HERE. I HAVE SOMETHING TO SHOW YOU.
WHAT IS IT?
IT'S A FRIENDSHIP STRING THE PRIESTES GAVE ME. SHE SAYS I SH TIE IT TO BOYS WHO I W TO BE MY BROTHERS
NO!
YOU RAN AWAY, SAYING YOU DID NOT WANT TO BE MY BROTHER! YOU RAN AWAY EVEN BEFORE I COULD TELL YOU THAT I WANTED TO TIE IT TO THE PUPPY.

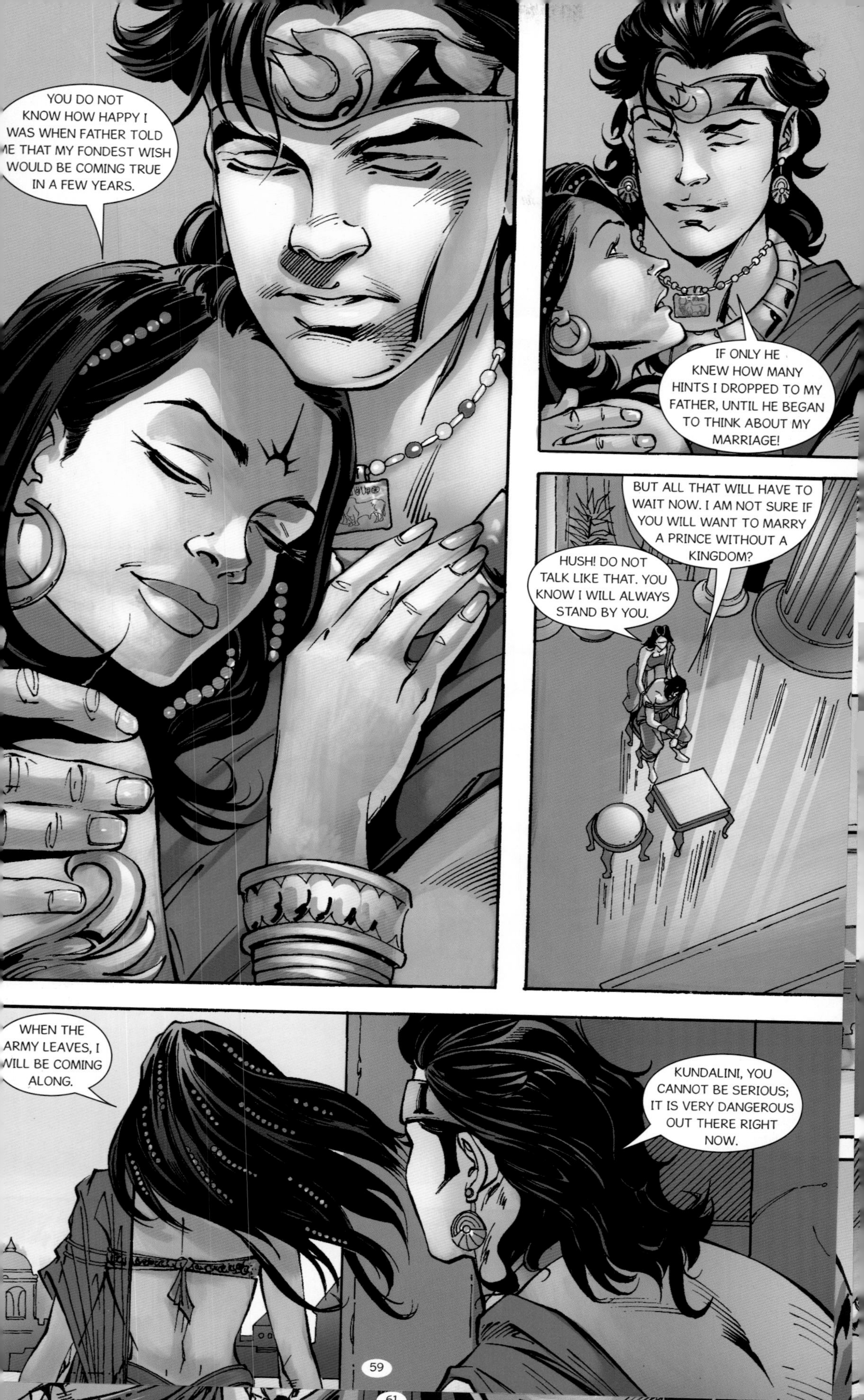
YOU DO NOT KNOW HOW HAPPY I WAS WHEN FATHER TOLD ME THAT MY FONDEST WISH WOULD BE COMING TRUE IN A FEW YEARS.
IF ONLY HE KNEW HOW MANY HINTS I DROPPED TO MY FATHER, UNTIL HE BEGAN TO THINK ABOUT MY MARRIAGE!
BUT ALL THAT WILL HAVE TO WAIT NOW. I AM NOT SURE IF YOU WILL WANT TO MARRY A PRINCE WITHOUT A KINGDOM?
HUSH! DO NOT TALK LIKE THAT. YOU KNOW I WILL ALWAYS STAND BY YOU.
WHEN THE ARMY LEAVES, I WILL BE COMING ALONG.
KUNDALINI, YOU CANNOT BE SERIOUS; IT IS VERY DANGEROUS OUT THERE RIGHT NOW.

THE KING HAS BEEN KILLED!

THE GODS HAVE LEFT US!

WE ARE DOOMED!

SO, MAHAVINDASA, I AM FINALLY RID OF YOU. I HAVE BROKEN HARAPPA INTO PIECES. NOW I MUST GO BACK TO SIND! I MUST RALLY MY ALLIES. I WILL SOON RULE ALL THESE KINGDOMS.

GET THE PALACE DOCTORS AND THE PRIESTESS HERE. FAST!

CALL KUNDALINI PLEASE.

GET THE PRINCESS HERE! NOW!

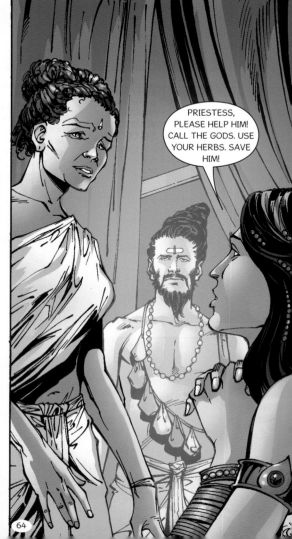

PRIESTESS, PLEASE HELP HIM! CALL THE GODS. USE YOUR HERBS. SAVE HIM!

FATHER!

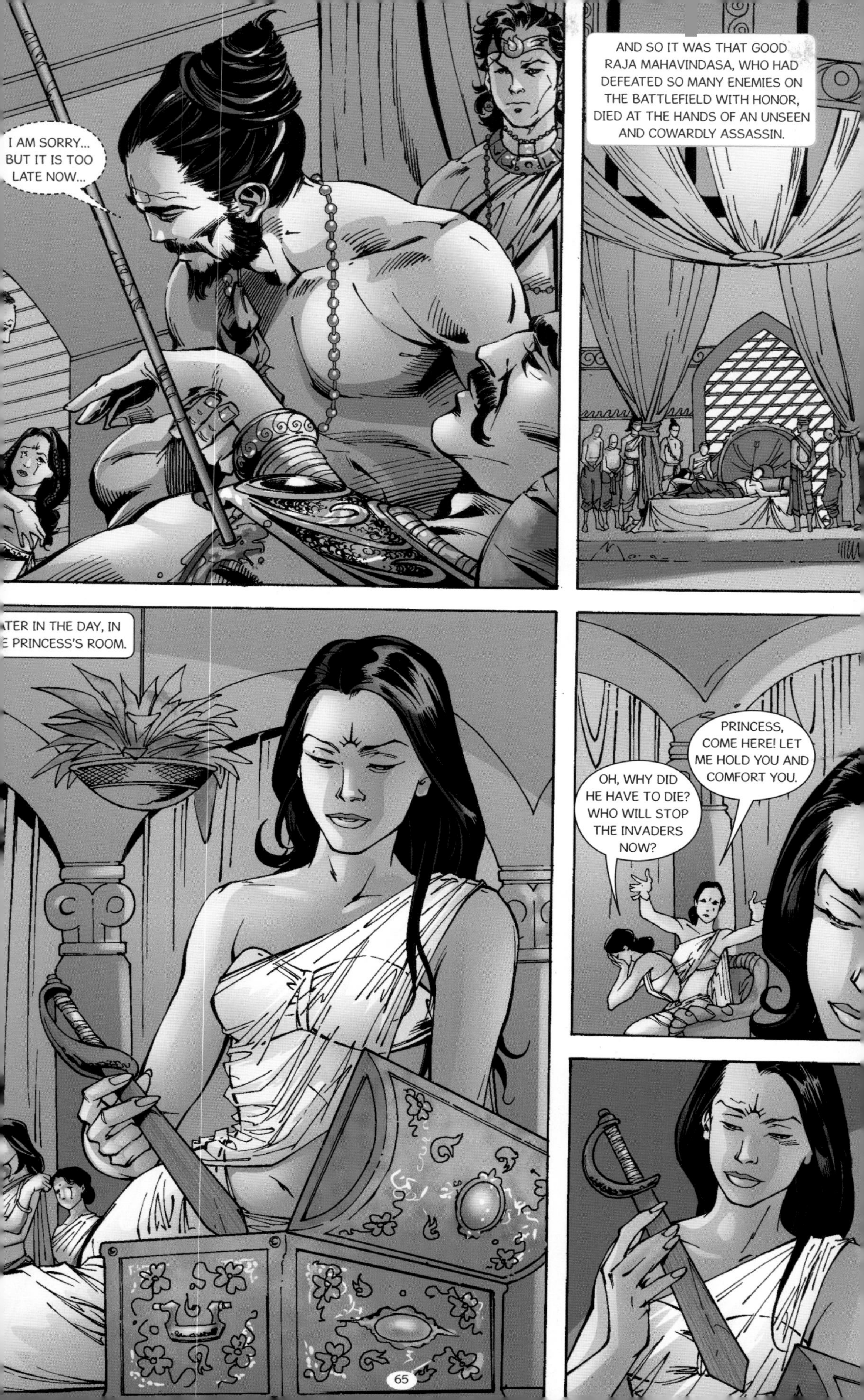
I AM SORRY... BUT IT IS TOO LATE NOW...
AND SO IT WAS THAT GOOD RAJA MAHAVINDASA, WHO HAD DEFEATED SO MANY ENEMIES ON THE BATTLEFIELD WITH HONOR, DIED AT THE HANDS OF AN UNSEEN AND COWARDLY ASSASSIN.
ATER IN THE DAY, IN E PRINCESS'S ROOM.
OH, WHY DID HE HAVE TO DIE? WHO WILL STOP THE INVADERS NOW?
PRINCESS, COME HERE! LET ME HOLD YOU AND COMFORT YOU.

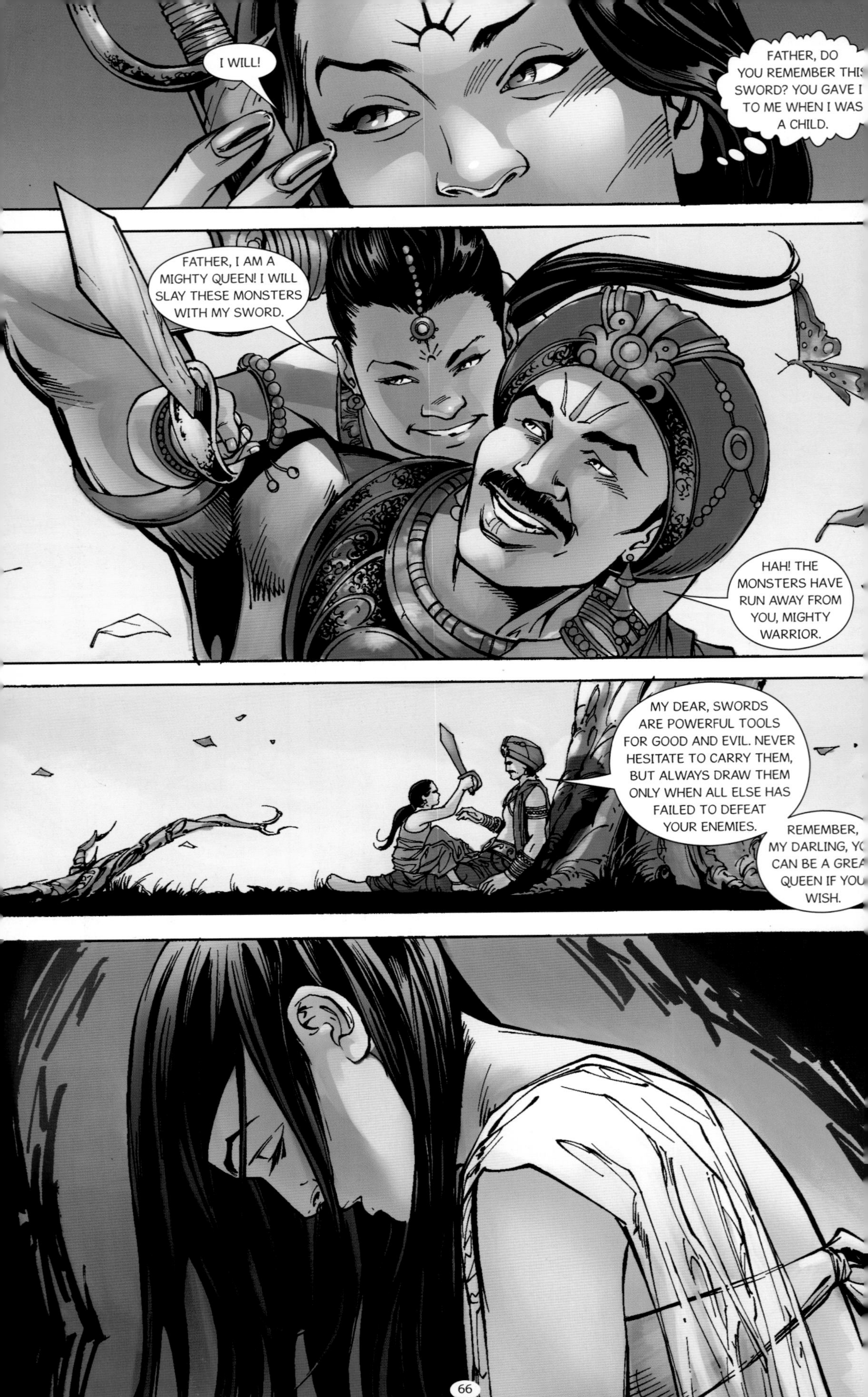
I WILL!
FATHER, DO YOU REMEMBER THIS SWORD? YOU GAVE I TO ME WHEN I WAS A CHILD.
FATHER, I AM A MIGHTY QUEEN! I WILL SLAY THESE MONSTERS WITH MY SWORD.
HAH! THE MONSTERS HAVE RUN AWAY FROM YOU, MIGHTY WARRIOR.
MY DEAR, SWORDS ARE POWERFUL TOOLS FOR GOOD AND EVIL. NEVER HESITATE TO CARRY THEM, BUT ALWAYS DRAW THEM ONLY WHEN ALL ELSE HAS FAILED TO DEFEAT YOUR ENEMIES.
REMEMBER, MY DARLING, YO CAN BE A GREA QUEEN IF YOU WISH.

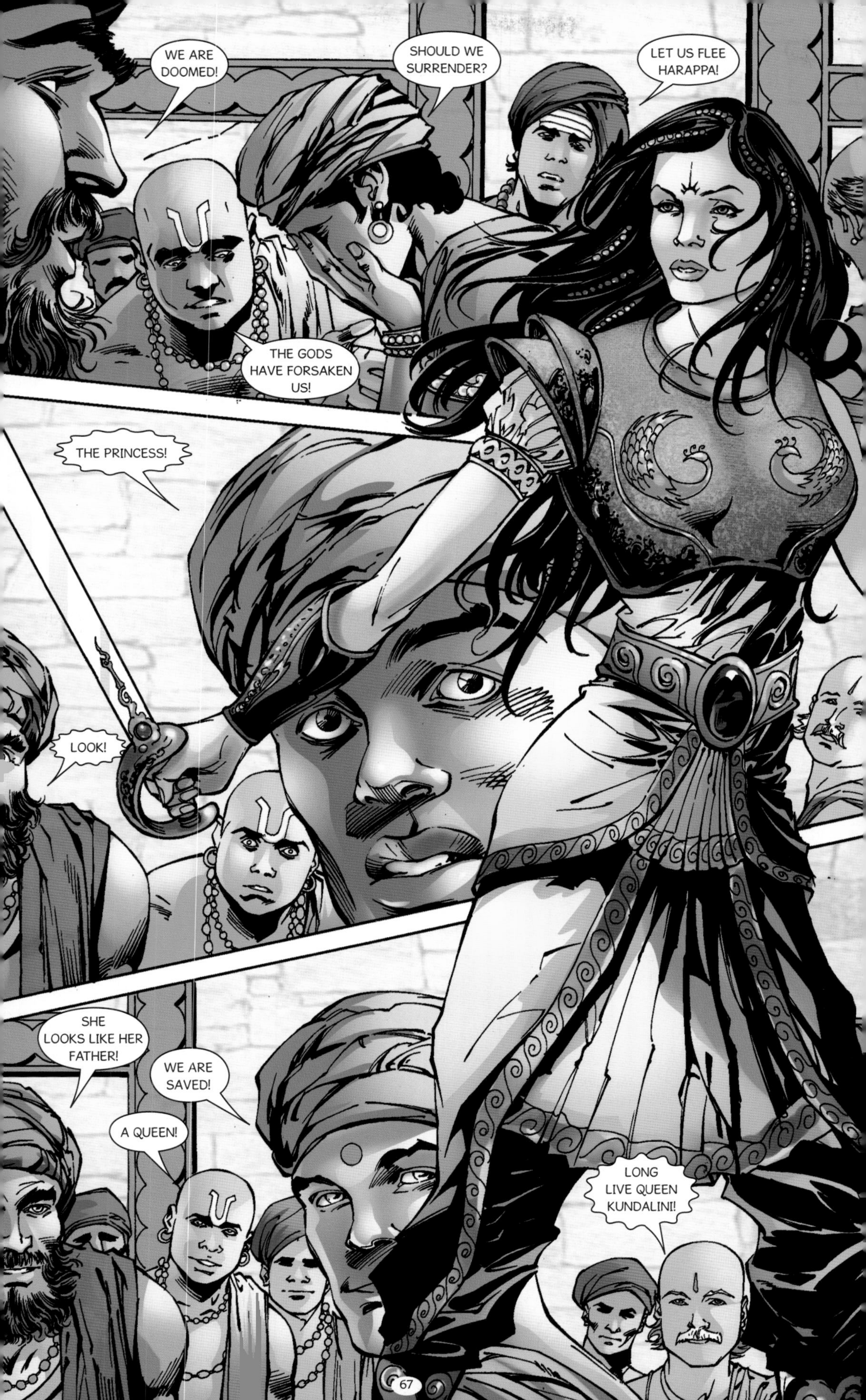
WE ARE DOOMED!
SHOULD WE SURRENDER?
LET US FLEE HARAPPA!
THE GODS HAVE FORSAKEN US!
THE PRINCESS!
LOOK!
SHE LOOKS LIKE HER FATHER!
WE ARE SAVED!
A QUEEN!
LONG LIVE QUEEN KUNDALINI!

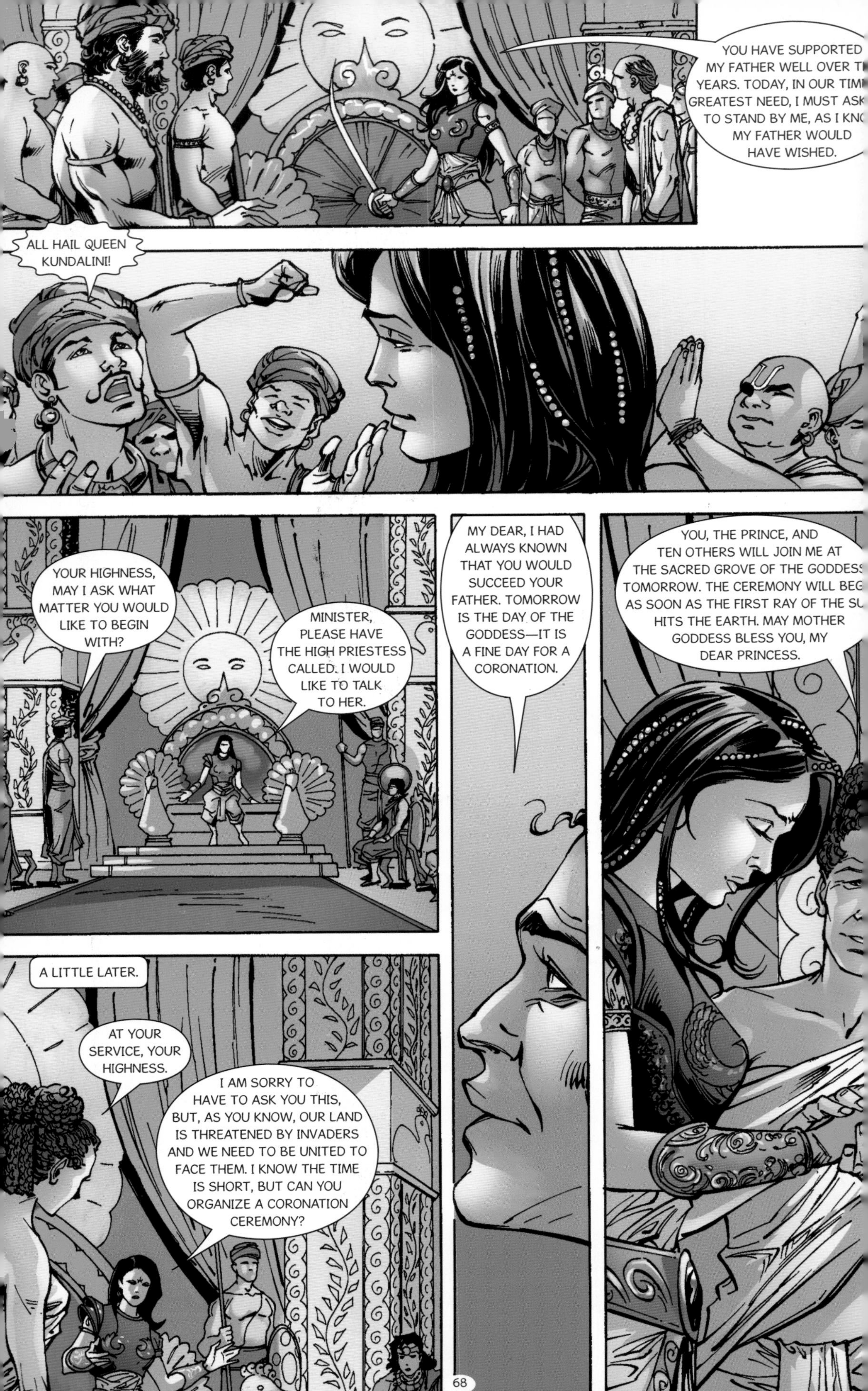
YOU HAVE SUPPORTED MY FATHER WELL OVER T YEARS. TODAY, IN OUR TIM GREATEST NEED, I MUST ASK TO STAND BY ME, AS I KN MY FATHER WOULD HAVE WISHED.
ALL HAIL QUEEN KUNDALINI!
YOUR HIGHNESS, MAY I ASK WHAT MATTER YOU WOULD LIKE TO BEGIN WITH?
MINISTER, PLEASE HAVE THE HIGH PRIESTESS CALLED. I WOULD LIKE TO TALK TO HER.
A LITTLE LATER.
AT YOUR SERVICE, YOUR HIGHNESS.
I AM SORRY TO HAVE TO ASK YOU THIS, BUT, AS YOU KNOW, OUR LAND IS THREATENED BY INVADERS AND WE NEED TO BE UNITED TO FACE THEM. I KNOW THE TIME IS SHORT, BUT CAN YOU ORGANIZE A CORONATION CEREMONY?
MY DEAR, I HAD ALWAYS KNOWN THAT YOU WOULD SUCCEED YOUR FATHER. TOMORROW IS THE DAY OF THE GODDESS—IT IS A FINE DAY FOR A CORONATION.
YOU, THE PRINCE, AND TEN OTHERS WILL JOIN ME AT THE SACRED GROVE OF THE GODDESS TOMORROW. THE CEREMONY WILL BEG AS SOON AS THE FIRST RAY OF THE SU HITS THE EARTH. MAY MOTHER GODDESS BLESS YOU, MY DEAR PRINCESS.

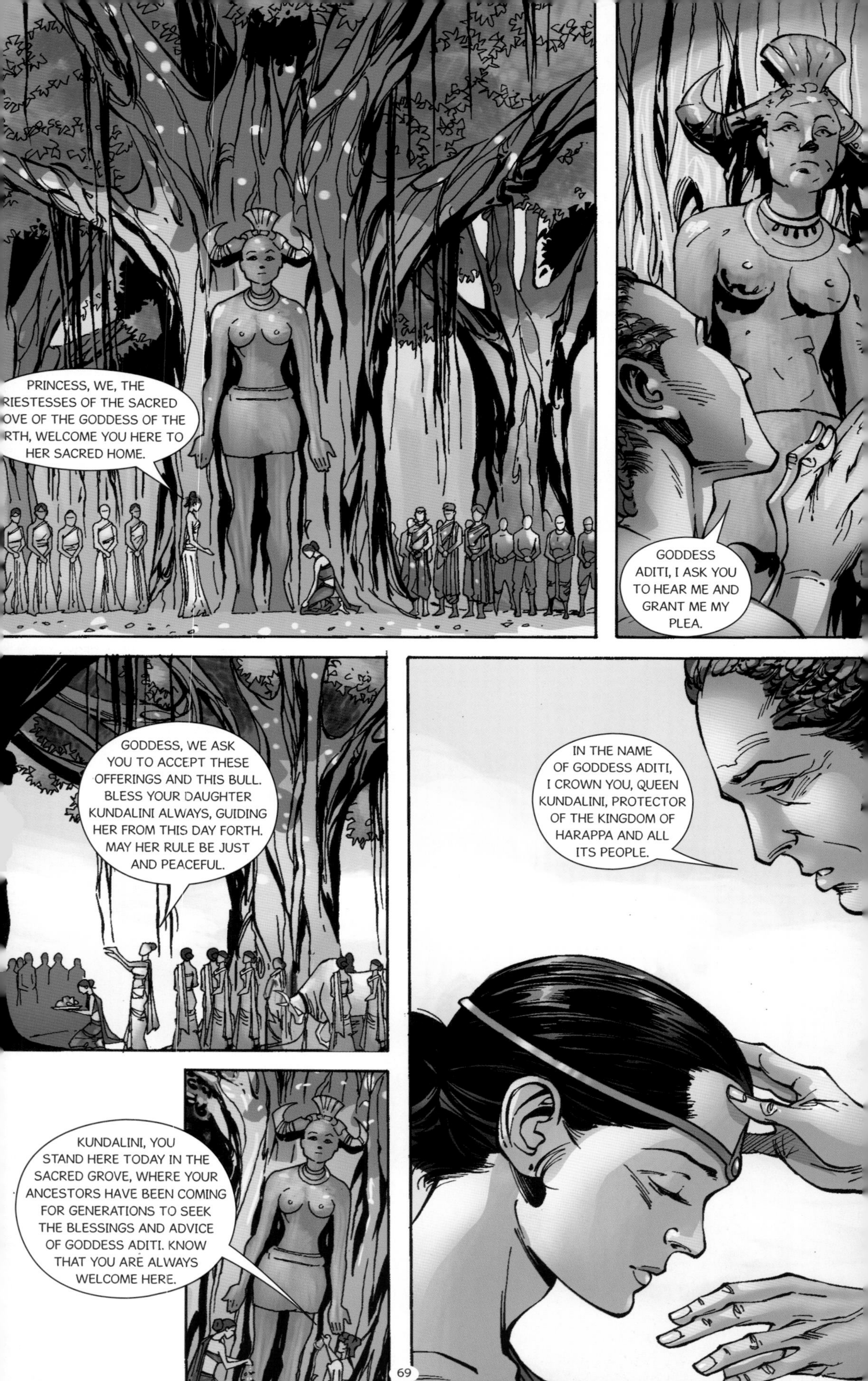
PRINCESS, WE, THE RIESTESSES OF THE SACRED OVE OF THE GODDESS OF THE RTH, WELCOME YOU HERE TO HER SACRED HOME.
GODDESS ADITI, I ASK YOU TO HEAR ME AND GRANT ME MY PLEA.
GODDESS, WE ASK YOU TO ACCEPT THESE OFFERINGS AND THIS BULL. BLESS YOUR DAUGHTER KUNDALINI ALWAYS, GUIDING HER FROM THIS DAY FORTH. MAY HER RULE BE JUST AND PEACEFUL.
IN THE NAME OF GODDESS ADITI, I CROWN YOU, QUEEN KUNDALINI, PROTECTOR OF THE KINGDOM OF HARAPPA AND ALL ITS PEOPLE.
KUNDALINI, YOU STAND HERE TODAY IN THE SACRED GROVE, WHERE YOUR ANCESTORS HAVE BEEN COMING FOR GENERATIONS TO SEEK THE BLESSINGS AND ADVICE OF GODDESS ADITI. KNOW THAT YOU ARE ALWAYS WELCOME HERE.

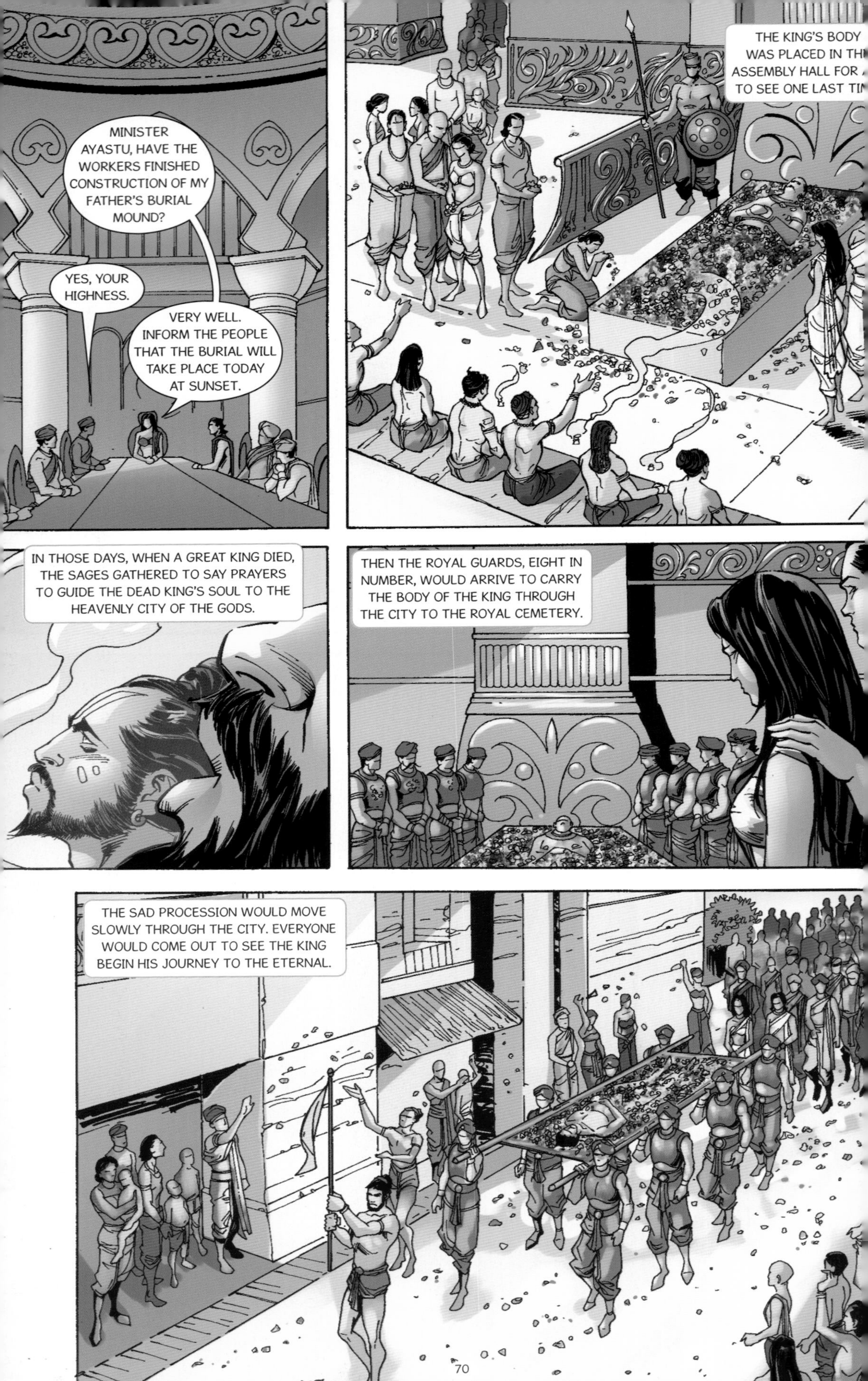
MINISTER AYASTU, HAVE THE WORKERS FINISHED CONSTRUCTION OF MY FATHER'S BURIAL MOUND?
YES, YOUR HIGHNESS.
VERY WELL. INFORM THE PEOPLE THAT THE BURIAL WILL TAKE PLACE TODAY AT SUNSET.
THE KING'S BODY WAS PLACED IN TH ASSEMBLY HALL FOR TO SEE ONE LAST TI
IN THOSE DAYS, WHEN A GREAT KING DIED, THE SAGES GATHERED TO SAY PRAYERS TO GUIDE THE DEAD KING'S SOUL TO THE HEAVENLY CITY OF THE GODS.
THEN THE ROYAL GUARDS, EIGHT IN NUMBER, WOULD ARRIVE TO CARRY THE BODY OF THE KING THROUGH THE CITY TO THE ROYAL CEMETERY.
THE SAD PROCESSION WOULD MOVE SLOWLY THROUGH THE CITY. EVERYONE WOULD COME OUT TO SEE THE KING BEGIN HIS JOURNEY TO THE ETERNAL.

THE ROYAL CEMETERY OF HARAPPA.

ALL GREAT RULERS IN THOSE DAYS WERE BURIED UNDER HIGH, CIRCULAR, MUD-BRICK BURIAL MOUNDS. IN THE CENTER FAR BELOW, WERE LARGE STONE WALLED CRYPTS INTO WHICH THE BODY WOULD BE PLACED.

OFFERINGS OF FOOD AND DRINK FAVORED BY THE DEAD KING WERE LOWERED DOWN TO EASE HIS JOURNEY INTO THE AFTERLIFE.

IN THOSE DAYS, GREAT PEOPLE WERE BURIED AND NOT CREMATED. CREMATION WAS RESERVED FOR COMMON PEOPLE AND PRIESTS.

AND SO, WITH THE SEALING OF THE CRYPT, THIS CHAPTER OF OUR STORY MUST END. GOING BACK TO THE WAR...

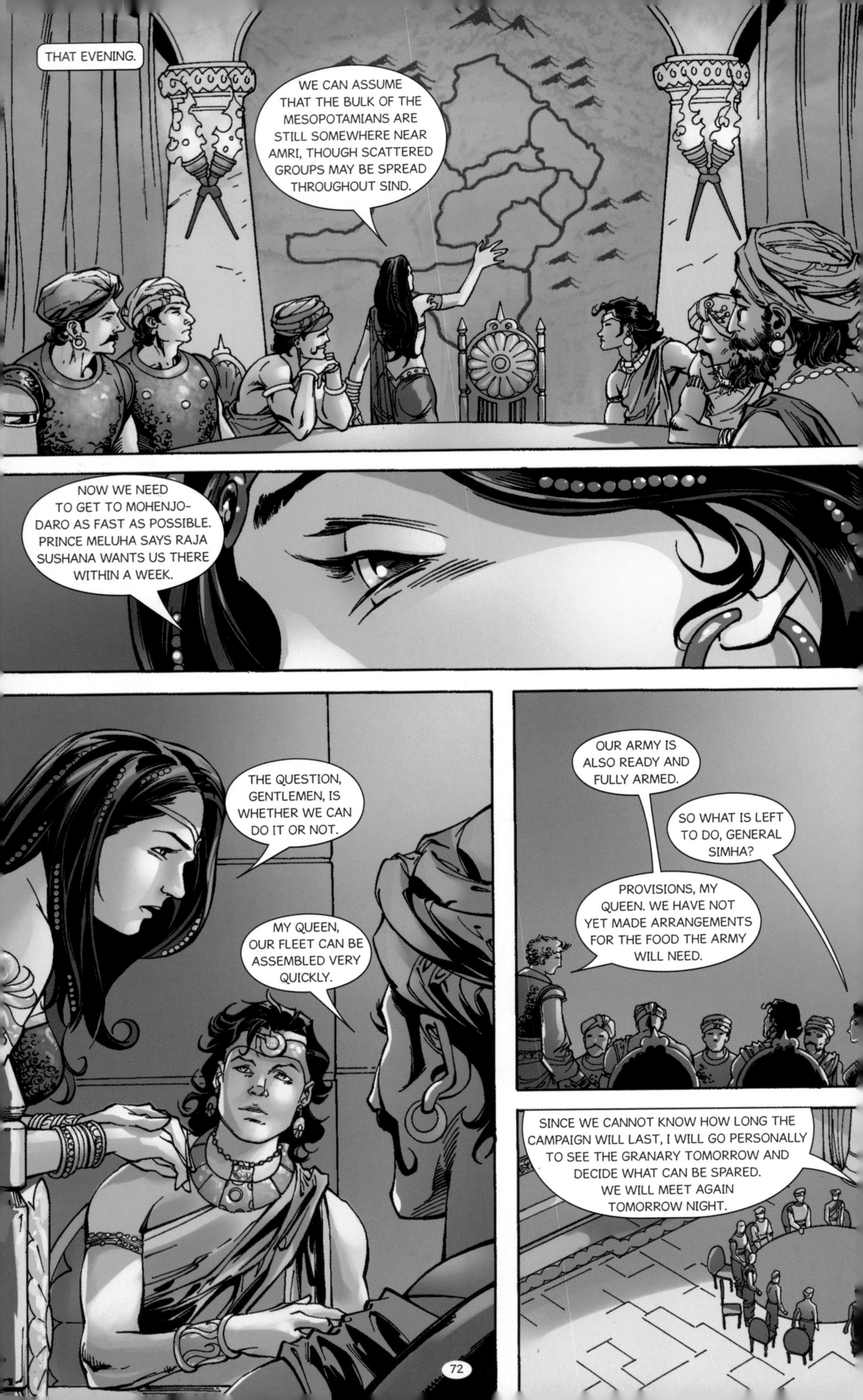
THAT EVENING.
WE CAN ASSUME THAT THE BULK OF THE MESOPOTAMIANS ARE STILL SOMEWHERE NEAR AMRI, THOUGH SCATTERED GROUPS MAY BE SPREAD THROUGHOUT SIND.
NOW WE NEED TO GET TO MOHENJO-DARO AS FAST AS POSSIBLE. PRINCE MELUHA SAYS RAJA SUSHANA WANTS US THERE WITHIN A WEEK.
THE QUESTION, GENTLEMEN, IS WHETHER WE CAN DO IT OR NOT.
MY QUEEN, OUR FLEET CAN BE ASSEMBLED VERY QUICKLY.
OUR ARMY IS ALSO READY AND FULLY ARMED.
SO WHAT IS LEFT TO DO, GENERAL SIMHA?
PROVISIONS, MY QUEEN. WE HAVE NOT YET MADE ARRANGEMENTS FOR THE FOOD THE ARMY WILL NEED.
SINCE WE CANNOT KNOW HOW LONG THE CAMPAIGN WILL LAST, I WILL GO PERSONALLY TO SEE THE GRANARY TOMORROW AND DECIDE WHAT CAN BE SPARED. WE WILL MEET AGAIN TOMORROW NIGHT.

THE NEXT DAY.

THIS IS OUR GRANARY COMPLEX. IN GOOD YEARS, WE STORE A VARIETY OF ESSENTIAL GRAINS HERE.

HOW LONG DO YOU KEEP THEM HERE?

MOST GRAINS CAN BE SAFELY STORED HERE FOR AT LEAST TWO YEARS, BUT IF THE CROP IS GOOD, WE CHANGE ALL THE STOCK.

THAT WAY YOU ALWAYS STORE FRESH GRAINS!

YOUR HIGHNESS, WELCOME!

THANK YOU, SUPERINTENDENT MAKAAN. I HOPE YOU HAVE ALL THE DETAILS OF THE STOCKS AVAILABLE NOW.

YES, YOUR HIGHNESS.

GOOD! TELL ME HOW MUCH WE HAVE STORED HERE AND HOW MUCH WE CAN SPARE WITHOUT RISKING THE LIVES OF OUR PEOPLE?

MY QUEEN, LAST YEAR'S HARVEST WAS VERY GOOD.

IN ADDITION, SO FAR THE GROWING SEASON HAS BEEN VERY GOOD.

IT IS UNLIKELY THAT WE WILL FACE ANY MAJOR PROBLEMS THIS YEAR.

VERY WELL. I WANT YOU TO ORGANIZE ENOUGH FOOD FOR TWO WEEKS FOR AN ARMY OF FIVE THOUSAND SOLDIERS. THE GRAINS AND SOLDIERS WILL BE FERRIED BY SHIP TO MOHENJO-DARO.

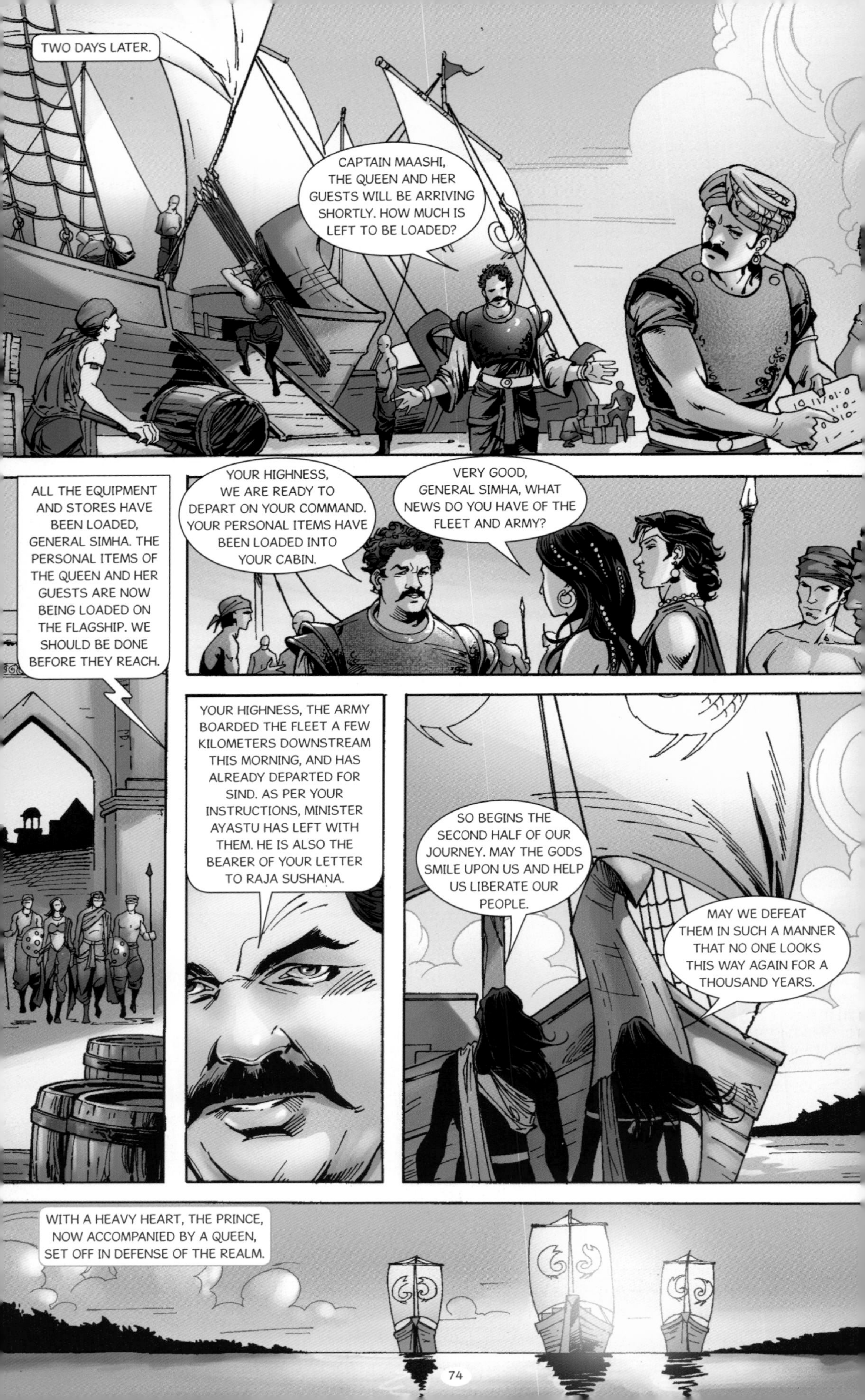
TWO DAYS LATER.
CAPTAIN MAASHI, THE QUEEN AND HER GUESTS WILL BE ARRIVING SHORTLY. HOW MUCH IS LEFT TO BE LOADED?
ALL THE EQUIPMENT AND STORES HAVE BEEN LOADED, GENERAL SIMHA. THE PERSONAL ITEMS OF THE QUEEN AND HER GUESTS ARE NOW BEING LOADED ON THE FLAGSHIP. WE SHOULD BE DONE BEFORE THEY REACH.
YOUR HIGHNESS, WE ARE READY TO DEPART ON YOUR COMMAND. YOUR PERSONAL ITEMS HAVE BEEN LOADED INTO YOUR CABIN.
VERY GOOD, GENERAL SIMHA, WHAT NEWS DO YOU HAVE OF THE FLEET AND ARMY?
YOUR HIGHNESS, THE ARMY BOARDED THE FLEET A FEW KILOMETERS DOWNSTREAM THIS MORNING, AND HAS ALREADY DEPARTED FOR SIND. AS PER YOUR INSTRUCTIONS, MINISTER AYASTU HAS LEFT WITH THEM. HE IS ALSO THE BEARER OF YOUR LETTER TO RAJA SUSHANA.
SO BEGINS THE SECOND HALF OF OUR JOURNEY. MAY THE GODS SMILE UPON US AND HELP US LIBERATE OUR PEOPLE.
MAY WE DEFEAT THEM IN SUCH A MANNER THAT NO ONE LOOKS THIS WAY AGAIN FOR A THOUSAND YEARS.
WITH A HEAVY HEART, THE PRINCE, NOW ACCOMPANIED BY A QUEEN, SET OFF IN DEFENSE OF THE REALM.

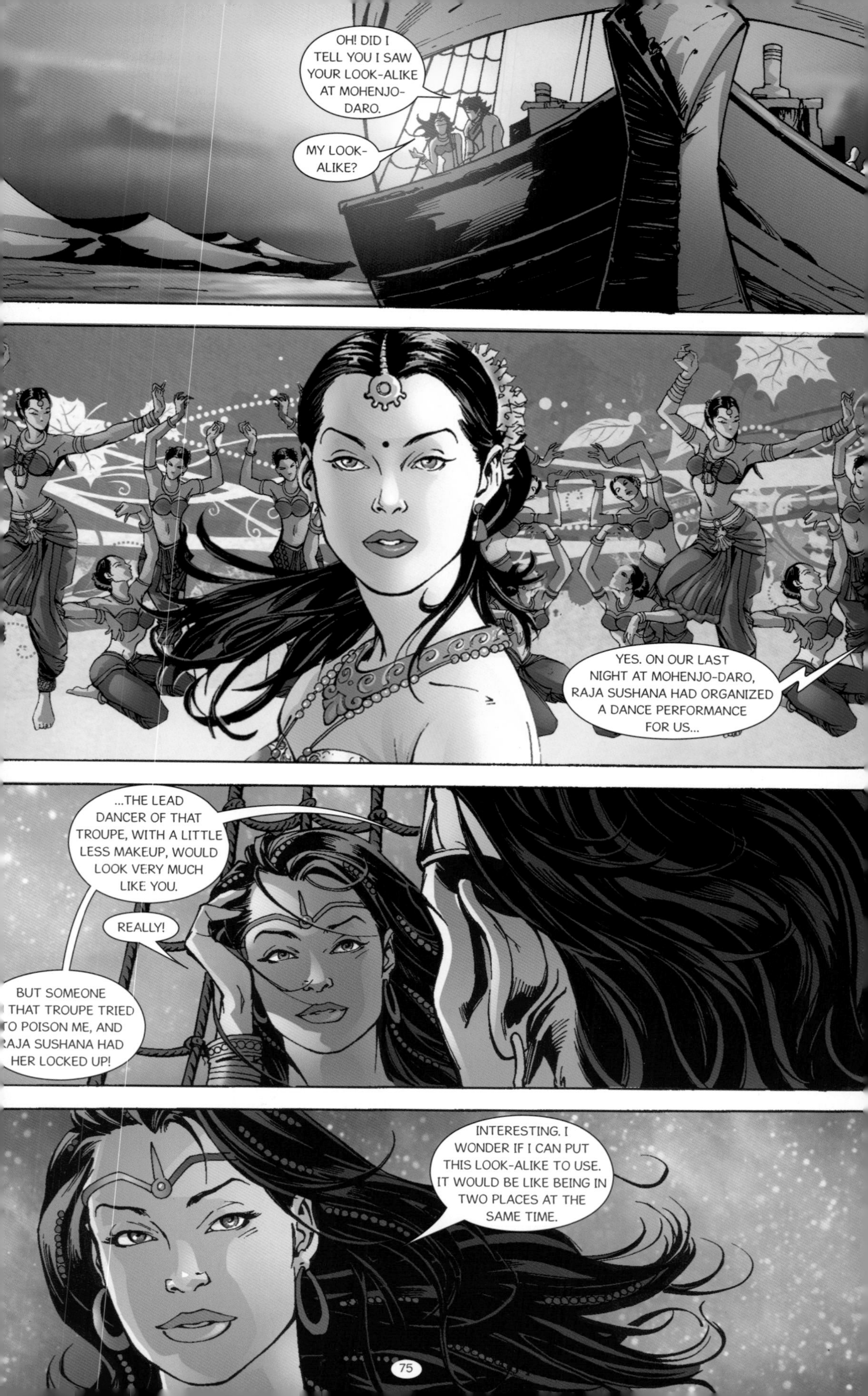
OH! DID I TELL YOU I SAW YOUR LOOK-ALIKE AT MOHENJO-DARO.
MY LOOK-ALIKE?
YES. ON OUR LAST NIGHT AT MOHENJO-DARO, RAJA SUSHANA HAD ORGANIZED A DANCE PERFORMANCE FOR US...
...THE LEAD DANCER OF THAT TROUPE, WITH A LITTLE LESS MAKEUP, WOULD LOOK VERY MUCH LIKE YOU.
REALLY!
BUT SOMEONE THAT TROUPE TRIED TO POISON ME, AND RAJA SUSHANA HAD HER LOCKED UP!
INTERESTING. I WONDER IF I CAN PUT THIS LOOK-ALIKE TO USE. IT WOULD BE LIKE BEING IN TWO PLACES AT THE SAME TIME.

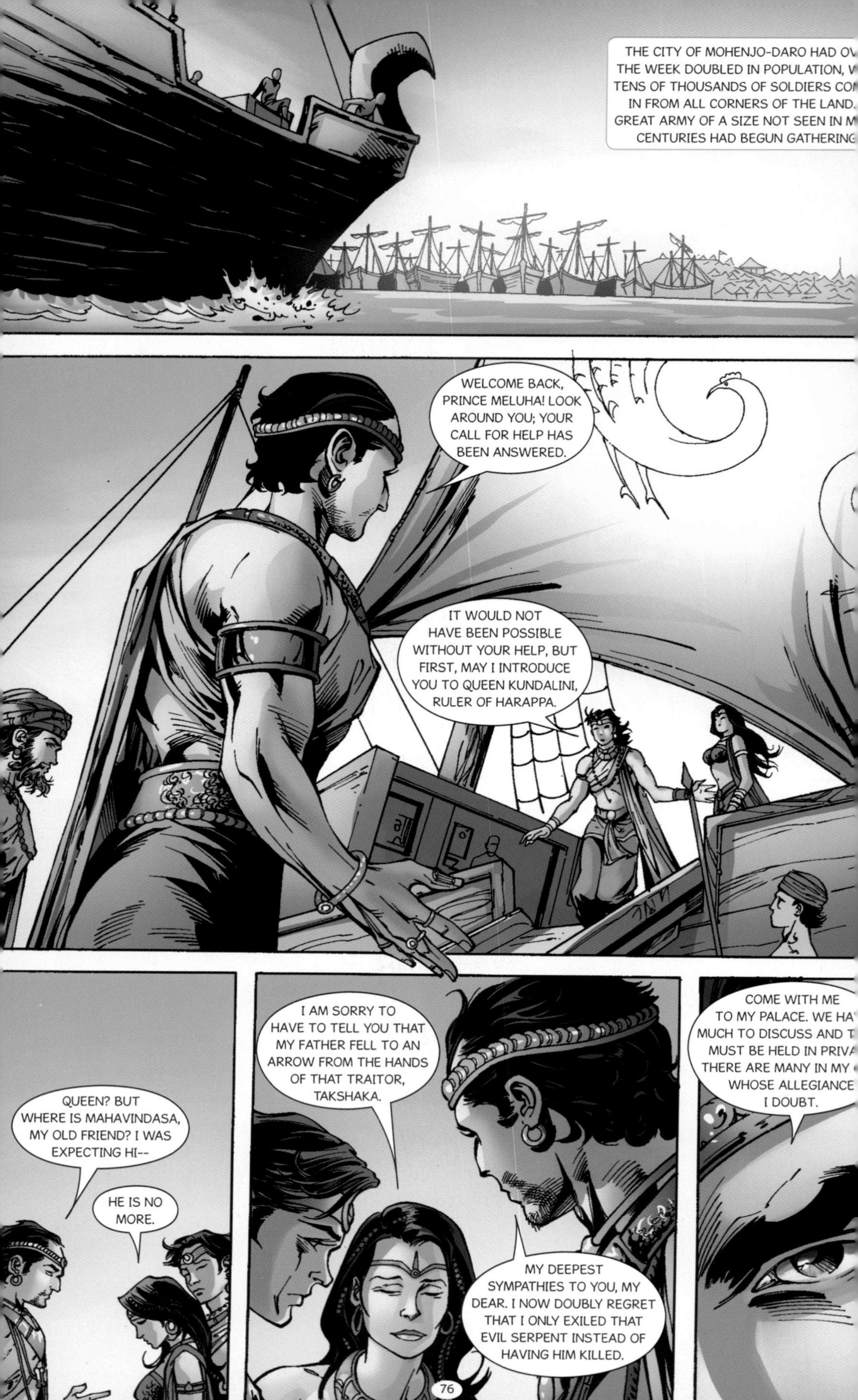
THE CITY OF MOHENJO-DARO HAD OV THE WEEK DOUBLED IN POPULATION, TENS OF THOUSANDS OF SOLDIERS CO IN FROM ALL CORNERS OF THE LAND. GREAT ARMY OF A SIZE NOT SEEN IN CENTURIES HAD BEGUN GATHERING
WELCOME BACK, PRINCE MELUHA! LOOK AROUND YOU; YOUR CALL FOR HELP HAS BEEN ANSWERED.
IT WOULD NOT HAVE BEEN POSSIBLE WITHOUT YOUR HELP, BUT FIRST, MAY I INTRODUCE YOU TO QUEEN KUNDALINI, RULER OF HARAPPA.
QUEEN? BUT WHERE IS MAHAVINDASA, MY OLD FRIEND? I WAS EXPECTING HI--
HE IS NO MORE.
I AM SORRY TO HAVE TO TELL YOU THAT MY FATHER FELL TO AN ARROW FROM THE HANDS OF THAT TRAITOR, TAKSHAKA.
MY DEEPEST SYMPATHIES TO YOU, MY DEAR. I NOW DOUBLY REGRET THAT I ONLY EXILED THAT EVIL SERPENT INSTEAD OF HAVING HIM KILLED.
COME WITH ME TO MY PALACE. WE HA MUCH TO DISCUSS AND T MUST BE HELD IN PRIVA THERE ARE MANY IN MY WHOSE ALLEGIANCE I DOUBT.

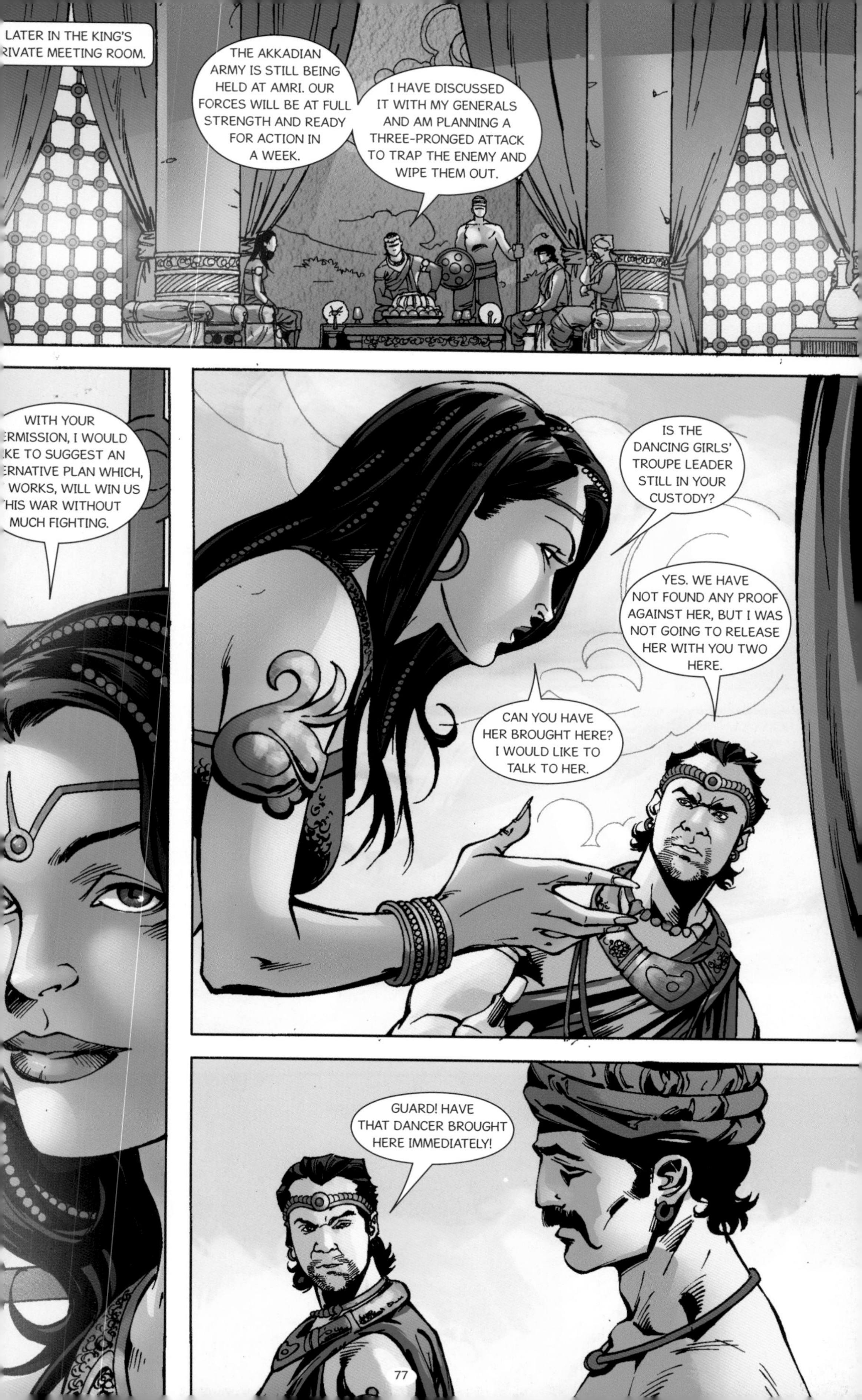
LATER IN THE KING'S
RIVATE MEETING ROOM.
THE AKKADIAN ARMY IS STILL BEING HELD AT AMRI. OUR FORCES WILL BE AT FULL STRENGTH AND READY FOR ACTION IN A WEEK.
I HAVE DISCUSSED IT WITH MY GENERALS AND AM PLANNING A THREE-PRONGED ATTACK TO TRAP THE ENEMY AND WIPE THEM OUT.
WITH YOUR
ERMISSION, I WOULD
KE TO SUGGEST AN
ERNATIVE PLAN WHICH,
WORKS, WILL WIN US
HIS WAR WITHOUT
MUCH FIGHTING.
IS THE DANCING GIRLS' TROUPE LEADER STILL IN YOUR CUSTODY?
YES. WE HAVE NOT FOUND ANY PROOF AGAINST HER, BUT I WAS NOT GOING TO RELEASE HER WITH YOU TWO HERE.
CAN YOU HAVE HER BROUGHT HERE? I WOULD LIKE TO TALK TO HER.
GUARD! HAVE THAT DANCER BROUGHT HERE IMMEDIATELY!

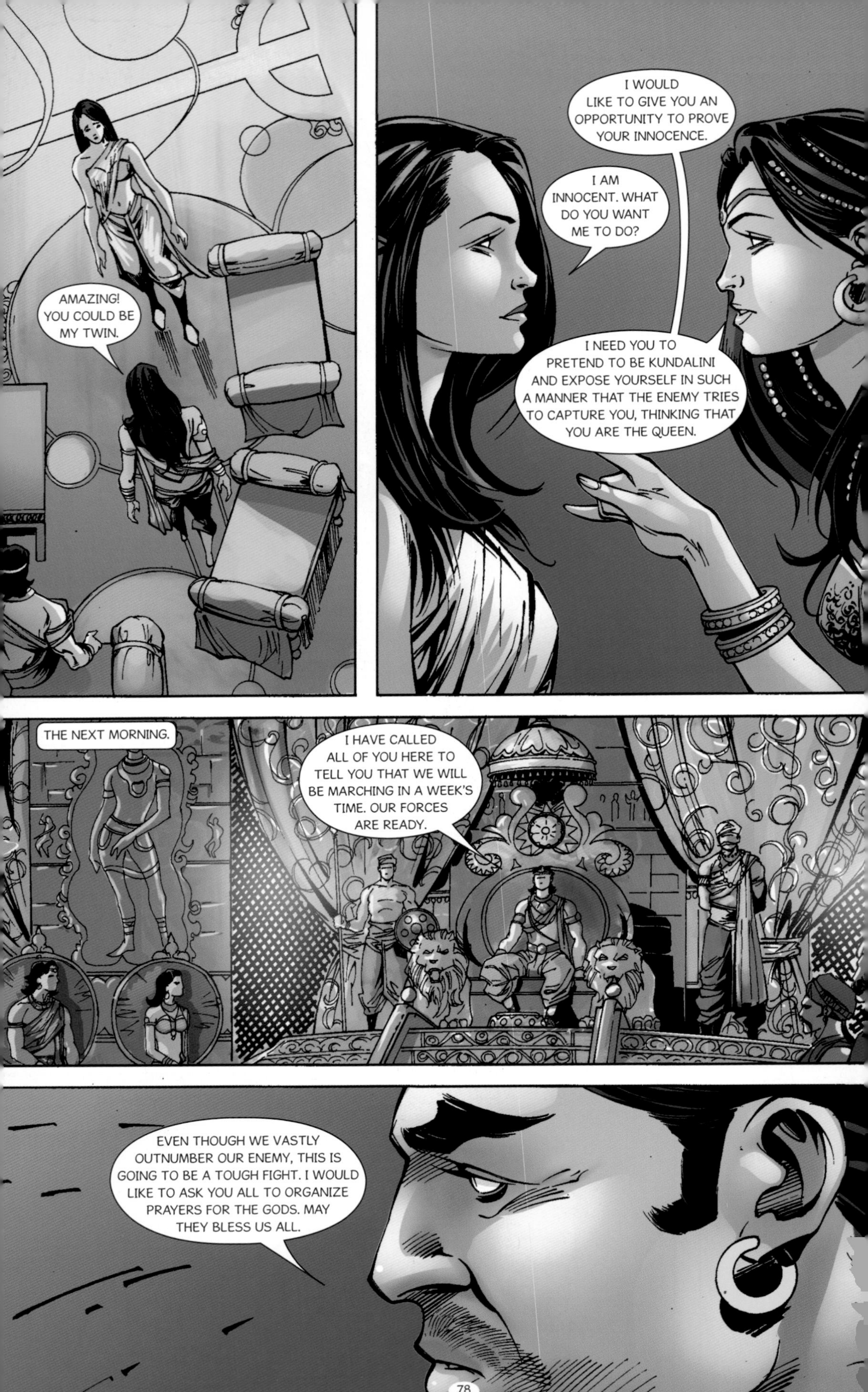
AMAZING! YOU COULD BE MY TWIN.
I WOULD LIKE TO GIVE YOU AN OPPORTUNITY TO PROVE YOUR INNOCENCE.
I AM INNOCENT. WHAT DO YOU WANT ME TO DO?
I NEED YOU TO PRETEND TO BE KUNDALINI AND EXPOSE YOURSELF IN SUCH A MANNER THAT THE ENEMY TRIES TO CAPTURE YOU, THINKING THAT YOU ARE THE QUEEN.
THE NEXT MORNING.
I HAVE CALLED ALL OF YOU HERE TO TELL YOU THAT WE WILL BE MARCHING IN A WEEK'S TIME. OUR FORCES ARE READY.
EVEN THOUGH WE VASTLY OUTNUMBER OUR ENEMY, THIS IS GOING TO BE A TOUGH FIGHT. I WOULD LIKE TO ASK YOU ALL TO ORGANIZE PRAYERS FOR THE GODS. MAY THEY BLESS US ALL.

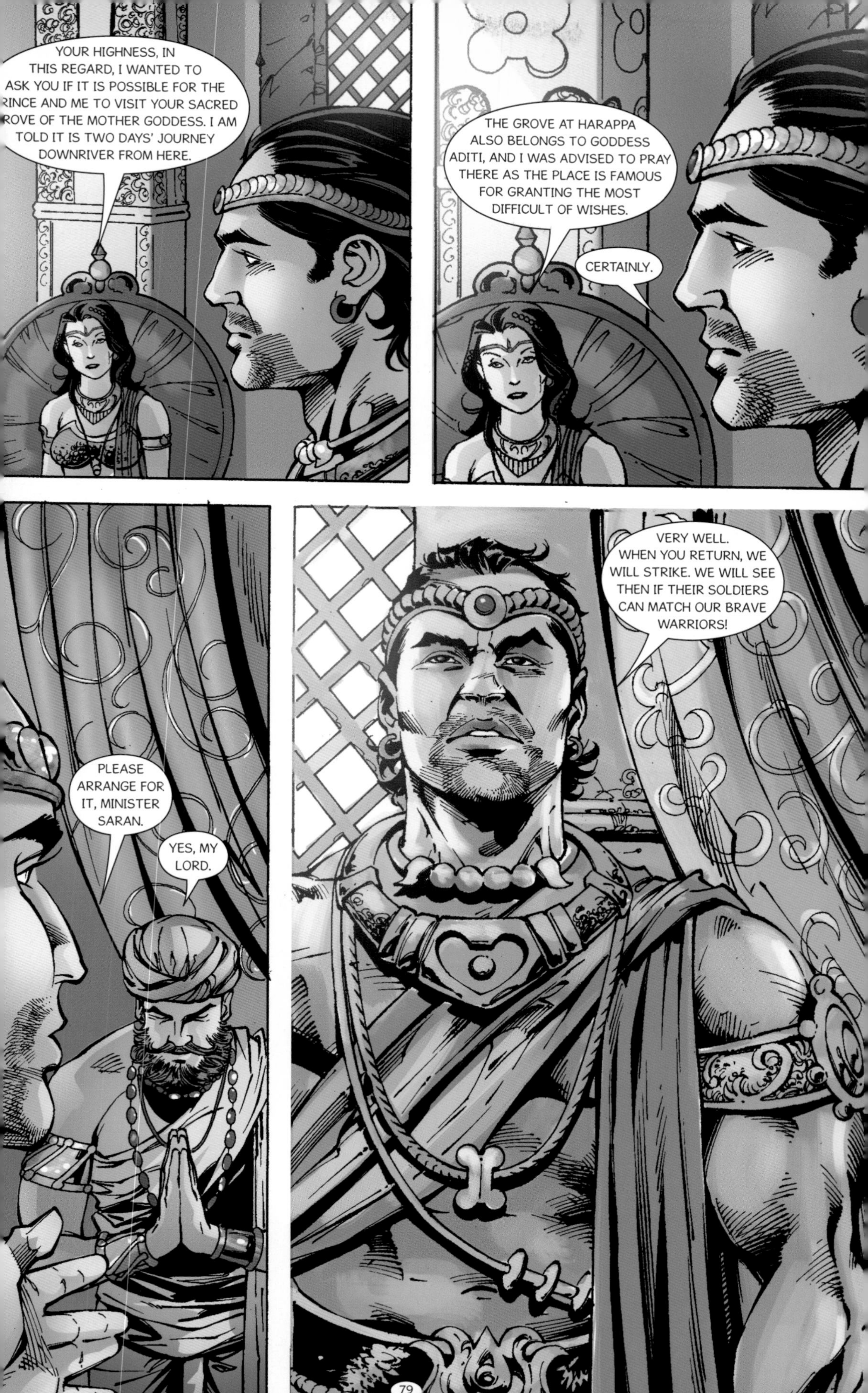
YOUR HIGHNESS, IN THIS REGARD, I WANTED TO ASK YOU IF IT IS POSSIBLE FOR THE RINCE AND ME TO VISIT YOUR SACRED ROVE OF THE MOTHER GODDESS. I AM TOLD IT IS TWO DAYS' JOURNEY DOWNRIVER FROM HERE.
THE GROVE AT HARAPPA ALSO BELONGS TO GODDESS ADITI, AND I WAS ADVISED TO PRAY THERE AS THE PLACE IS FAMOUS FOR GRANTING THE MOST DIFFICULT OF WISHES.
CERTAINLY.
PLEASE ARRANGE FOR IT, MINISTER SARAN.
YES, MY LORD.
VERY WELL. WHEN YOU RETURN, WE WILL STRIKE. WE WILL SEE THEN IF THEIR SOLDIERS CAN MATCH OUR BRAVE WARRIORS!

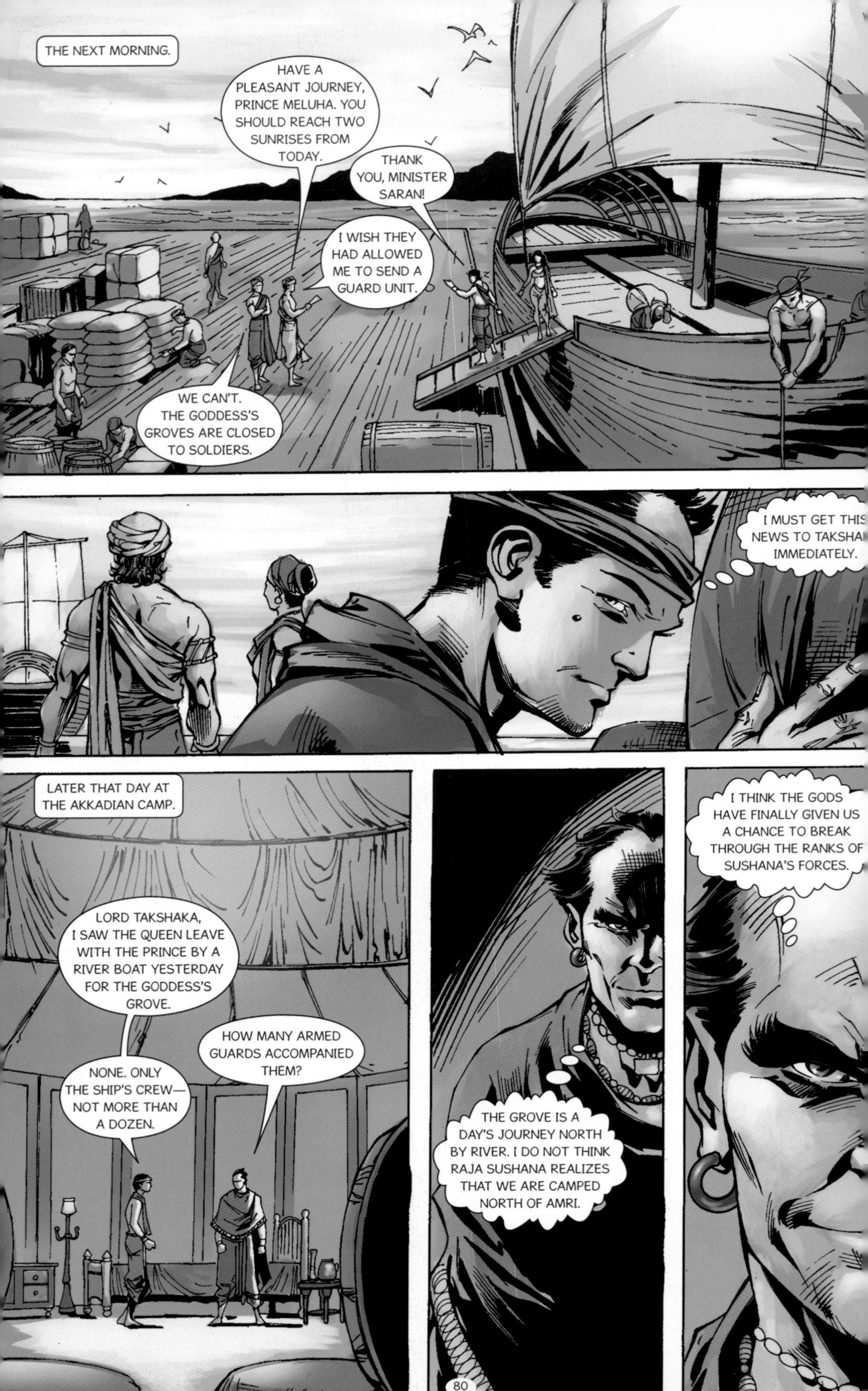
THE NEXT MORNING.
HAVE A PLEASANT JOURNEY, PRINCE MELUHA. YOU SHOULD REACH TWO SUNRISES FROM TODAY.
THANK YOU, MINISTER SARAN!
I WISH THEY HAD ALLOWED ME TO SEND A GUARD UNIT.
WE CAN'T. THE GODDESS'S GROVES ARE CLOSED TO SOLDIERS.
I MUST GET THIS NEWS TO TAKSHA IMMEDIATELY.
LATER THAT DAY AT THE AKKADIAN CAMP.
LORD TAKSHAKA, I SAW THE QUEEN LEAVE WITH THE PRINCE BY A RIVER BOAT YESTERDAY FOR THE GODDESS'S GROVE.
HOW MANY ARMED GUARDS ACCOMPANIED THEM?
NONE. ONLY THE SHIP'S CREW— NOT MORE THAN A DOZEN.
THE GROVE IS A DAY'S JOURNEY NORTH BY RIVER. I DO NOT THINK RAJA SUSHANA REALIZES THAT WE ARE CAMPED NORTH OF AMRI.
I THINK THE GODS HAVE FINALLY GIVEN US A CHANCE TO BREAK THROUGH THE RANKS OF SUSHANA'S FORCES.

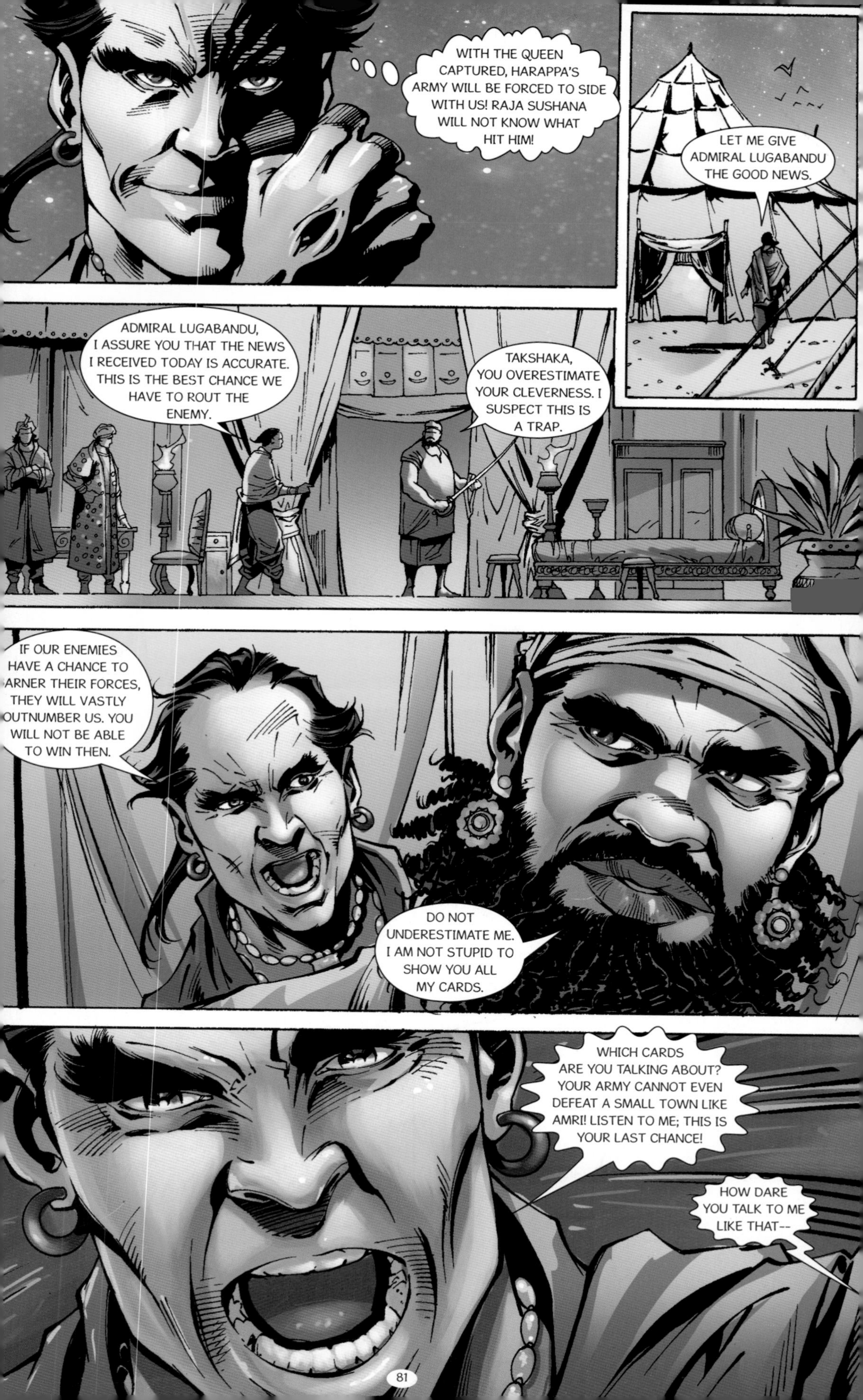
WITH THE QUEEN CAPTURED, HARAPPA'S ARMY WILL BE FORCED TO SIDE WITH US! RAJA SUSHANA WILL NOT KNOW WHAT HIT HIM!
LET ME GIVE ADMIRAL LUGABANDU THE GOOD NEWS.
ADMIRAL LUGABANDU, I ASSURE YOU THAT THE NEWS I RECEIVED TODAY IS ACCURATE. THIS IS THE BEST CHANCE WE HAVE TO ROUT THE ENEMY.
TAKSHAKA, YOU OVERESTIMATE YOUR CLEVERNESS. I SUSPECT THIS IS A TRAP.
IF OUR ENEMIES HAVE A CHANCE TO ARNER THEIR FORCES, THEY WILL VASTLY OUTNUMBER US. YOU WILL NOT BE ABLE TO WIN THEN.
DO NOT UNDERESTIMATE ME. I AM NOT STUPID TO SHOW YOU ALL MY CARDS.
WHICH CARDS ARE YOU TALKING ABOUT? YOUR ARMY CANNOT EVEN DEFEAT A SMALL TOWN LIKE AMRI! LISTEN TO ME; THIS IS YOUR LAST CHANCE!
HOW DARE YOU TALK TO ME LIKE THAT--

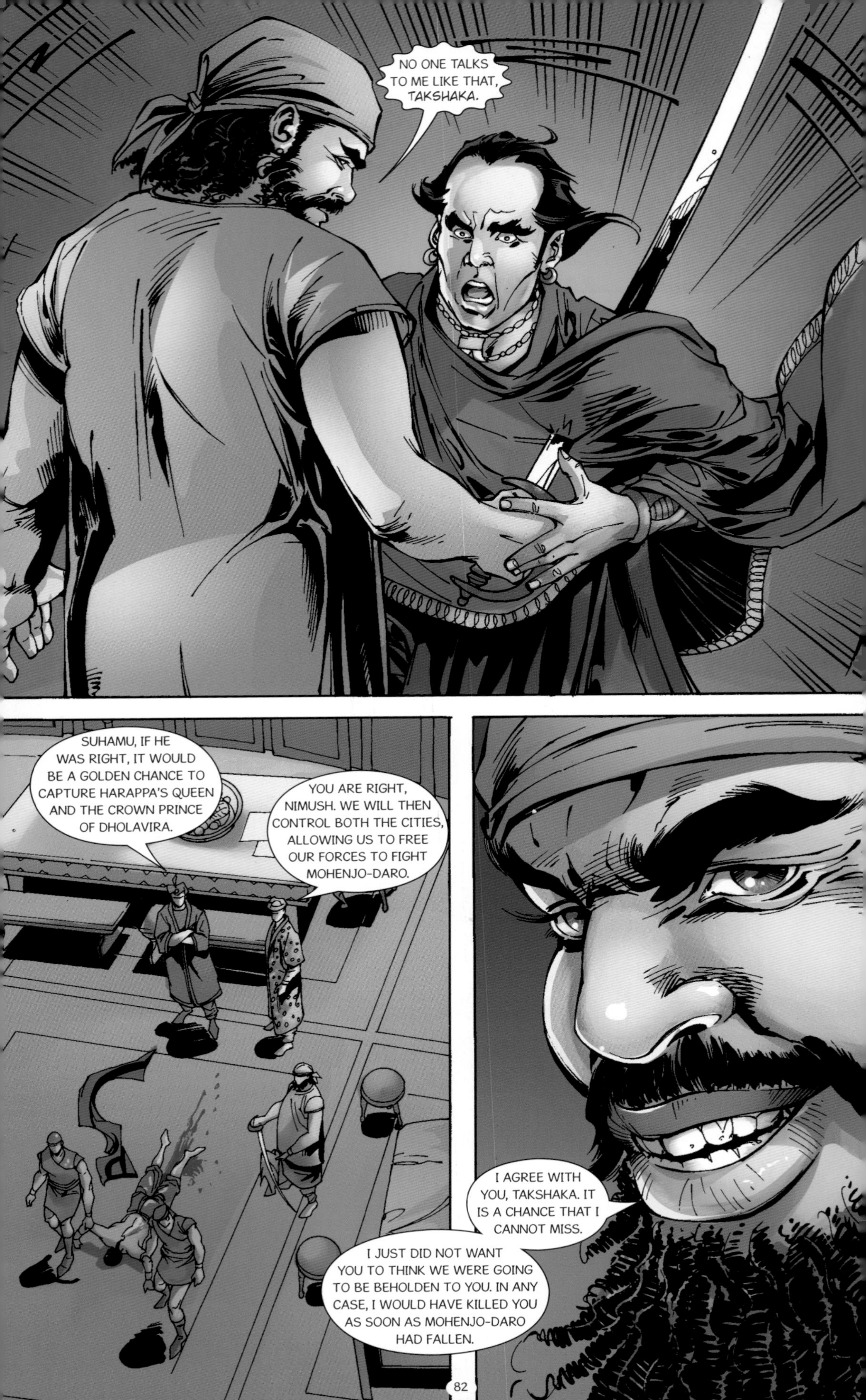
NO ONE TALKS TO ME LIKE THAT, TAKSHAKA.
SUHAMU, IF HE WAS RIGHT, IT WOULD BE A GOLDEN CHANCE TO CAPTURE HARAPPA'S QUEEN AND THE CROWN PRINCE OF DHOLAVIRA.
YOU ARE RIGHT, NIMUSH. WE WILL THEN CONTROL BOTH THE CITIES, ALLOWING US TO FREE OUR FORCES TO FIGHT MOHENJO-DARO.
I AGREE WITH YOU, TAKSHAKA. IT IS A CHANCE THAT I CANNOT MISS.
I JUST DID NOT WANT YOU TO THINK WE WERE GOING TO BE BEHOLDEN TO YOU. IN ANY CASE, I WOULD HAVE KILLED YOU AS SOON AS MOHENJO-DARO HAD FALLEN.

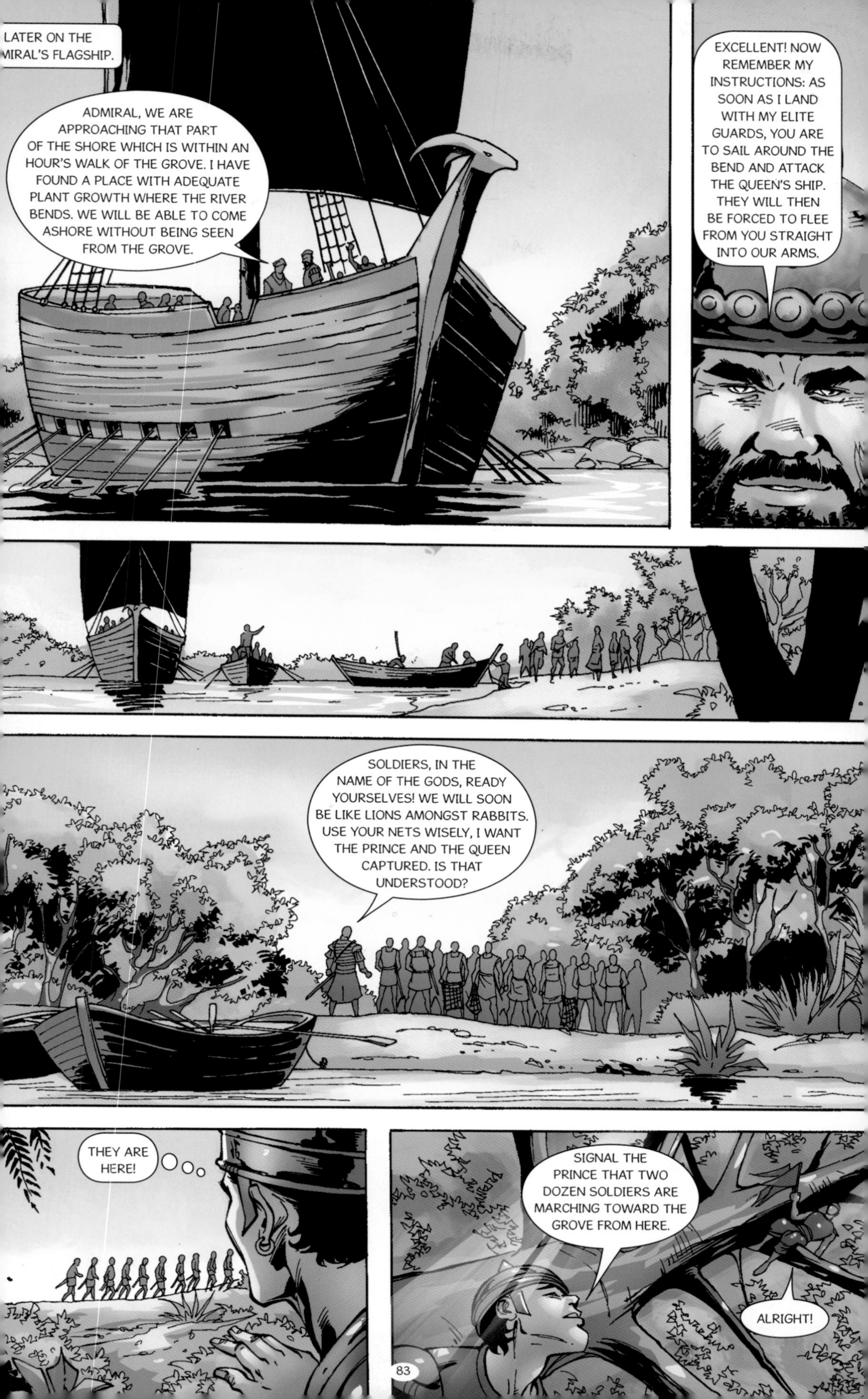

LATER ON THE
MIRAL'S FLAGSHIP.
ADMIRAL, WE ARE APPROACHING THAT PART OF THE SHORE WHICH IS WITHIN AN HOUR'S WALK OF THE GROVE. I HAVE FOUND A PLACE WITH ADEQUATE PLANT GROWTH WHERE THE RIVER BENDS. WE WILL BE ABLE TO COME ASHORE WITHOUT BEING SEEN FROM THE GROVE.
EXCELLENT! NOW REMEMBER MY INSTRUCTIONS: AS SOON AS I LAND WITH MY ELITE GUARDS, YOU ARE TO SAIL AROUND THE BEND AND ATTACK THE QUEEN'S SHIP. THEY WILL THEN BE FORCED TO FLEE FROM YOU STRAIGHT INTO OUR ARMS.
SOLDIERS, IN THE NAME OF THE GODS, READY YOURSELVES! WE WILL SOON BE LIKE LIONS AMONGST RABBITS. USE YOUR NETS WISELY, I WANT THE PRINCE AND THE QUEEN CAPTURED. IS THAT UNDERSTOOD?
THEY ARE HERE!
SIGNAL THE PRINCE THAT TWO DOZEN SOLDIERS ARE MARCHING TOWARD THE GROVE FROM HERE.
ALRIGHT!

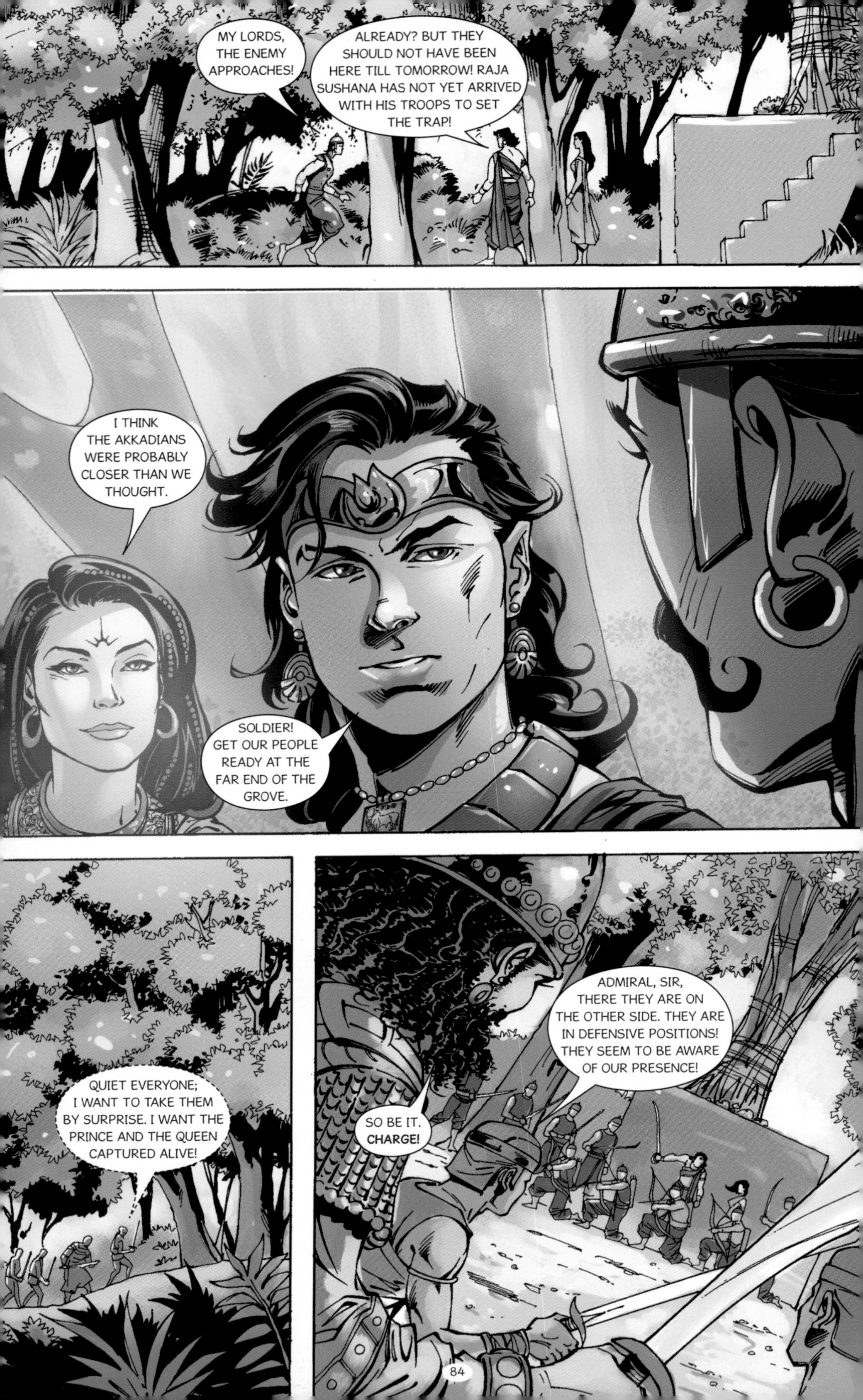
MY LORDS, THE ENEMY APPROACHES!
ALREADY? BUT THEY SHOULD NOT HAVE BEEN HERE TILL TOMORROW! RAJA SUSHANA HAS NOT YET ARRIVED WITH HIS TROOPS TO SET THE TRAP!
I THINK THE AKKADIANS WERE PROBABLY CLOSER THAN WE THOUGHT.
SOLDIER! GET OUR PEOPLE READY AT THE FAR END OF THE GROVE.
QUIET EVERYONE; I WANT TO TAKE THEM BY SURPRISE. I WANT THE PRINCE AND THE QUEEN CAPTURED ALIVE!
ADMIRAL, SIR, THERE THEY ARE ON THE OTHER SIDE. THEY ARE IN DEFENSIVE POSITIONS! THEY SEEM TO BE AWARE OF OUR PRESENCE!
SO BE IT. CHARGE!

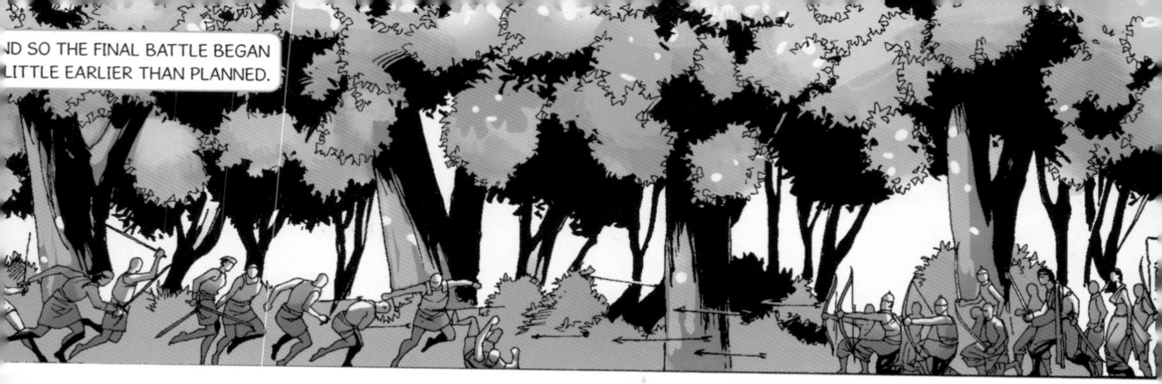
ND SO THE FINAL BATTLE BEGAN
LITTLE EARLIER THAN PLANNED.

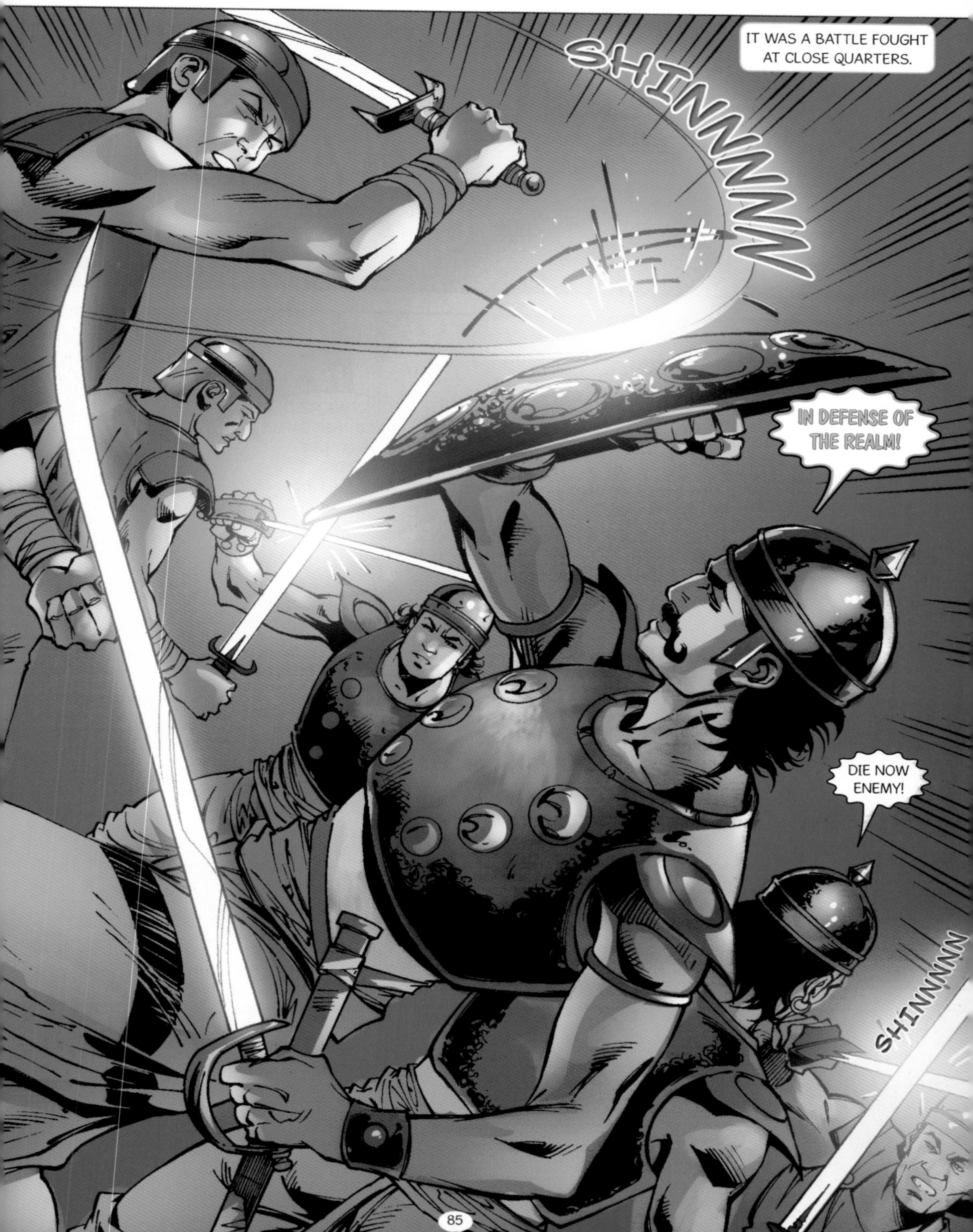
IT WAS A BATTLE FOUGHT
AT CLOSE QUARTERS.
SHINNNNNN
IN DEFENSE OF
THE REALM!
DIE NOW
ENEMY!
SHINNNNN

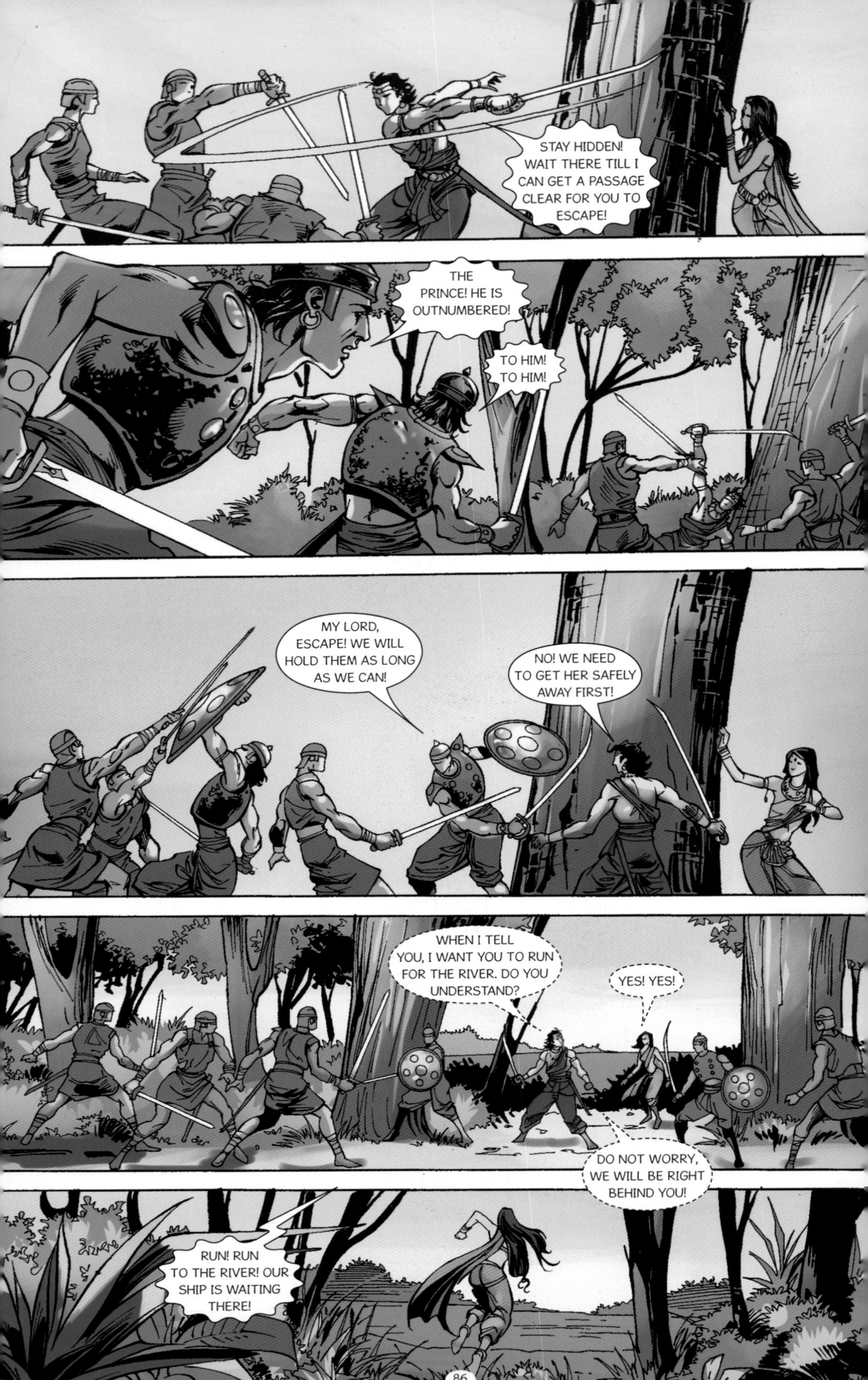
STAY HIDDEN! WAIT THERE TILL I CAN GET A PASSAGE CLEAR FOR YOU TO ESCAPE!
THE PRINCE! HE IS OUTNUMBERED!
TO HIM! TO HIM!
MY LORD, ESCAPE! WE WILL HOLD THEM AS LONG AS WE CAN!
NO! WE NEED TO GET HER SAFELY AWAY FIRST!
WHEN I TELL YOU, I WANT YOU TO RUN FOR THE RIVER. DO YOU UNDERSTAND?
YES! YES!
DO NOT WORRY, WE WILL BE RIGHT BEHIND YOU!
RUN! RUN TO THE RIVER! OUR SHIP IS WAITING THERE!

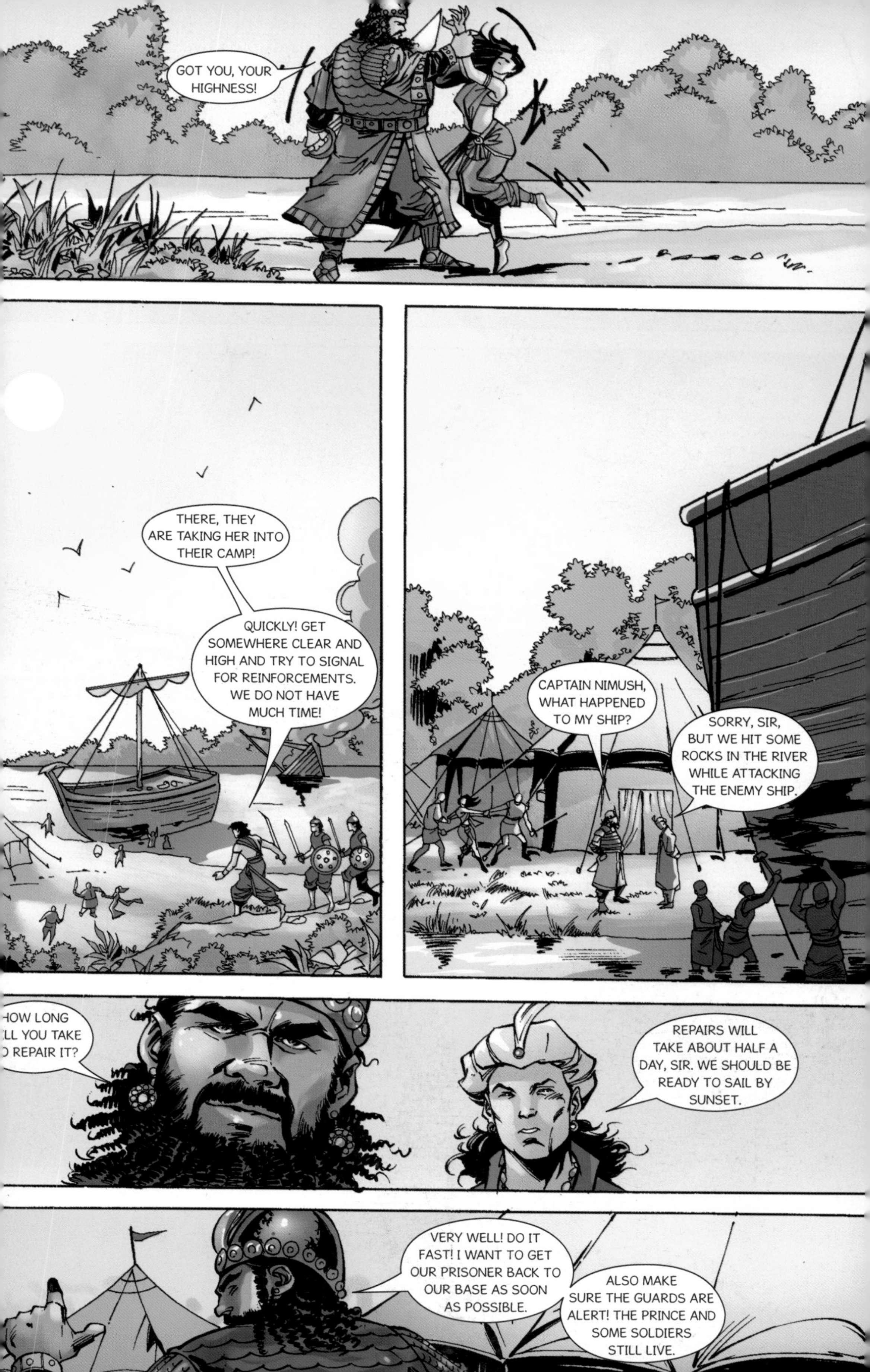
GOT YOU, YOUR HIGHNESS!
THERE, THEY ARE TAKING HER INTO THEIR CAMP!
QUICKLY! GET SOMEWHERE CLEAR AND HIGH AND TRY TO SIGNAL FOR REINFORCEMENTS. WE DO NOT HAVE MUCH TIME!
CAPTAIN NIMUSH, WHAT HAPPENED TO MY SHIP?
SORRY, SIR, BUT WE HIT SOME ROCKS IN THE RIVER WHILE ATTACKING THE ENEMY SHIP.
OW LONG LL YOU TAKE O REPAIR IT?
REPAIRS WILL TAKE ABOUT HALF A DAY, SIR. WE SHOULD BE READY TO SAIL BY SUNSET.
VERY WELL! DO IT FAST! I WANT TO GET OUR PRISONER BACK TO OUR BASE AS SOON AS POSSIBLE.
ALSO MAKE SURE THE GUARDS ARE ALERT! THE PRINCE AND SOME SOLDIERS STILL LIVE.

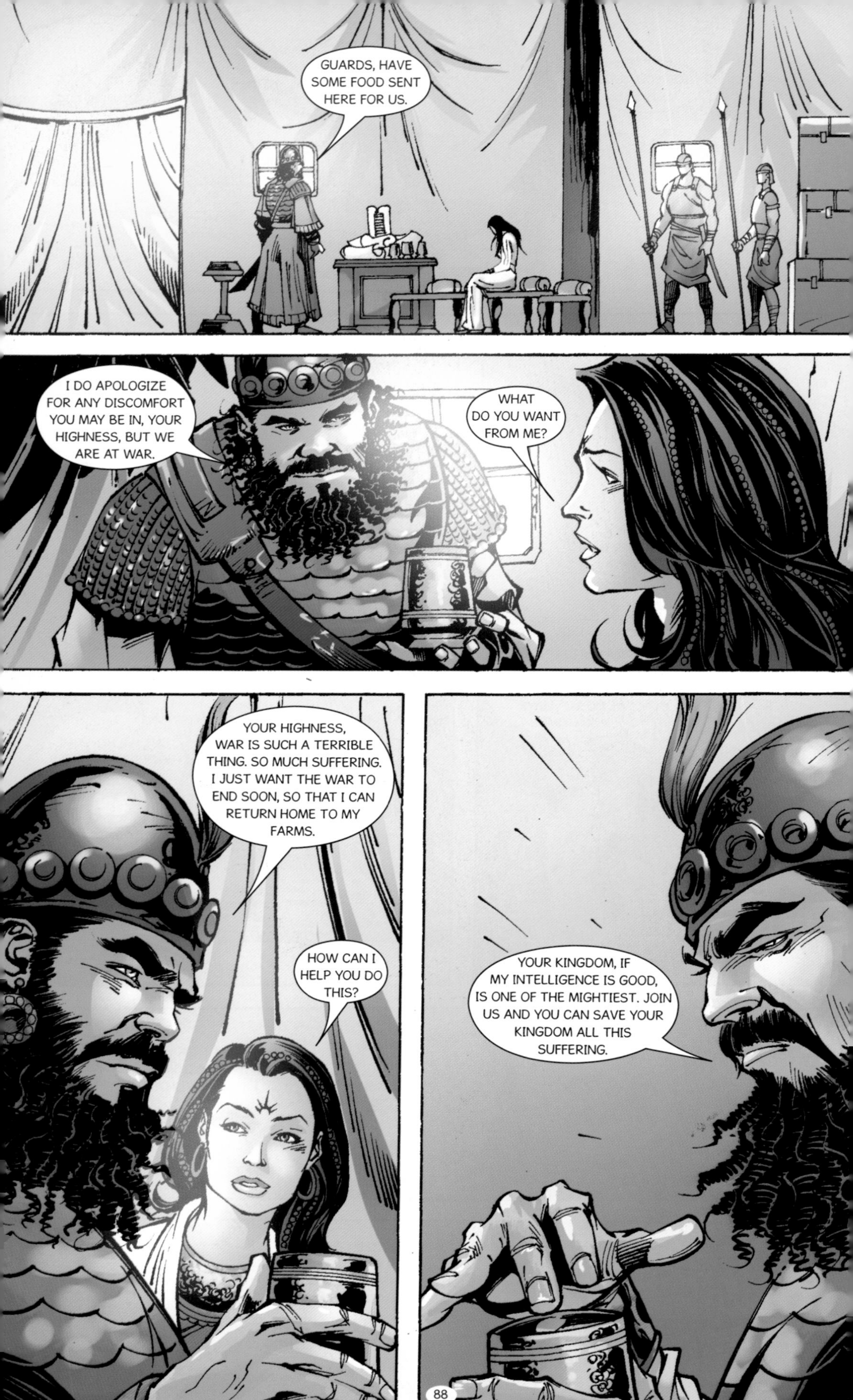
GUARDS, HAVE SOME FOOD SENT HERE FOR US.
I DO APOLOGIZE FOR ANY DISCOMFORT YOU MAY BE IN, YOUR HIGHNESS, BUT WE ARE AT WAR.
WHAT DO YOU WANT FROM ME?
YOUR HIGHNESS, WAR IS SUCH A TERRIBLE THING. SO MUCH SUFFERING. I JUST WANT THE WAR TO END SOON, SO THAT I CAN RETURN HOME TO MY FARMS.
HOW CAN I HELP YOU DO THIS?
YOUR KINGDOM, IF MY INTELLIGENCE IS GOOD, IS ONE OF THE MIGHTIEST. JOIN US AND YOU CAN SAVE YOUR KINGDOM ALL THIS SUFFERING.

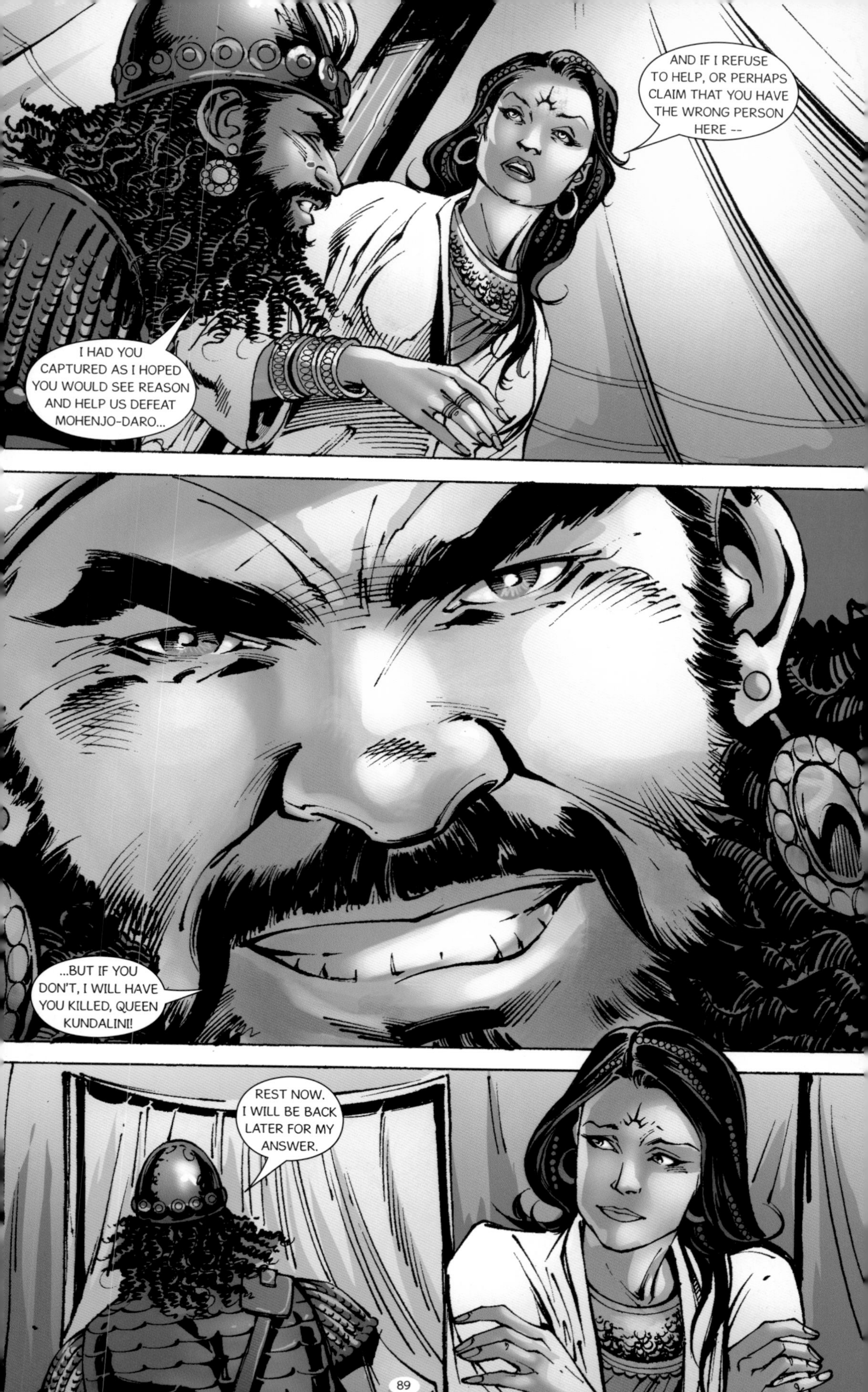
AND IF I REFUSE TO HELP, OR PERHAPS CLAIM THAT YOU HAVE THE WRONG PERSON HERE --
I HAD YOU CAPTURED AS I HOPED YOU WOULD SEE REASON AND HELP US DEFEAT MOHENJO-DARO...
...BUT IF YOU DON'T, I WILL HAVE YOU KILLED, QUEEN KUNDALINI!
REST NOW. I WILL BE BACK LATER FOR MY ANSWER.

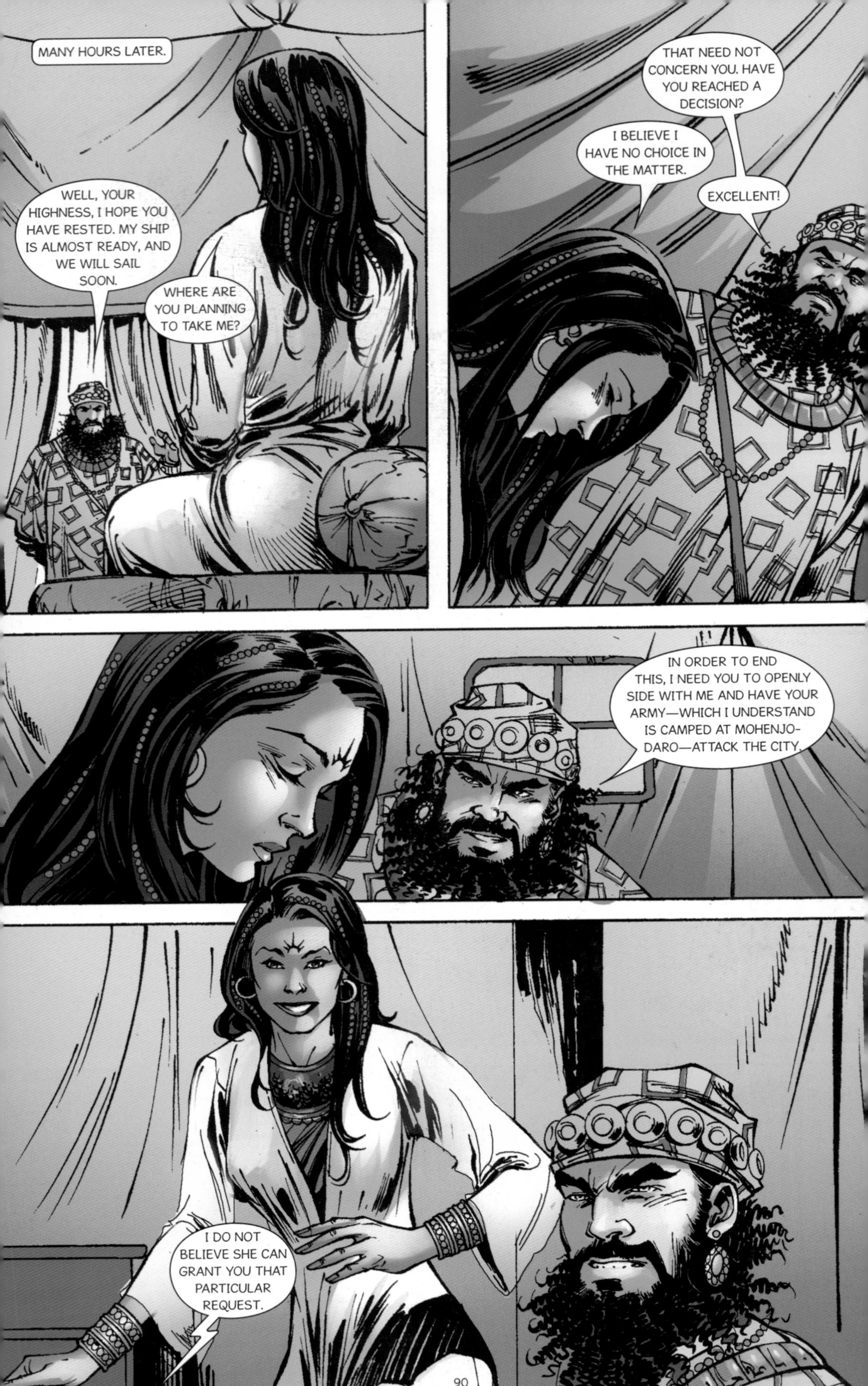
MANY HOURS LATER.
WELL, YOUR HIGHNESS, I HOPE YOU HAVE RESTED. MY SHIP IS ALMOST READY, AND WE WILL SAIL SOON.
WHERE ARE YOU PLANNING TO TAKE ME?
THAT NEED NOT CONCERN YOU. HAVE YOU REACHED A DECISION?
I BELIEVE I HAVE NO CHOICE IN THE MATTER.
EXCELLENT!
IN ORDER TO END THIS, I NEED YOU TO OPENLY SIDE WITH ME AND HAVE YOUR ARMY—WHICH I UNDERSTAND IS CAMPED AT MOHENJO-DARO—ATTACK THE CITY.
I DO NOT BELIEVE SHE CAN GRANT YOU THAT PARTICULAR REQUEST.

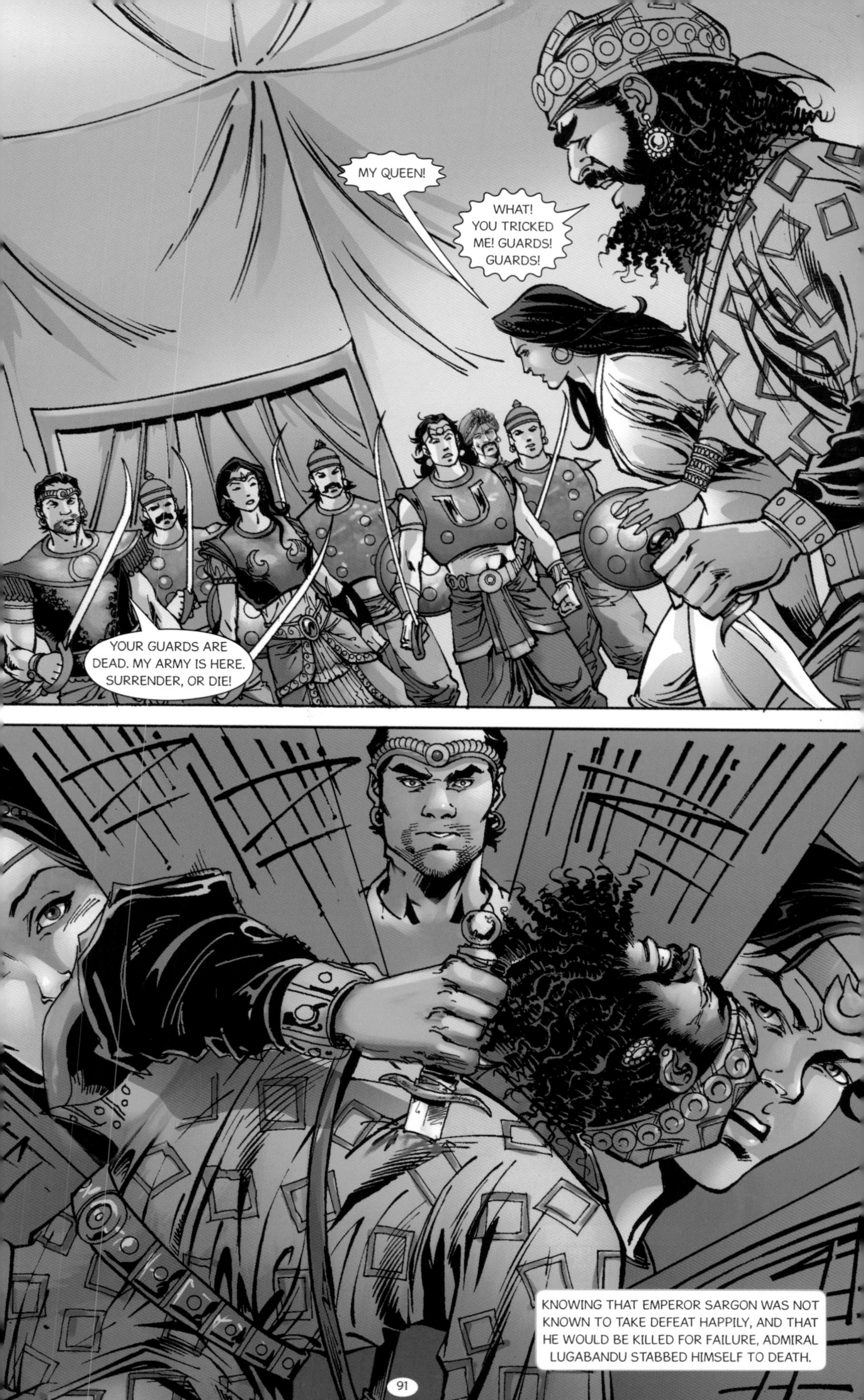
MY QUEEN!
WHAT! YOU TRICKED ME! GUARDS! GUARDS!
YOUR GUARDS ARE DEAD. MY ARMY IS HERE. SURRENDER, OR DIE!
KNOWING THAT EMPEROR SARGON WAS NOT KNOWN TO TAKE DEFEAT HAPPILY, AND THAT HE WOULD BE KILLED FOR FAILURE, ADMIRAL LUGABANDU STABBED HIMSELF TO DEATH.

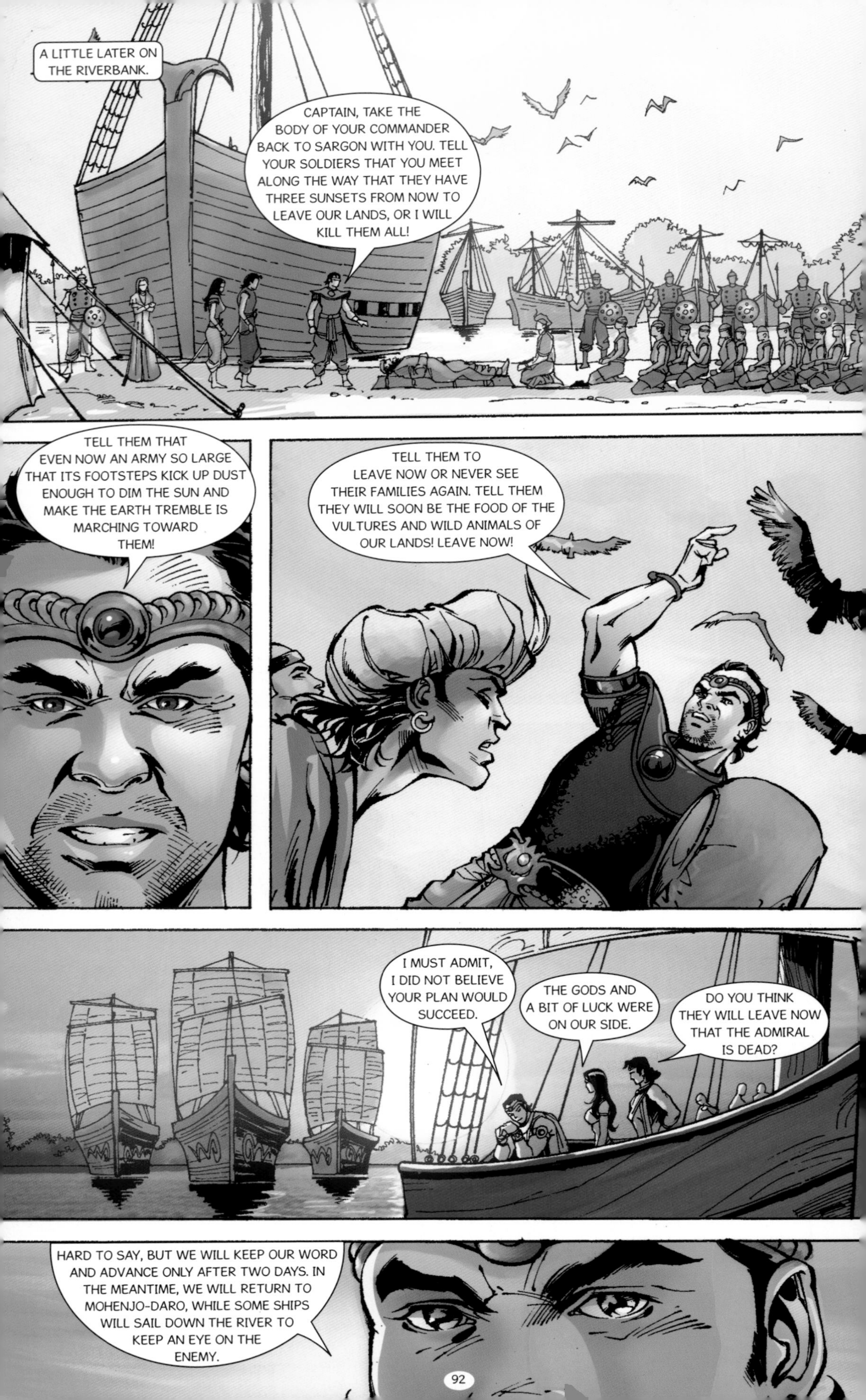
A LITTLE LATER ON THE RIVERBANK.
CAPTAIN, TAKE THE BODY OF YOUR COMMANDER BACK TO SARGON WITH YOU. TELL YOUR SOLDIERS THAT YOU MEET ALONG THE WAY THAT THEY HAVE THREE SUNSETS FROM NOW TO LEAVE OUR LANDS, OR I WILL KILL THEM ALL!
TELL THEM THAT EVEN NOW AN ARMY SO LARGE THAT ITS FOOTSTEPS KICK UP DUST ENOUGH TO DIM THE SUN AND MAKE THE EARTH TREMBLE IS MARCHING TOWARD THEM!
TELL THEM TO LEAVE NOW OR NEVER SEE THEIR FAMILIES AGAIN. TELL THEM THEY WILL SOON BE THE FOOD OF THE VULTURES AND WILD ANIMALS OF OUR LANDS! LEAVE NOW!
I MUST ADMIT, I DID NOT BELIEVE YOUR PLAN WOULD SUCCEED.
THE GODS AND A BIT OF LUCK WERE ON OUR SIDE.
DO YOU THINK THEY WILL LEAVE NOW THAT THE ADMIRAL IS DEAD?
HARD TO SAY, BUT WE WILL KEEP OUR WORD AND ADVANCE ONLY AFTER TWO DAYS. IN THE MEANTIME, WE WILL RETURN TO MOHENJO-DARO, WHILE SOME SHIPS WILL SAIL DOWN THE RIVER TO KEEP AN EYE ON THE ENEMY.

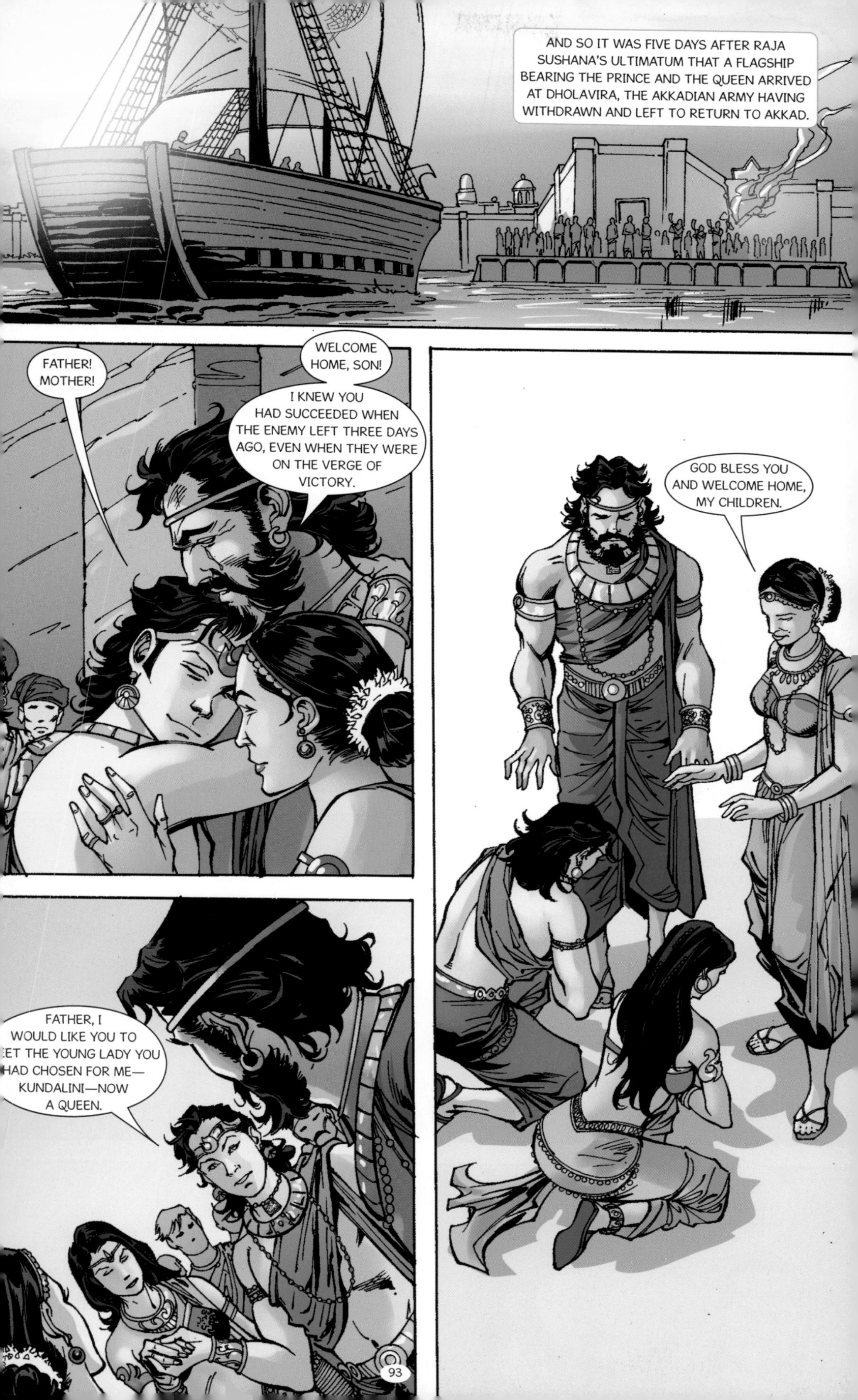
AND SO IT WAS FIVE DAYS AFTER RAJA SUSHANA'S ULTIMATUM THAT A FLAGSHIP BEARING THE PRINCE AND THE QUEEN ARRIVED AT DHOLAVIRA, THE AKKADIAN ARMY HAVING WITHDRAWN AND LEFT TO RETURN TO AKKAD.
FATHER! MOTHER!
WELCOME HOME, SON!
I KNEW YOU HAD SUCCEEDED WHEN THE ENEMY LEFT THREE DAYS AGO, EVEN WHEN THEY WERE ON THE VERGE OF VICTORY.
FATHER, I WOULD LIKE YOU TO ET THE YOUNG LADY YOU HAD CHOSEN FOR ME— KUNDALINI—NOW A QUEEN.
GOD BLESS YOU AND WELCOME HOME, MY CHILDREN.

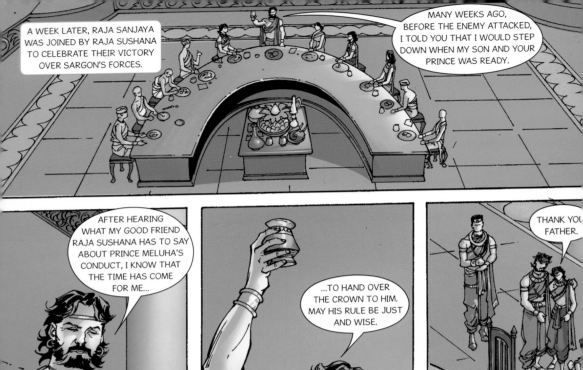

A WEEK LATER, RAJA SANJAYA WAS JOINED BY RAJA SUSHANA TO CELEBRATE THEIR VICTORY OVER SARGON'S FORCES.

MANY WEEKS AGO, BEFORE THE ENEMY ATTACKED, I TOLD YOU THAT I WOULD STEP DOWN WHEN MY SON AND YOUR PRINCE WAS READY.

AFTER HEARING WHAT MY GOOD FRIEND RAJA SUSHANA HAS TO SAY ABOUT PRINCE MELUHA'S CONDUCT, I KNOW THAT THE TIME HAS COME FOR ME...

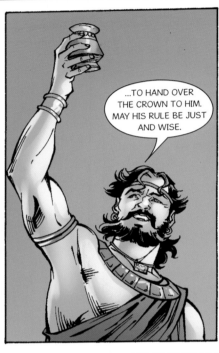

...TO HAND OVER THE CROWN TO HIM. MAY HIS RULE BE JUST AND WISE.

THANK YOU FATHER.

TOMORROW WILL BE A GREAT DAY; WE WILL FIRST ANOINT OUR NEW KING AND THEN MARRY OUR KING TO HIS QUEEN!

MAY THE GODS BLESS THIS UNION OF TWO INDIVIDUALS AND TWO KINGDOMS. MAY PROSPERITY ALWAYS REIGN.

94

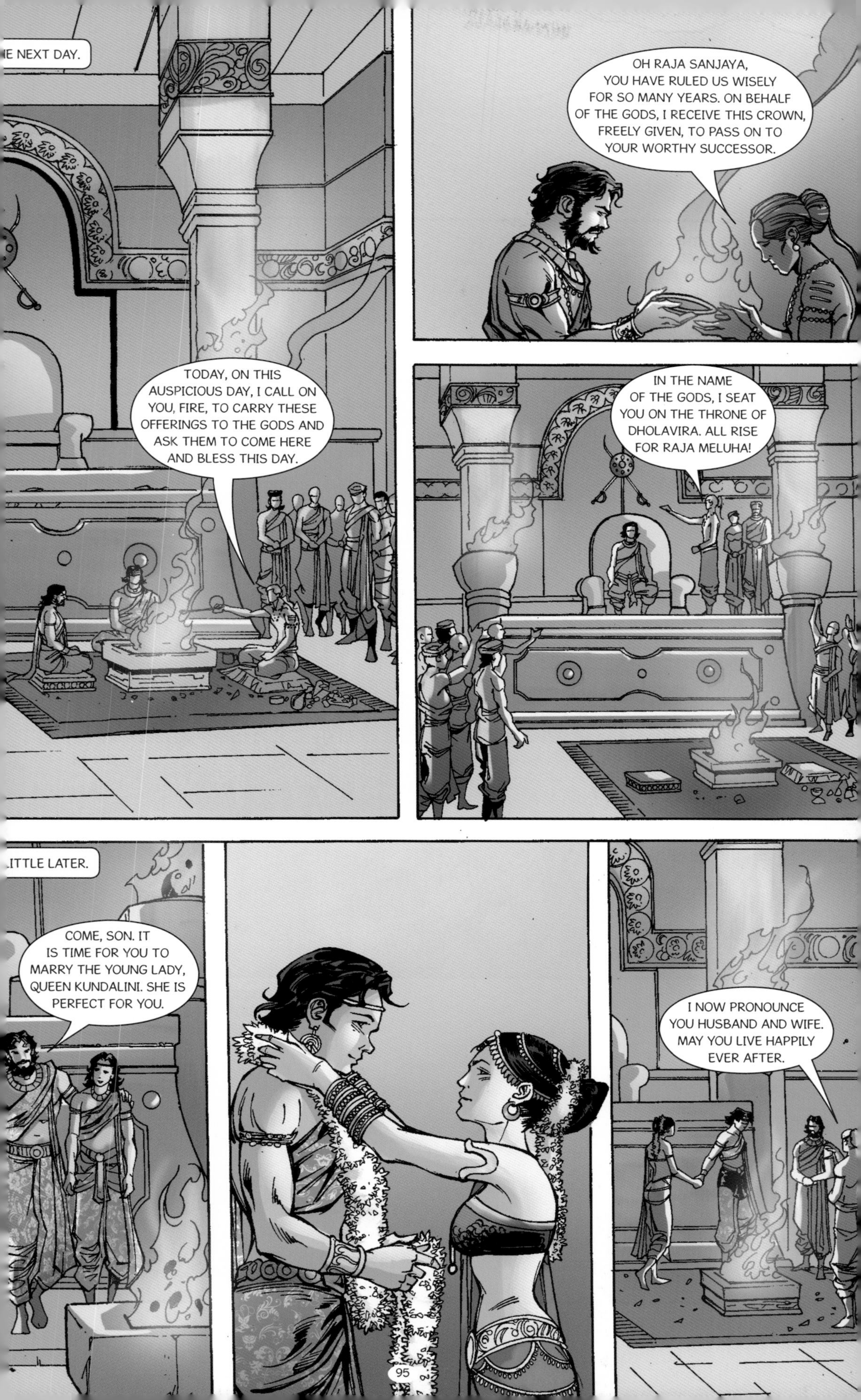

E NEXT DAY.
TODAY, ON THIS AUSPICIOUS DAY, I CALL ON YOU, FIRE, TO CARRY THESE OFFERINGS TO THE GODS AND ASK THEM TO COME HERE AND BLESS THIS DAY.
OH RAJA SANJAYA, YOU HAVE RULED US WISELY FOR SO MANY YEARS. ON BEHALF OF THE GODS, I RECEIVE THIS CROWN, FREELY GIVEN, TO PASS ON TO YOUR WORTHY SUCCESSOR.
IN THE NAME OF THE GODS, I SEAT YOU ON THE THRONE OF DHOLAVIRA. ALL RISE FOR RAJA MELUHA!
.ITTLE LATER.
COME, SON. IT IS TIME FOR YOU TO MARRY THE YOUNG LADY, QUEEN KUNDALINI. SHE IS PERFECT FOR YOU.
I NOW PRONOUNCE YOU HUSBAND AND WIFE. MAY YOU LIVE HAPPILY EVER AFTER.

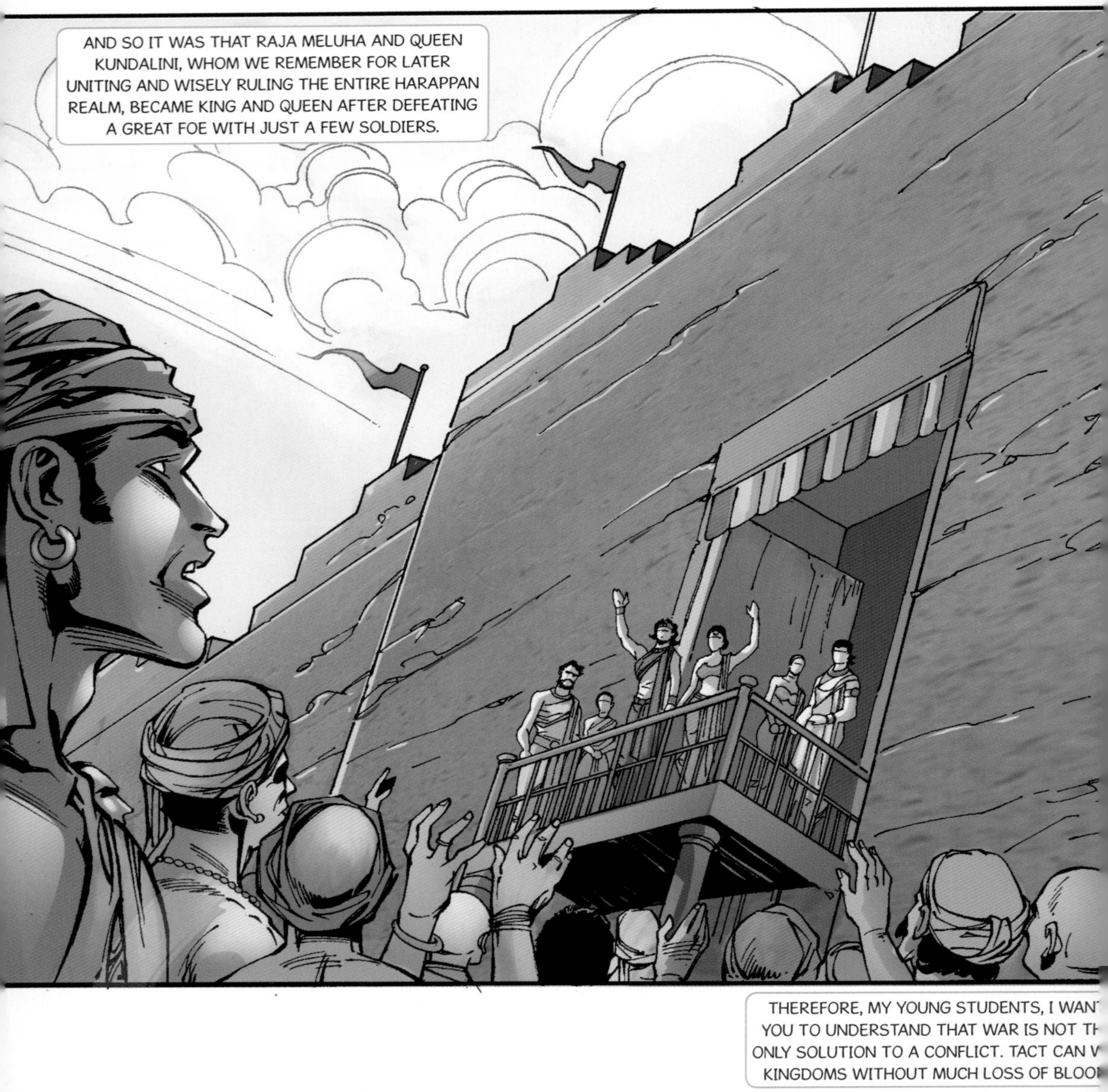
AND SO IT WAS THAT RAJA MELUHA AND QUEEN KUNDALINI, WHOM WE REMEMBER FOR LATER UNITING AND WISELY RULING THE ENTIRE HARAPPAN REALM, BECAME KING AND QUEEN AFTER DEFEATING A GREAT FOE WITH JUST A FEW SOLDIERS.
THEREFORE, MY YOUNG STUDENTS, I WAN
YOU TO UNDERSTAND THAT WAR IS NOT TH
ONLY SOLUTION TO A CONFLICT. TACT CAN W
KINGDOMS WITHOUT MUCH LOSS OF BLOO

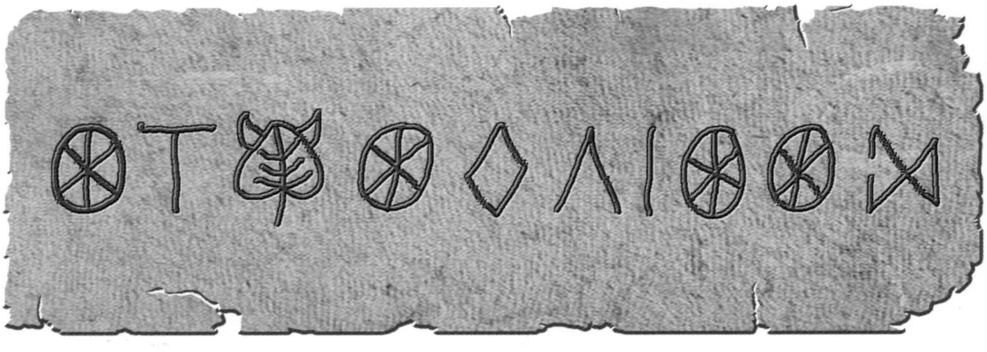

THE WRIGHT BROTHERS

www.campfire.co.in

tten by Lewis Helfand

strated by Sankha Banerjee

This is the story of how the Wright Brothers find a way to change the world for the better.

Orville and Wilbur Wright were just two seemingly average brothers from the American city of Dayton, Ohio, without even a high school diploma. Both were content living as local businessmen, printing newspapers and building bicycles. Like so many others, the two creative and inventive brothers harbored a secret fantasy since childhood, a dream to be able to fly.

In the late 1800s, the world's leading scientists were trying to construct a machine that could soar above the earth. One by one, these brilliant scientists failed, some even falling to their deaths, victims of their own winged contraptions. So, how could Orville and Wilbur even think of succeeding when no one else could?

But succeed they did. This is the story of their lives, the risks they take, and their unwillingness to accept defeat despite facing multiple failures.

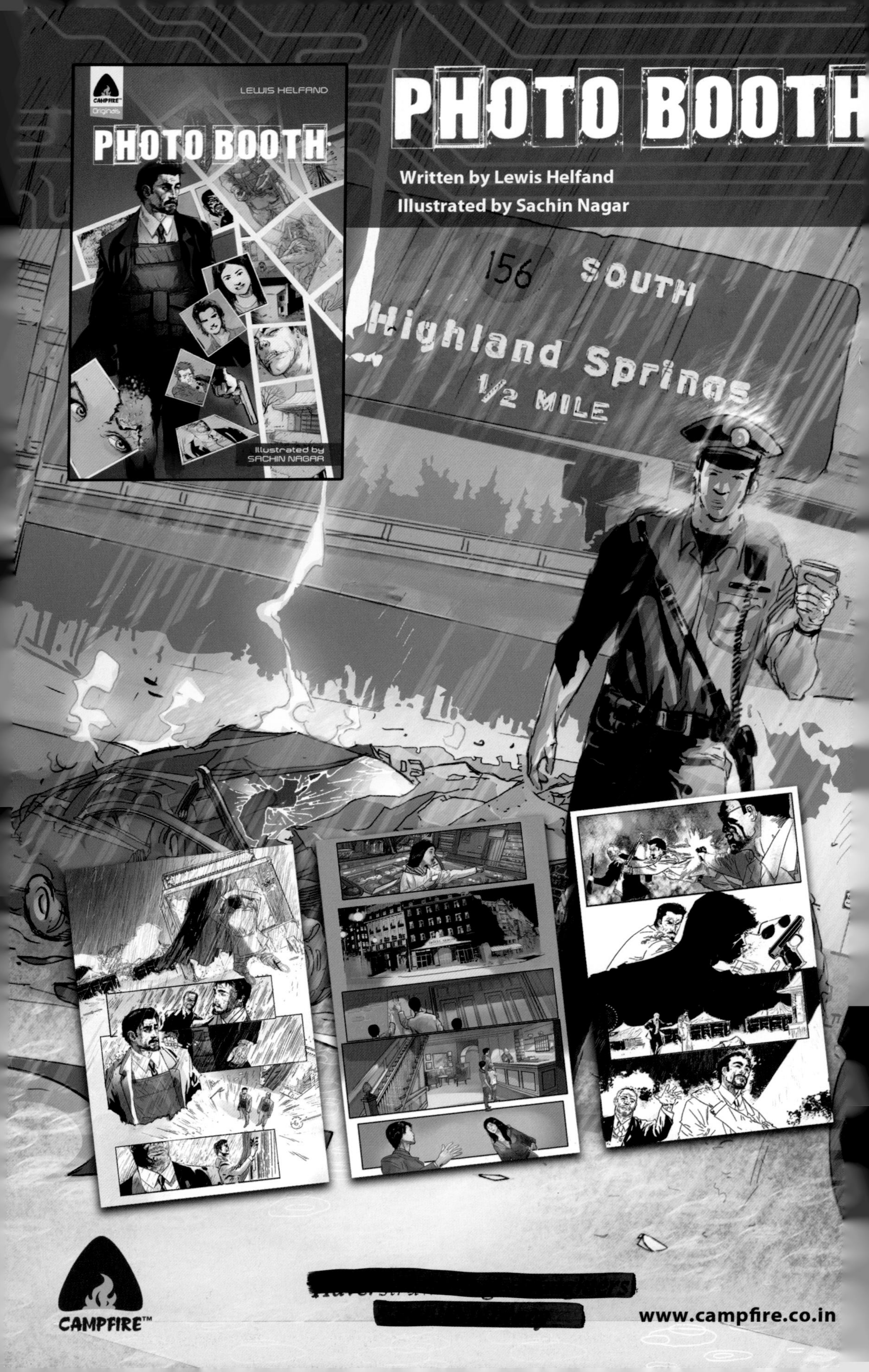
CAMPFIRE Originals
LEWIS HELFAND
PHOTO BOOTH
Illustrated by SACHIN NAGAR
PHOTO BOOTH
Written by Lewis Helfand
Illustrated by Sachin Nagar
156 SOUTH
Highland Springs
1/2 MILE
CAMPFIRE™
[redacted]
www.campfire.co.in

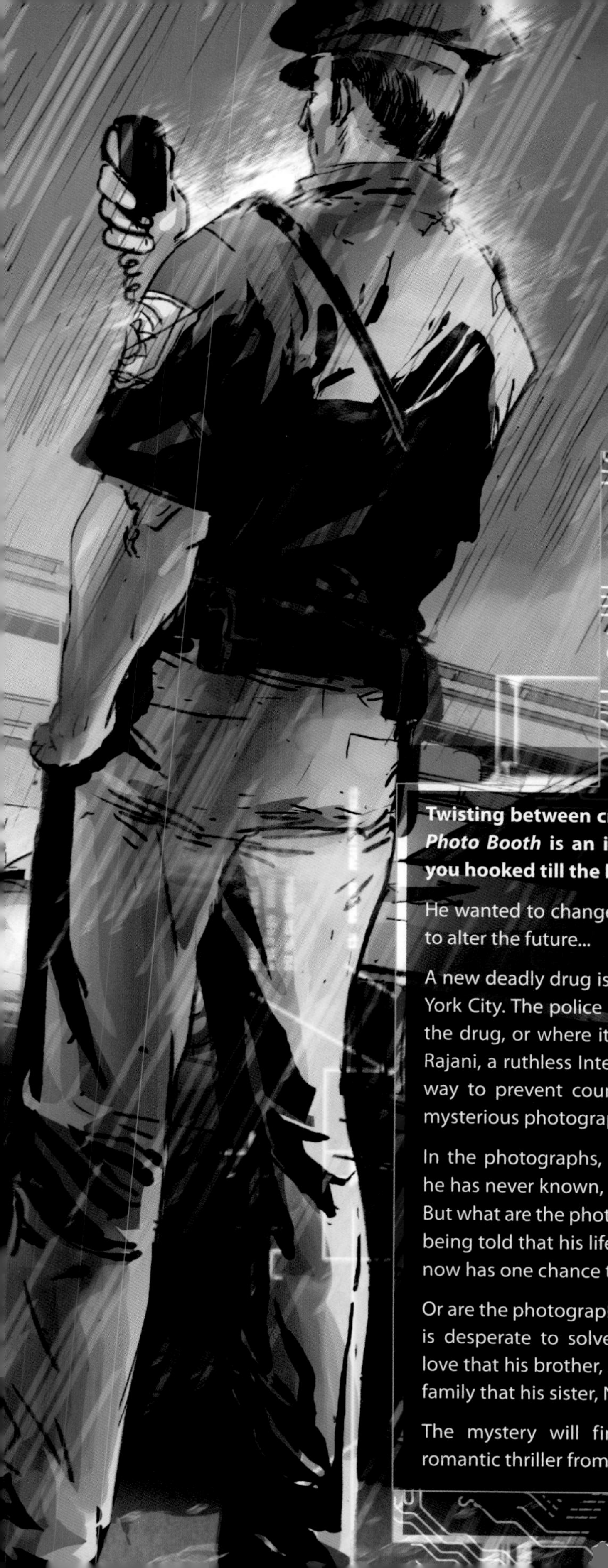

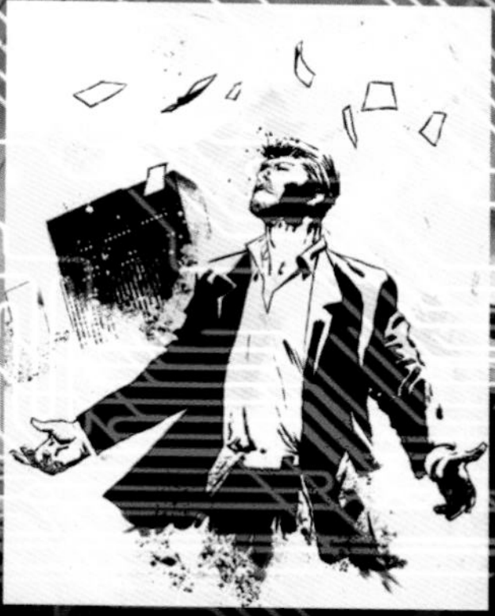

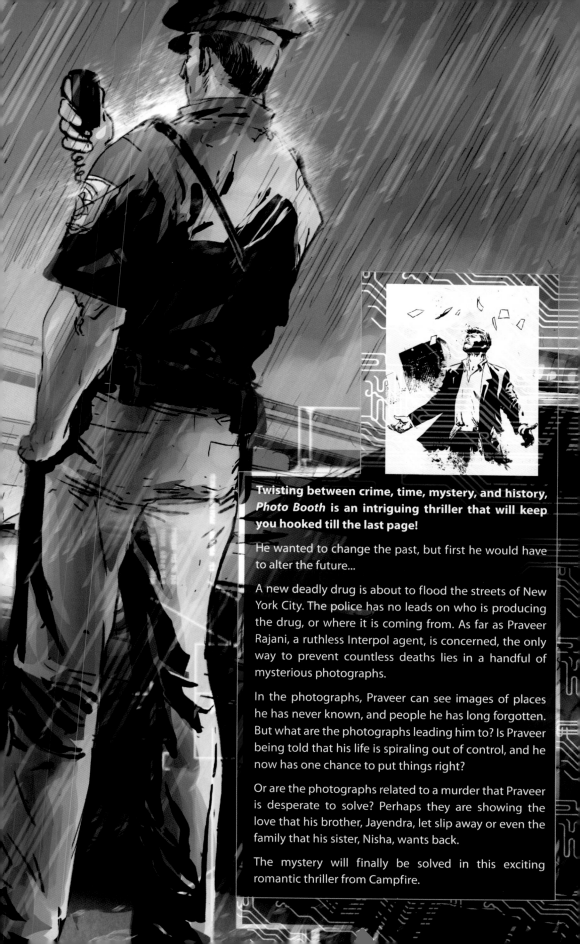

Twisting between crime, time, mystery, and history, *Photo Booth* is an intriguing thriller that will keep you hooked till the last page!

He wanted to change the past, but first he would have to alter the future...

A new deadly drug is about to flood the streets of New York City. The police has no leads on who is producing the drug, or where it is coming from. As far as Praveer Rajani, a ruthless Interpol agent, is concerned, the only way to prevent countless deaths lies in a handful of mysterious photographs.

In the photographs, Praveer can see images of places he has never known, and people he has long forgotten. But what are the photographs leading him to? Is Praveer being told that his life is spiraling out of control, and he now has one chance to put things right?

Or are the photographs related to a murder that Praveer is desperate to solve? Perhaps they are showing the love that his brother, Jayendra, let slip away or even the family that his sister, Nisha, wants back.

The mystery will finally be solved in this exciting romantic thriller from Campfire.

GLOSSARY

Akkad: A lost ancient city, believed to lie in central Iraq, which was once the capital of a large empire founded by Sargon. It was also known as Agade.

Alexander: The Greek King Alexander the Great (356 B.C.–323 B.C.) invaded India in 326 B.C. and fought many battles with the tribes and kingdoms of western India.

Amri: An ancient city in the southern province of Sind, Pakistan, that existed from 3500 B.C. to1500 B.C.

Aria: An ancient name for the land of Ariana in Afghanistan.

Ashram: A retreat center used by ascetics to meditate or teach pupils.

Citadel: Many of the large Indus towns and cities have elevated mounds or divisions with their own fortification, that are referred to as citadels by archeologists.

Dholavira: Located on Khadir Island in Kutch, India, this ancient city was inhabited from 3100 B.C. to1500 B.C. It was one of the five largest Indus cities.

Dhruva: The ancient Indian name (popularly used now) for the star Thuban—the second last star in the tail of the constellation Ursa Major.

Dilmun: The ancient name of the island of Baharain. It was a major trading port and an ancient Mesopotamian cemetery.

Ganweriwala Ther: Located in the Cholistan Desert of Pakistan, this ancient city was inhabited from c.3100 B.C. to 2000 B.C. It was one of the five largest Harappan cities, and once lay on the delta of the River Saraswati (modern River Ghaggar/Hara) where it met a large lake.

God Ea: Mesopotamian god of the Wind and Earth.

Goddess Aditi: Indian goddess of the Earth; Mother Earth.

Harappa: Located on the banks of the River Ravi in the province of Punjab in Pakistan, it was one of the most famous and largest Indus cities that has been extensively excavated. It existed from from c.3500 B.C to1700 B.C.

Harappans: A name often applied to the people of the Indus Valley Civilization, which existed from 2550 B.C. to1950 B.C. Archeologists believe its ancient name may have been Meluha.

Kutch: The island district of Gujarat, India. It was once said to have been made up of seven islands. It was colonized by people from Sind around 3100 B.C.

Lal Daro: An ancient town and fortified outpost, that lies within the delta of the River Indus. It gets its name which means 'Red Mound', from the burned red mud bricks that it is made up of.

Magan: The ancient land on both sides of the entrance to the Persian Gulf. It includes the U.A.E., northern Oman, and parts of the Makran Coast of Iran and Pakistan. It was a major source of copper during those times.

Mahuwa: A tree growing extensively in parts of western India from which a strong liquor is made.

Malwa: A high plateau in central India crisscrossed by many rivers. Today, most of this plateau is part of the Indian state of Madhya Pradesh.

Mohenjo-daro: Located on the banks of the River Indus in the Sind province, Pakistan, it was one of the most famous and largest Indus cities, and has been extensively excavated. It was founded sometime before 3100 B.C. and existed till 2000 B.C., when it was abandoned. It was later reoccupied briefly during Buddhist times when a stupa and monastery were built on its citadel mound.

Naphtha: An ancient Greek term for the oil that used to ooze out of the ground in parts of the Middle East.

Pashupati: An ancient Indian god, probably tribal in origin. He is the 'Protector of Cattle' and is today another name for the Hindu god, Shiva.

Raja Rai Por (Porus): The ruler of a kingdom between the rivers Chenab and Jhelum in modern Punjab Province, Pakistan. He fought a famous battle with Alexander the Great in 326 B.C., in which he lost.

Rakhigarhi: Located in the state of Haryana in India, it was one of the five largest Indus cities. It was occupied from c.3500 B.C. to 2000 B.C.

Rann of Kutch: This extensive salt pan, which becomes a shallow sea during the monsoon, separates Kutch from the Sind province. It was once a shallow, navigable sea.

River Nara: A dry river channel that runs parallel and to the east of the River Indus in Sind, Pakistan. It is believed to either mark an ancient eastern course of the River Indus or the channel of the River Saraswati.

River Ravi: This is one of the tributaries of the River Indus. The city of Harappa lies on its banks.

River Sutlej: A tributary of the River Indus.

River Sindhu: The ancient name of the modern River Indus.

Sapta Rishi: The Indian name for the constellation of Ursa Major, or the Big Dipper.

Saran: A fortified outpost on the northern shore of Khadir Island, about two kilometers from Dholavira.

Sargon: The greatest ruler of the ancient city of Akkad, Sargon lived from 2334 B.C. to 2279 B.C. He was known as Sargon the Great, and vastly expanded the Akkadian Empire.

Shishupala: The Indian name for the constellation Ursa Minor, or the Little Dipper.

Sind: The southern province of modern Pakistan through which the River Indus flows.

Varanasi: A holy city located in central India.

Zebu Bull: A variety of *Bos indicus*, the type of cattle common throughout India.

THE CIVILIZATION THAT WAS

AFGHANISTAN
Islamabad
Indus
PAKISTAN
Harappa
Kalibanga
Mehrgarh
Pirak
Sukkur
Indus
Ghaggar-Hakra
Rakhigarhi
Lakhanjo Daro
Ganweriwala
Farmana
Khairpur
Mohenjo Daro
Kot Diji
Thar Desert Sites
Delhi
INDIA
Arabian Sea
Dholavira
Narmada

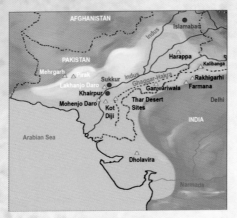

Almost 4000 years ago, when most cultures consisted of nomadic forest dwellers, a great civilization, which can boast of the earliest known accounts of urban planning, developed along the River Indus in the Indian subcontinent. It is known as the Indus Valley Civilization. Its two great cities were Harappa and Mohenjo-daro. Let's find out some more fascinating information about them.

HOW THEY LIVED

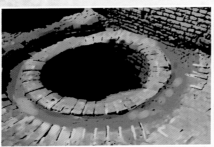

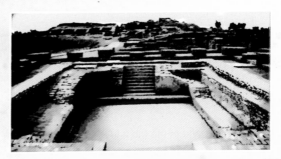

The people of this civilization lived in well-planned cities. Their houses were built of mud bricks, burne bricks, and chiseled stones. Each house had a courtyard, a private well, and a bathroom. Some citie had large public baths that were generally used for religious bathing. The most famous one is the Grea Bath in Mohenjo-daro. In many places, citadels were built. Carved stone gateways and fortified wal surrounded them. The citadels also had a huge range of water reservoirs around them.

THEIR JEWELRY

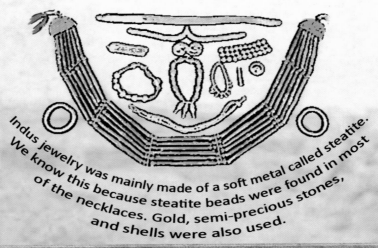

Indus jewelry was mainly made of a soft metal called steatite. We know this because steatite beads were found in most of the necklaces. Gold, semi-precious stones, and shells were also used.

THE PUZZLING DISCOVERIES

The River Indus used to flood regularly. When it did, cities in the Indus Valley Civilization were rebuilt on top of the ones destroyed. Archeologists have discovered several such rebuilt cities. However, what is puzzling is that each of the later cities were built a little less skillfully. The most well-planned and skillful one was at the bottom. Seems like builders grew less able in perfection over time!

Though the Indus Valley is the largest of all the four ancient civilizations (Egyptian, Mesopotamian, and Chinese being the other three), very little is known about it. Archeologists have found four hundred distinct symbols on many well-carved seals. The seals bear carvings of animals, figures, and symbols of religious life along with a script that archeologists have not been able to decipher. The seals may have been used in trade as many of them have been discovered in Mesopotamian sites. Till the time a Rosetta stone is found, discovering more information about this civilization would be really tricky.

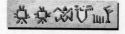

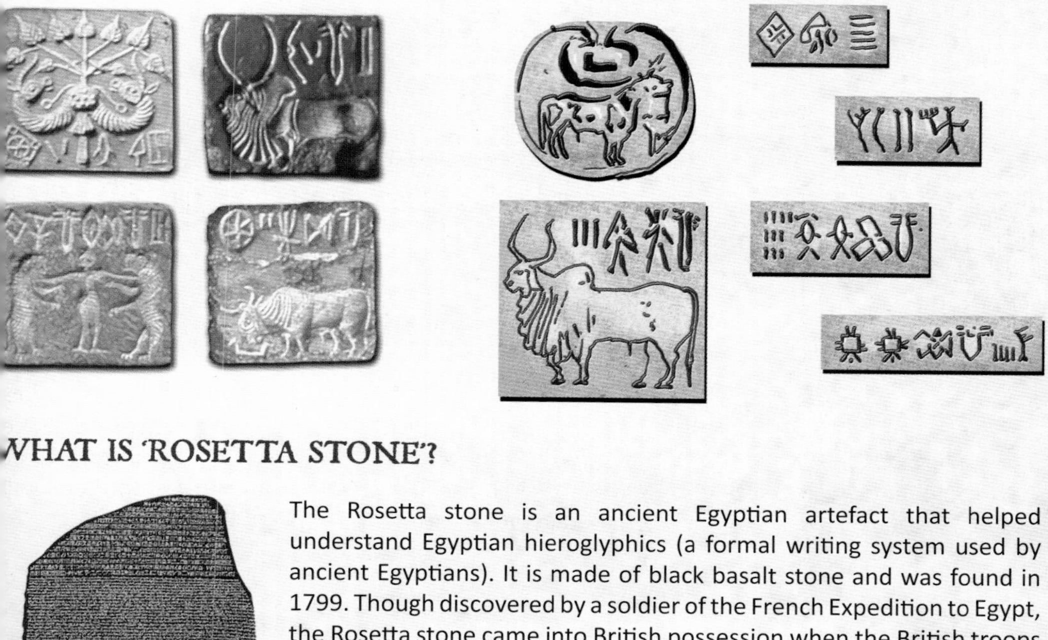

WHAT IS 'ROSETTA STONE'?

The Rosetta stone is an ancient Egyptian artefact that helped understand Egyptian hieroglyphics (a formal writing system used by ancient Egyptians). It is made of black basalt stone and was found in 1799. Though discovered by a soldier of the French Expedition to Egypt, the Rosetta stone came into British possession when the British troops defeated the French in 1801. It is the most visited object in the British Museum. The term 'Rosetta stone' also means a clue, breakthrough, or discovery that provides crucial knowledge for solving a problem.

DID YOU KNOW?

- The name 'India' has been derived from the River Indus, the valleys around which were home to the early settlers of the Indus Valley Civilization.

- Sindhu is the ancient name of the River Indus.

- The Indus Valley Civilization is also known as the Harappan, Indus-Saraswati, and Hakra Civilization.

Available now

Putting the fun back into readi[ng]

Explore the latest from Campfire at

www.campfire.co.in